What on earth was she getting herself into?

Lily's stomach clenched as she walked through the bedroom door. What was she doing alone with a man? Granted, Dylan wasn't a complete stranger and he had saved her life. But it had been years since she'd known him, and these were such extreme circumstances.

She struggled to grasp the implications. "Why don't we just tell the man we're not married?"

"It was his mistake to begin with. Why correct him? It's better we muddy our trail. If the Maddock gang catches wind that we've stayed in the area, Forrestor saying he put up a married couple will attract less attention."

"You can have the bed," she said with a pretend air of truce.

Suspicious of her offer, he anchored a hand on his lean hips. Sunlight caught the bristles on his cheeks, painting them gold. "There's enough room for two."

* * *

Klondike Fever
Harlequin® Historical #891—April 2008

KATE BRIDGES

KLONDIKE FEVER

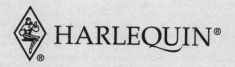

HARLEQUIN®

TORONTO • NEW YORK • LONDON
AMSTERDAM • PARIS • SYDNEY • HAMBURG
STOCKHOLM • ATHENS • TOKYO • MILAN • MADRID
PRAGUE • WARSAW • BUDAPEST • AUCKLAND

ISBN-13: 978-0-373-29491-6
ISBN-10:   0-373-29491-3

KLONDIKE FEVER

DON'T MISS THESE OTHER NOVELS AVAILABLE NOW:

#892 NO PLACE FOR A LADY—Louise Allen
Miss Bree Mallory has no time for the pampered aristocracy!
She's too taken up with running the best coaching company on
the roads. But an accidental meeting with an earl
changes everything....
Join Louise Allen's unconventional heroine as she shocks Society!

#893 A SINFUL ALLIANCE—Amanda McCabe
Marguerite is exceptionally beautiful—and entirely deadly!
Sent by a king to assassinate the gorgeous Nicolai, she finds
herself torn between royal duty and ardent desire....
*Award-winning Amanda McCabe brings us scandal
and seduction at the Tudor court!*

#894 THE WANTON BRIDE—Mary Brendan
With disgrace just a breath away, Emily ached for Mark's strong
arms to comfort her. Yet she held a secret—one that would surely
prevent *any* gentleman from considering her as a suitable bride....
Can Mary Brendan's hero's passion overcome Emily's fears?

This book is dedicated to all the new writers out there who are working hard at making their prose sparkle and their stories soar. Who stay up late at night, miss family outings, spend money on paper and ink and stamps instead of small luxuries for themselves, in hopes that one day their manuscripts will sell. You already enrich the world with your imagination and devotion.

Chapter One

~~~⌇⌇⌇~~~

Yukon wilderness
August 1898

Dylan Wayburn recognized her before she recognized him.

She dressed differently, he thought. An odd mix of blatant beauty and hidden treasure. And after five years, instead of recognition in her eyes, there was dismissal. Dylan lowered the brim of his Stetson and hoped it would stay that way.

He studied her through half-closed eyes.

Miss Lilybeth Cromwell had always been self-conscious of a man's attention. Yet the top button of her square neckline, scooped low like many high-society dresses, was half undone. It riveted the faces of all four men in the stagecoach. They waited for the button to slip completely and grace them with more of her bosom. Even the old lady seated beside Dylan was sniffing into a handkerchief and staring. Funny thing was, Lilybeth wore a black silk shawl around her shoulders, covering up the brilliant blue dress beneath.

Dylan never could understand that about women. She put that revealing dress on this morning and now she was trying to hide it.

Lilybeth was as far from demure as her flowing red hair and full lips would allow. But then again, Miss Lilybeth Cromwell was not the shy, nameless adolescent he'd once known. She was Klondike Lily, the wealthiest woman in the Yukon.

Rumor had it, the gold nuggets on her claim were the size of grizzly claws.

Dylan tried to ignore her. He shoved a shoulder against the hard boards and peered out the window.

No sound of anything unusual. Still nothing to look at for the hundreds of miles between Dawson City and the tent town of Whitehorse except acres of spruce and aspen and the occasional cottonwood. A ridge of mountains engulfed the river valley. The turquoise waters of the Yukon River gushed on the other side of their coach.

They hit another rut. The six passengers swayed in unison and Dylan's gaze bobbed back to Lily.

Her button inched closer to release. He swallowed mighty hard, turned away again and stared at the outside shadows—two men driving a team of twelve horses. A strongbox locked in between them. A stack of luggage.

No one else had voiced it, but Dylan was well aware they were carrying a cache of gold. He knew it the instant he'd seen the number of horses on the team this morning. He'd been following the gold but he hadn't been looking forward to meeting up with Lily again. Sooner or later, he knew they would, seeing how much gold she owned and how attractive that made her to thieves. And that, of course, was the reason he was here.

Beneath his boots, he felt the weight of the gold shift, tucked somewhere into a secret iron trap beneath the floorplanks. The stash was fairly well balanced, but on the odd turn, it slid an inch or two to the right, making the iron wheels on his side of the coach creak.

Mud wagon was a more appropriate term for the contraption they were riding in. A far cry from a civilized stagecoach in a civilized part of the world.

Twenty-eight days and nights he'd been traveling alone. Hiding behind scrub bush, eating berries when he couldn't light a fire to attract attention, letting the scratch grow on his jaw, ensuring his holster and Colt revolvers were visible to all.

He'd be damned if he'd allow one inconsequential woman to blow his cover. If necessary, he could take down the two men sitting on either side of her.

Still, Dylan bristled with caution. He hoped she wouldn't do anything reckless that might jeopardize the coming ambush and what he had to do to protect everyone inside the coach.

Lily adjusted her skirts and turned away from the bodyguard sitting on her right. His breath smelled of breakfast sausages. Heat glued their shoulders together. She usually preferred a window seat when she traveled, whether by train or wagon or ship, but her two secret bodyguards, provided by the stage depot three hours ago, insisted on flanking her.

She wiggled, panting for a pocket of air that wasn't scented with either man's breath. Envy gripped her as she stared at the formidable stranger slumped across from them. He sat beside the curtain and its rustling breeze. Why, with his dark Stetson perched low over his face, the mysterious man who seemed impressed with his own sense of danger hardly needed all the fresh air blowing his way. He was sleeping, for Lord's sake, not even able to fully appreciate the gust!

And here she was, gasping.

There were some things money still couldn't buy.

In fact, a lot of things.

Oh, here it came…a pinch of pine. Summer cedar.

She inhaled. Perhaps she'd get to the town of White-horse in one sane piece, after all. Then on to Skagway, Alaska, where her sister had last been sighted.

She smelled whisky again, hailing from the sleeping stranger. How could a person take to drink so early in the morning?

Lily slid her hanky beneath her heavy wall of hair. She dabbed the moisture. If she hadn't been in such a hurry to leave, she would have pinned her hair into a bun. Despite the heat, it wasn't proper to go anywhere without a shawl.

Look how the stranger slid forward, silently demanding more space around him than any other passenger.

Weathered blue jeans covered his long legs. Expensive guns rested on lean hips. His crisp white shirt and suede vest made him look like an outlaw who was trying to behave. She glared at the broad shoulders and how many extra inches they occupied, inches that right-fully belonged to the older woman beside him and her elderly husband squeezed next to her, the Sawyers.

And why hadn't the selfish man bothered to shave? Was it too much to ask for a man to look decent? His shaggy brown hair could use a cut. He was traveling alone, but surely he hadn't thought the coach would be empty from Dawson City to Whitehorse. They were in the middle of a gold rush!

Klondike fever, she called it. A burning inside the bellies of some men and women. A yearning to attain something grand, something they'd never seen or touched before.

They could have all the gold they could carry out of Dawson, if they struck it rich. The newly opened dirt path along the rivers between the Yukon and Alaska was no more than a hacked rut, but it was the only land route between Canada and the United States. Most folks still traveled by the waterways.

Heavens to God, look at him. Even his cowboy boots were obnoxiously large. She had half a mind to shake the living—

A dark eye peered at her from beneath his cowboy hat.

Heat rose to her cheeks.

Go ahead, tell him how much space he takes up! How his knees are just an inch away from her body-guard's. A bodyguard whose seat she had paid for. Why, she had literally paid for three seats in this coach, while he had only paid for one.

Air…she needed air….

The sound of gunshots lurched her forward, and suddenly she forgot all about the seating arrangements.

Her button finally came undone, but Dylan had no time to savor Lily. His pulse leaped at the blast of gunfire. He lunged for his Colts.

The old woman beside him shrieked, "No!"

"Hit the floor," Dylan shouted and the Sawyers slid to their knees.

One of the drivers toppled from above the stagecoach, blood trickling off his left boot. He fell to the moving dirt.

Lily turned to her bodyguards. "Do something!" she urged.

Their guns were already halfway up, but Dylan was faster at pointing his six-shooters. "Toss your weapons."

Fury etched their faces. They dropped their guns.

Lily trembled. "Blazes," she whispered at Dylan, her skin pale against her wild auburn hair.

He knelt on the seat and peered out the window. The stagecoach careened down the trail, rocking everyone back and forth. They clutched their seats to hang on.

Hooves thundered in the grass. Five masked men galloped within yards of the coach, gaining fast. With steady aim, Dylan hit one chest, then another. Gravely wounded, the men toppled over their horses.

Dylan was well aware what was happening inside the coach, too. One of the bodyguards whipped out a hidden pistol.

Dylan twisted around, shot at the man's wrist, and as the other bodyguard rushed him, Dylan shoved his boots into the man's gut and heaved as hard as he could. The man crashed through the door and out to the rolling ground. The door slapped open and closed.

More gunshots sounded outside. The coach slowed.

"Damn," said Dylan. The slowing meant his side was losing. Hidden gold shifted beneath his boots and the right wheels creaked.

Lily's blue eyes widened. "What do you want?"

Dylan kept his gun pointed at the injured man beside her, who was clutching a bloody wrist. "Your hired men are part of the gang trying to rob you."

"Go to hell!" the bodyguard hollered.

Lily recoiled, unsure of who to look at, unsure of who to trust.

Dylan nudged the old man on the floor. "You all right?"

The gent moaned and helped his wife to her seat.

Lily kept her startled sights on Dylan. Her eyes flickered with recognition. Her mouth slackened. She was about to speak.

"Don't say it," he whispered.

"But you're—"

"Don't say it."

She blinked rapidly and clutched her beaded handbag. Her lips went white. Her chin quivered. Her posture lost its strength.

Her remaining bodyguard lunged at Dylan with a knife. Dylan knocked the blade out of the ravaged hands and kicked the son of a bitch straight through the flapping door and onto the grass.

The old couple gasped.

Color rushed back to Lily's cheeks. She took in

everything around her as the coach came to a shuddering stop.

"Pretend you're with me," Dylan said.

"But—"

"You either trust me or you don't." He locked on to her frantic expression.

With the Sawyers back beside him, Dylan took a chance and jumped to Lily's side. She didn't fuss when he peered out the open door. Ready for hell.

Silence swelled around them. The elderly couple clung together. With his guns lowered, Dylan sat frozen next to Lily. He listened to her rapid breathing.

Gulls cawed above the rushing river to his right. Sunshine bore down on the coach, casting a looming shadow to his left. Slowly, footsteps sounded on the crush of pebbles and two shadows trudged toward the open coach door. Dylan motioned everyone inside to remain calm and quiet.

"Whaddya got up there, old man?" They couldn't see him, but they could hear the stranger booming at the driver, known only as Yul.

"Whatever you want, you can have," Yul replied.

Good. Don't fight.

Two rough-looking men shoved their Enfield revolvers into the coach window. In their forties. Muscled. Greased-back hair. When Dylan recognized them, a bold chill raced up the back of his neck. Beneath the grime and bristles, they both had the thick nose of the Maddock brothers, the cowlick on the right side of their foreheads. The nasty gleam in the small dark eyes Dylan would never forget. Kirk and Sloan Maddock. The ones who'd captured him three years ago in

Alberta District. The ones who'd stoked the goddamn fire…. Did they recognize him? His hair was overgrown and he was in dire need of a shave himself.

He'd shot and maybe killed two of their men. How would they retaliate?

Old-lady Sawyer sobbed.

"Well, well, well." The heavier man, with a half-grown beard, cocked his gun at Dylan.

Dylan tossed his Colts to the floor and put his arm protectively around Lily.

The other brother, slimmer with a red welt on his forehead, stared at Lily's undone button. Dylan lowered her shawl over her chest to protect her.

"What do you want?" Dylan gritted his teeth.

"Come on out. Where we can see ya."

The desire for revenge pounded through Dylan, but he restrained himself. He got out first, then helped Lily and the Sawyers, sticking closest to her.

The man with the beard, Kirk, motioned them to get away from the coach. "Where you keepin' it?" he asked Lily.

"I—I don't know what you mean."

"Klondike Lily." He whistled. "Not only as rich as sunshine. You're a looker."

The other slime, who appeared to be scaring the wits out of Yul by pointing his trigger at him, leered in her direction, too. "Ow, darlin'."

"Tell them," Dylan commanded her.

"Pardon me?" she asked.

The coach sat perched at an angle, leaning over toward the men who stood at the edge of the river. Were the Maddocks blind? All they had to do was look at the coach to see the gold had shifted to the back wheel.

Dylan slid an arm around Lily and squeezed. "Tell them."

She pressed her lips together, and glared from one man to the other.

When she didn't offer it, Dylan did.

"It's hidden in the bottom of the coach," he said to her look of dismay. "Trapdoor."

Come on Lily give them the key.

As if reading his mind, Lily whipped it out from her corset and flung it at their feet.

Sloan picked it up and chuckled. "Still warm."

Dylan backed away slightly, guiding Lily to where the older couple was standing. He had to time this precisely, expertly, or they'd all be gunned down in cold blood.

"Hey, hey." The man with the welt came over.

Dylan's heart raced. Was he suspicious?

The slime took out a pair of handcuffs.

"That's not necessary." Dylan tried to stop him, but short of getting a gun in the belly for his troubles, there wasn't anything he could do. Yet.

Sloan handcuffed Dylan and Lily together. The cuffs felt cool and tight on his thick wrist. They were preparing to take Dylan and Lily with them.

"How dare you," she said. "Take the gold and leave us alone."

"Shut up. We'll take what we want." He reached low, beneath her skirts. The other man handed him a long chain he'd retrieved from their saddlebags.

Sloan motioned to Dylan. "Give me your foot."

Dylan muttered, not wanting to obey, but the other man still had a gun aimed at them.

He stood still as he and Lily were chained together at their ankles and secured with a lock. More chains were hanging out of the saddlebags. Why so many? Why not do away with all the passengers on the spot? Not that Dylan was complaining.

Kirk's heavy boots thudded into the stones as he stepped to the coach and leaned over the seat, searching for the hidden trapdoor. Greedy bastard.

"Found it!"

When the thinner brother turned around in glee and walked toward the coach, it was the opening Dylan was looking for.

He lowered himself swiftly to the ground, yanking Lily with him, picked up a heavy boulder and heaved it at the left side of the coach.

The stagecoach shuddered, and in one mighty swoop, crashed over the river's edge and down on the two killers. They were pinned beneath a busted wheel, gurgling water and a ton of gold.

They hadn't even had time to scream.

Stunned, the witnesses watched the waves settle.

The horses, still attached to the overturned coach, reared in panic. They had to be released, and fast.

The man holding the gun at Yul stood motionless, staring with his eyeballs nearly popping out of his head at how the other two had disappeared. "Son of a—" He rushed Dylan.

Old-man Sawyer was already aiming his shiny pistol. He pulled the trigger and the murderous bastard crumpled.

"Thank you." Dylan didn't care where the old couple had been hiding the gun. He was only grateful they had.

Dylan pulled Lily along as he leaped to calm the horses. Mrs. Sawyer was dumbstruck but, with her husband's urging, rushed to the animals, their only means of escape.

Yul addressed Dylan. "I can't believe you turned the tables on 'em, mister. Who are you?"

Lily stared at him. She seemed to know who he was.

The horses tried to buck. Lily shuffled with Dylan as he released the team. Yul helped separate them.

"We've gotta run," hollered Dylan. "Keys to our locks are somewhere under the coach, but there's no time to look."

"The vermin are trapped," said Yul. "I'll get—"

"No! Unleash the horses! Get us four! Go!"

"What's the hurry? They can't hurt us any—"

Then they saw it. Over the ridge, four more men galloped toward them. A tunnel of dust whipped behind them like a menacing tornado. Devils on horseback.

"The gang's bigger than you think," Dylan shouted. "Untie the horses!"

Like magic, the stage driver singled out four.

Dylan raced to help the old couple up on two, dragging Lily with him.

Yul mounted his with ease.

"Go!" Dylan hoisted Lily by the waist and tried to shove her up onto a black mare that was tied to a bay, while shouting to the others. "Don't wait for us! They'll stop to get the gold. When they see their men, they'll want our blood. Go!"

Lily slid off the mare's side for the third time. Frantically, she tried to claw her way up again. "I can't get up."

"Pull harder." But it wasn't working. Their horses were spooked and going 'round in circles. And it was near impossible for two people chained together to mount as one.

Yul and the Sawyers tore off into the wilderness.

Dylan, steady as a knife in the wind, calculated the distance between himself and the approaching gang. Five hundred yards.

With a mighty hand, he slapped the bay and then the black mare. The horses raced into the woods, scaring the other horses with them, so Dylan and Lily were left with none, standing among the bushes.

She gasped at what he'd done.

"Without horses, they can't haul away the gold," he explained.

He used his left hand to grab her right. Clenched as one, they ran. He picked his guns off the grass and shuffled toward the river.

"They'll think we *all* got away on horses."

"They'll kill us."

"Only if they know where we are."

Dylan held tight to Lily's hand. They splashed through the river up to higher land, then down a gully. Their feet landed at different times, and due to their chains, they toppled head over skirts. Barely looking up, they jumped to their feet. Trees engulfed them.

Their hearts pounded in unison as they raced along the stones, flying through the air with the wind at their faces and danger at their heels.

Chapter Two

"They wanted to tie all the passengers together." Dylan's voice roared above the river to reach her ears. "That's why all the chains."

One step behind him, Lily hurled over boulders and brush. Her throat burned. Mud caked the hemlines of her satin dress and petticoats. Her silk shawl, knotted at her waist, slapped against her backside as she ran. After thirty minutes of running and walking and running again, they'd gotten the proper sense of balance. The most difficult thing was how to coordinate their shackled wrists as they ran with their ankles chained.

"Watch out!" He ducked beneath the trees, trying to hold branches away from her body.

One whipped her in the face. Its thorns scratched her cheek. The sting didn't stop her. She cupped her cheek with her free hand, determined to keep pace alongside her new companion.

Her old companion.

Blazes, what was he to her anymore?

A stranger.

He looked like a scruffy drifter. The smell of whisky caught her nostrils. My, how the mighty had fallen.

But he had been there to help her.

Dylan turned his dark face toward her, his brow shielded from the noon sun by his Stetson. "They had the chains and handcuffs ready on the horse. Did you see them?"

She panted, gazing up at the lean cut of his profile. How could he run so fast and talk at the same time? "No."

"They meant to take us with them."

What was he getting at?

"Maybe for ransom," he explained.

She didn't have the breath to talk. They wanted her gold, but once they got it, what more did they want? Did they think she had more?

The stitch in her side pounded up her ribcage. She tried pinching her stomach to stop it, but her right hand was tied to his left and she didn't have the strength to slow him down.

She dragged her feet, barely able to continue.

"Just a bit further," he urged. "I think our trick worked. They don't suspect we got away on foot."

He slowed his pace and the stitch in her side slowed its pounding.

Gently, he set her down on a patch of soft grass, hidden from the road by a circle of pines. He sat beside her.

Squinting through the needles past his heaving chest, Lily couldn't see anyone. No one chasing them.

There was just a long patch of river, wooded slopes, and the warm Yukon wind blowing through the green and golden grasses. They'd run about a mile.

With great relief, she leaned her back in the grass. Safe for now. She drank the air.

He removed the canteen slung over his square shoulders. When in tarnation had he managed to get that? She had feared for her very life, yet he'd attended to so many little details around him, you'd think…you'd think he himself might be one of the Maddock gang.

She'd heard of the bloody gang, like everyone else in Dawson City. A handful of men who tormented the weak. They robbed fragile old men who'd struck gold in the Klondike and weren't physically able to defend themselves. And women like herself.

She trembled. How could she be sure Dylan was telling the truth when he'd said her bodyguards were on the wrong side of the law? Maybe he was the liar.

She blinked up at him, fearing for her life. Her heart struck like a fist against her ribs.

What kind of man had Dylan become? How had he known so much about where her gold was hidden? And how had he managed to escape the Maddocks when so few had? Had their convenient escape been planned, so he could now lead her to her own grave?

No. They would have shot her right there. They didn't need her any longer. They had her gold, didn't they?

A sob rushed up her throat.

Her gold. It didn't matter. It did not matter.

She was chained to Dylan Wayburn. She gazed up the length of his muscled body. Darker. Meaner. Stronger than ever. How long had it been?

"Five years," he said, as if he could read her mind.

He fingered the brim of his Stetson. Rich brown hair touched his shoulders. He removed the cap of his canteen. As he did, the sleeve on his right hand slid up a few inches, revealing what looked to be a birthmark an inch wide…or perhaps a tattoo…no, neither.

She couldn't take her eyes off it. It was branded into his flesh. Two arches that crossed over each other. Sweet Lord. Was it a cattle brand? When she'd known him years ago, he had lived peacefully on his family property—the mansion, the stables.

Dylan had been the most robust and wayward of the three bachelors—the youngest, always good for laughter and practical jokes. What on earth had happened?

What was the horrible mark on his wrist? It made her queasy.

Dylan held the canteen toward her and offered her the first drink.

She didn't make a move toward it for fear of what it held. "Poison?"

His eyes flickered. The lines around his mouth compressed. "That's why you think I'm here? To kill you?"

Dylan stiffened with the accusation. He watched Lily as she contemplated him. Her cheek was scratched and bleeding. Dammit, he'd just now noticed. The slender muscles of her throat moved as she swallowed. Her clear blue eyes sank into his. Five hard years.

If she truly thought he was here to do her in, she had a lot of guts waiting calmly for his answer.

To prove his intentions, he lifted his canteen and guzzled the first mouthful.

Then he set it on the grass by her boots and reached for the hidden derringer at the back of his waist. She flinched as it came toward her, obviously once again thinking the worst.

"The gun's for you." He showed her it was loaded. "One bullet. I've got more you can store in your handbag."

He turned the weapon grip-out and she gingerly slid her fingers over the pearl inlay.

"You can use it on me. Or you can hold onto it and pray you never need it. Choice is yours. But if you do decide to blast me, I'd suggest you wait till after I get us unchained."

She pressed her lips together in annoyance.

"Otherwise—" he tugged on the handcuffs "—dead weight."

Then, to her look of shock, he lifted the edge of her dress.

She tried to claw her way up the grass. "No!"

Ignoring her outburst, he found a clean patch of fabric, poured water onto it and patted her bloody cheek.

She didn't fight him; it must have felt too good. She took over holding and dabbing the fabric, closing her eyes in relief. His gaze skimmed over her lifted skirts to her pristine white petticoats and feminine boots.

She saw him looking and he spun his face the other direction.

He studied the stream. No sign of humans behind or ahead of them.

An elk a hundred yards ahead lowered its head to

graze. Behind it, almost hidden, a magnificent herd of a hundred more roamed the pastures. Their coats were glossy velvet.

Lily followed his gaze and they sat for a minute, silent, wondering what the hell to do.

The thin flask of whisky he'd tucked into the inside of his vest pressed against his ribs. He wasn't drinking it, he was using it to rub into his face. The smell always kept people at a distance, so they rarely asked questions and he could keep his cover.

Lily sniffed and turned away, as though the odor bothered her. She lowered her leg onto the grass. "Your father would be proud you opted not to kill me."

"Truly funny." But he didn't care to laugh.

He stared over the distant mountains. They were a mix of grassy slopes, some with shrubs, others just vertical rocky ridges dusted with powdered snow. Without turning his head, he asked her, "I'd appreciate if you did up all your buttons."

She must have looked down, for she let out a soft gasp. Then she hauled his wrist up with her own to fiddle with her blouse.

His hand was a lot closer than he wished it, and he couldn't stop himself from imagining the soft flesh he'd glimpsed earlier. The round swell of her bosom. A peek at the virgin-white lace of her corset. A tiny beauty mark partway down her right breast.

Hell.

Just hell.

It was hard enough working on his own, chasing the Maddock gang hundreds of miles in all directions. How was he supposed to do it with her?

"Enough of a rest?" he asked.

"I've only just caught my breath." She lifted the canteen to her lips.

"At least you can talk and move at the same time now."

She sputtered the water. "No need for insults."

"It's a matter of truth."

"Truth. Is that important to you?"

He slid his teeth together and ignored the question, instead rising to his feet. He dragged her up with him. "All set?"

She gave him back the canteen and peered around his shoulders to the countryside. A cloudless blue sky. The sun was strong. She didn't have a hat and he told himself to stick close to the trees and shade. Otherwise, she'd wind up with one hell of a headache later.

"How far do you think to the nearest cabin?" She peered south, the same direction as the stagecoach had been heading.

"You're looking in the wrong direction."

"What do you mean?"

"Look north. We're going back from where we came. We're going after the Maddock gang."

Horrified, she stared at him. Then she chuckled with disbelief. "Truly funny." She flung his own sarcastic remark back to him.

"We'll follow the river a ways. It's the only clear-cut path leading anywhere. I imagine, with all that gold, they'll want to spend some. There's no civilization in this part of the world where they can spend it. Except Dawson City where we came from. Or White-horse to the other side. Beyond that, there's Alaska, but it's a hell of a journey away."

"Well, I'd like to get where I was going. White-horse. Then Alaska. Skagway, Alaska."

He started moving. She didn't. The chains clinked at their ankles as he pulled her, but she resisted, tugging at the heavy iron.

He huffed. "My moving requires you to move, too."

"There are two of us here. And I vote we get as far away from those filthy animals as possible."

Shoulder to shoulder and thigh to thigh with her, Dylan peered down at the soft bead of sweat forming on her upper lip. Her icy blue eyes glistened with red-hot temper.

"Your vote doesn't count," he said.

With a flash of anger, she opened her mouth and glared.

He crossed his arms, looking straight ahead at the clear water and rounded stones along the shoreline of the Yukon River. He could outlast her. The last five years of his life had been devoted to just that. Surviving. Training. Outlasting.

Her shoulders slackened somewhat. "What made you suspect my bodyguards?"

"It all pieced together."

"What?"

"One of 'em signaled to the other when you weren't looking."

"How come you noticed?"

"It's in my nature, I guess," he said, hoping she'd be satisfied with that.

She exhaled and tried to turn away, but her movement caused the chains to shorten, snapping his leg.

"Stop yanking away like that. I'll topple right over you. You'll get hurt."

She stilled.

The heat of the sun's rays hit his cheek.

She swiped her loose wavy hair with her free hand. "So you're telling me…the stage depot set me up?"

"It's amazing how little money it takes to sway some people."

"Why did you help me?"

"It was either give them the gold or our lives. I made the logical choice."

"It's not logical for some people…you just said so. You recognized me. That's why you came to my rescue. Some stupid sense of guilt."

"Yeah." Let her believe it. There was no sense telling her the truth. He didn't feel guilty about the past. Not one iota. He might be stuck with her, but he'd get his job done in spite of her.

"Wait a minute," she said. "There's a hefty reward for the capture of the Maddock brothers. I saw the wanted posters nailed to every post in town."

"So there is."

"I should've known gold was driving you, too."

He flinched at the insult, but didn't deny it. Allowing her to believe he was after the reward money could help him with his cover.

"They think we fled on horses," he said. "They won't suspect we left on foot. They'd never in a thousand years believe we'd turn around and chase them down."

"Are you insane?"

"There's a lot of brush along the riverbed. We'll go far."

"You're mad! It wasn't your gold, it was mine. And

I say we think of our lives first. I say we go the other way. You take me to Whitehorse and I'll get to Alaska on my own from there. Let the law take care of chasing these men and returning my gold. Rumors are, the Mounties are already closing in."

He was well aware of how close—or how far, depending how you looked at it—the Mounties were on closing in.

"Just like that, I'm supposed to take you where you want?"

"That's right. You're a gentleman and I'm a…a lady trapped by circumstance."

He grumbled.

"You are still a gentleman, aren't you?"

He wouldn't be goaded.

"In case you hadn't noticed," she continued, "I was leaving town for good. Those were my suitcases on the front of the coach. All my possessions."

"And all your gold? All of it?"

She furrowed her brows but didn't answer.

"What's in Alaska?"

"My…my sister."

Her honesty surprised him. He tilted back his Stetson. "Ah, the infamous younger sister I never met. The one solely in your charge. The one you did everything for. Or so you said."

"Amanda. You must have known her name was Amanda."

"And how is…Amanda?"

"Amanda is…she's…she's missing." Lily's thick lashes fluttered as she turned away toward the trickling water. Her square neckline, scooped low and ringed with a sliver of feminine white lace, clung to her breasts.

Despite the harshness of his words, her predicament touched a soft part of him.

"Let's take one thing at a time." He scoured the riverbanks for a thick sharp stone.

Spotting one, he pulled her over. "Stand here. The water's gushing and will cover up the sound."

He arranged their feet and planted a flat rock beneath the chains, then smacked the iron links with the sharp stone.

She flinched with every strike. He set the chains back again and again, smashing down with all his might. Twenty minutes later, with biceps aching, he was almost through the metal.

"A couple more times should do it."

But it needed another seven before the chains finally snapped. She nearly toppled over at the release.

"You all right?"

He let her unwrap the loops of iron first, then he did his.

"What about the handcuffs?"

"There's not enough slack between the links to smash them with a rock. I'll have to think of something else. In the meantime, let's keep walking."

She stayed put. "Not until you tell me what your interest is in all of this."

Not a chance in hell. He'd never disclose himself to her.

He was a Mountie officer. Working in disguise as a drifter and drinker. But secretly sworn to police the territory.

Telling her who he was would not only jeopardize his safety, but hers as well if the Maddock gang caught wind she was traveling with the law.

Dylan ran his fingers over the burn on his wrist. She didn't need to know that, three years ago, Bolton Maddock had ordered his brothers, Kirk and Sloan, to use a cattle iron and brand him like an animal.

Free from the shackles at his feet, Dylan felt his power return. "I'm a lot bigger than you. If I have to, I'll drag you all the way behind me."

He gave her a yank, but blazes, she was strong and wouldn't budge. How long would he have to put up with this? With her?

Chapter Three

Lily glared at the strength in his face and the determination in the set lines of his mouth. Dylan Wayburn may have been rich at one time, but he wasn't anymore.

Now he had to use force, instead of money, to get his way.

She'd been using money herself for the past four months, and it was astounding how much—and who—it could buy. Too bad she couldn't use its power now. Had she lost it all, never to share it with her sister? The thought hit with a pang of sorrow.

Staring up at the hardened man panting down at her, she figured she'd be stupid to put up a fight. With a fling of her skirts, she followed his lead along the riverbed.

He had kicked and shot her two bodyguards without a second thought. He had overrun the other two men with a simple toss of a rock. Yes, she had his pistol weighing down her handbag, but if he attacked her, she'd never be able to reach it in time. Maybe he knew that.

The sun baked her shoulders. They continued walking.

After two hours of silence, her feet were raw inside her boots, her lips parched.

"More water, please." She stopped, and he gave her the canteen.

"You don't seem to care much about your gold."

She stiffened. He tossed insults at her as fast as other men tossed compliments.

"Is that what you believe?"

She guzzled water.

How long had she and Amanda dreamed of striking it rich? Two years ago, when they'd first heard the rumors of a goldstrike in the Yukon, she and Amanda had dreamed of a life full of adventure.

Instead, it had been so difficult last year when they had originally set out. First being tossed back and forth on the ocean to Alaska, retching her stomach contents every time she tried to swallow food. Then her argument with Amanda…the stupid battle…the awful separation. Finally, when it was too late, searching and searching the trails for her only family.

Shame crept up Lily's face. As the eldest, she should have known better. Nine years ago, at fifteen years of age, Lily had been left to care for her ten-year-old sister.

On the trail to Alaska, Lily should have ignored her sister's outbursts and realized the hurtful words were simply the result of not enough food or sleep. Amanda had called her a bully for wanting to continue to Dawson when all Amanda wanted to do was rest in Alaska. She said she'd hated every minute of traveling with Lily and hated the whole country.

After Amanda abandoned her, Lily went on a fruitless search. Despite Lily's despair, what could she do except go on alone? Perhaps, she might eventually run into her sister. In Lily's private daydreams, she fancied all would turn out well. But there'd been no Amanda. When Lily had arrived in Dawson City, she'd panned for gold and struck it within a week.

Now, four months later, as the richest woman in the Klondike, Lily had already witnessed enough groveling and greed to last her a decade. In that short time, she'd received exactly seven marriage proposals. More than a dozen solicitations of sexual favors. *And* they wanted her gold.

She pushed those thoughts away, but then that familiar ache of emptiness gripped her. It usually came at bedtime when she had too much time to think, not in the middle of the day. At night, sometimes blissful sleep came quickly. Other times she lay awake for hours, tortured by her own imagination and wrenching fear for her younger sister, now barely nineteen.

Something about this moment, standing in a territory so vast and untamed and beautiful, emphasized her loneliness. Mountains engulfed their lush valley. Water as clear as ice surged past her boots. The scent of summer grass and moss filled her head.

Was Amanda safe? Did she have enough to eat? If she had succumbed on the trail, Lily wouldn't be able to take the news.

But the rumor about Amanda that had recently come to her ears…dear Lord.

Maybe it wasn't Amanda. Maybe it was another slender young woman with ropes of blond hair.

Amanda couldn't be part of the Maddock gang. She just couldn't.

If that rumor was true, they'd be two sisters on opposite ends of the earth in all the ways that mattered.

Nausea shuddered through her. They'd been brought up in such strict beliefs that everything on the trail, everything improper they had done, including Lily's private transgressions that she would never reveal to another soul, brought a sense of shame. Was her sister living as a heartless criminal? Hadn't it been up to Lily, as her guardian, to counsel her and help her make wise choices?

Lily sank the empty canteen into the clear fresh river water, filled it and handed it back to her savior… or was he her captor?

"Of course I want the gold." She opened her handbag, removed a linen handkerchief, flipped it over her head and anchored the cloth around her hair to protect her from the blistering sun. Her nose was beginning to prick with the heat. Her fair skin could never take much sun.

"I'd like to see them strung up by their heels for what they did to me in that stagecoach. For what they did to the others—the poor drivers and that old couple."

"Yul knows his way around these parts. He'll do fine. The Sawyers can shoot and ride. The driver who fell was only nicked in the boot. Yul will double-back to help. He'll bring him back to Dawson."

Dylan's profile, his wide Stetson, shadowed her face.

"Would you like my hat? The sun might—"

"This'll do fine." She adjusted the kerchief.

Her eyes grew accustomed to his shadow. She craned her neck to study the turn of his lips, the straight nose and the groove of defiance nestled between his eyebrows. The breadth of his shoulders blocked out the mountains. His gold belt buckle glistened in the sun. Still, the smell of whisky wafted over her. He was a drinker, but his eyes were clear and sharp. It baffled her.

"How come you know so much about people?" she asked.

"Like I said. I keep my eyes open."

"But in Vancouver—"

"In Vancouver, I was young."

"Not the last time I saw you."

A muscle at his jawbone flickered. "You still can't forgive me for that kiss."

She puckered her lips, yanked her chained hand from his and trudged onward. There were things in her life she would never talk about again.

He hopped over a boulder and unexpectedly, a flask of whisky slipped from beneath his vest onto her path. The glass bounced off the wet stones.

He laughed in relief as he bent over to reach for it. "Didn't break."

Without blinking, she kept moving, stepping on the glass bottle and crushing it.

"Oh, I'm sorry."

He gaped at it and then her. "Why'd you do that?"

Because she didn't want her life balancing in the hands of a drinker. The clearer his head, the better. Besides, the smell of whisky coming from him was overpowering.

"Terribly sorry," she repeated when he wouldn't budge along. "Dear me."

He groaned, staring at the shards of glass stuck between glossy brown stones. "You broke it."

She gulped and rubbed the back of her hot neck, feeling a tad guilty. Under normal circumstances, she wouldn't care if he drank himself silly. But she was hand-cuffed to the alcoholic. He'd been a big drinker in Vancouver, too, sometimes coming home with his brothers, hooting and carousing so hard they woke the staff.

"I said I was sorry."

"I don't think you are."

She moved along, her shimmering blue skirts skimming over grass. "Let's not make this out to be more than it is."

Finally, he followed when she tugged. "You did that on purpose," he declared.

She sputtered. "Of course. I—I ordered that bottle to fall from your vest. I conjured the image in my mind and like magic, it happened. Let me see…if I close my eyes and think hard, maybe I can summon another stage-coach."

Frustrated, he shoved his Stetson past his brow. For whatever reason, he bit down on his wretched tongue.

Hmmm. She hadn't completely thought it through. She'd seen the flask and had jumped at the opportunity to deprive him of the powerful liquid. But what did she have on her hands now? A drunkard who might go through the shakes? Would he crave the fermented juice? Heavens, might he get violent?

Churning with the horrid possibilities, she trudged along. She could kick hard to defend herself. She'd always been a good kicker at male staff who had wandering fingers.

Twenty minutes later, a thin thread of smoke appeared hundreds of yards ahead. She squinted at the tiny dot on a mountainside. A cabin. The possibility of help perked her spirits.

Dylan brought his firm hand up across her chest to keep her still. He motioned to the clearing ahead. Two of their horses grazed on the slopes fifty paces to their right. It was the black mare and the jittery bay, still tethered together.

Freedom. But she and Dylan were handcuffed. How were they supposed to capture the two mares?

She turned back to the cabin. A new fear trembled through her. Perhaps the people inside weren't friends, but enemies.

Moments later, Dylan heard Lily's stomach growling from hunger, almost as loud as his own. On this trek, having horses could mean the difference between exhaustion and survival.

Dylan leaned into her temple. Her hair was moist with heat. "Follow my lead. Don't say a word."

She nodded.

Calmly, Dylan walked out from the trees, not focusing on the horses, but staring off to the side. Lily glided beside him, careful not to make their handcuffs click together. The black mare noticed immediately. Her ears twitched. She raised her head. The bay turned her face in their direction, too. Skittish, likely still upset by the gunfire and overturning of the stagecoach, the bay reared then galloped.

The black one startled, too. They tore off, tied together.

Dylan's heart jumped. Sweat pooled at his neck. Had they lost them?

He didn't react. He would allow the mares to calm down on their own.

He hummed as though he hadn't a care in the world. As though he and Lily were simply hiking through the woods, or perhaps pitching hay in the stables where the horses might have been accustomed.

Lily walked beside him, her head lowered toward the ground, pretending she was marching with purpose toward the slopes.

From his periphery, Dylan saw the horses stop a hundred feet away.

Dylan ripped out some tender shoots of grass. He passed them to Lily. She took them, seeming to know instantly what he intended. He collected more and then slowly approached the horses. Still humming, he walked past them then circled back, holding out the feed.

"Why, you two are tied together just like we are," he murmured to the black mare. He slid closer but still didn't lock eyes.

Lily held out the grass and the bay edged toward the gift, her nostrils twitching in the wind as though wondering how the people had come to be here, too.

When the mare crunched down on Lily's offering, Dylan and Lily stopped moving. He didn't immediately reach out to grab one, but allowed the horses to grow accustomed to human presence. His shoulders strained, ready to jump the animals, but instinct told him to go slow.

The bridle was just three feet from his left hand, but

it was the hand shackled to Lily. Would Lily have the finesse to follow his lead and go gently?

If they botched this attempt, the horses might startle and never return. Dylan read Lily's posture, the way she leaned into him a few inches, alert to her surroundings. She was waiting for him to make a move.

Gently, he raised his shackled hand, Lily lifted her arm gracefully with his, and he grabbed tight to the leather strap.

He smiled. Job well done.

He patted the mare's neck. "Well, now. Good afternoon."

Lily beamed, stroking the bay's nose. "It's good to see you again. Sorry about the commotion. It's over now."

They stood entranced by the animals for several minutes, getting reacquainted.

"We did it, Lily," Dylan held out the last of the grass. They had a chance, now, of catching up to the Maddock gang, of surviving the relentless wilderness.

Creases at the edges of her eyes indicated her relief and good humor.

It was the same smile that had captured him in Vancouver. As a young man, eager for female company, he had watched as one of the new kitchen servants, fifteen-year-old Lily Cromwell, six years younger than himself, served the rolls and marmalade. Breakfast had been her specialty.

He used to rise early and be one of the first down the stairs just to see the shy, gentle smile that dimpled her left cheek, but not her right. To see her blue, blue eyes and vivid red hair that caught the sun. Just to watch when she bowed her head, before she averted her gaze altogether to indicate she realized she shouldn't make eye contact with the Wayburn household.

With the Wayburn boys.

Now, as they stroked the horses in the strong Yukon sun, she averted her face as she always had.

"Whatever happened to Harrison?" she asked gently.

His heart rippled with sentiment.

"He was married last year."

She turned to stare at the mare's forehead. Freckles on the bridge of Lily's nose deepened and the lines around her soft pretty mouth strained, but those were the only reactions he detected.

But she couldn't look him in the eye, could she?

He steeled himself against the same flood of jealousy that always washed over him at the mention of his oldest brother.

She'd been so in love with Harrison.

But then, hadn't every young woman been riveted by Harrison's charm? They had all flocked to Harrison. The dances, the dinner parties, the riding groups in the country. But in the end, Harrison only had eyes—apparently—for the pretty breakfast maid who was never allowed to look at him directly. He'd compromised Lily in such a shameful way, letting her believe that marriage was approaching between them, kissing her in the library where anyone could walk in. In fact, their father had, and Harrison then denied any promise of marriage.

He knew she'd been shattered.

Dylan had privately beat the tar out of his older

brother for that. And then, when Lily had turned on Dylan because of *his* unexpected kiss, he and his father had had such a row, it had been the final factor in his decision to leave British Columbia.

"Who did he marry?" she asked.

Dylan supposed she couldn't help her curiosity. He watched her slender hand as it slid along the horse's reddish-brown coat.

"Annabelle Ainsworth."

Her lips trembled.

His heart roared.

It took a moment before Lily spoke again. "Lineage traced to Queen Victoria. He did well."

"Harrison always did well. Mostly at other people's expense."

She bowed her head and said no more.

Miss Lily Cromwell had been his family servant. Dirt poor. She came from generations of servants. Everything she'd made of her life now, she'd done on her own.

Such a far cry from his own wealthy heritage— parents who'd come from England, holding deeds to properties before they'd even set foot on Canadian soil.

Now their fortunes were reversed. He was living off the land like a penniless drifter. She was Klondike Lily, with more gold than he could ever comprehend.

Except that the Maddock brothers had just stolen every glittering ounce.

Chapter Four

How could they possibly defend themselves while bound together? Lily's stomach rumbled again, but hunger was the least of her worries. They had to face whoever was in the cabin, but their wrists were handcuffed.

Dylan scoured the landscape for something to pick the lock with. Lily trudged up the slope toward the nearing cabin. Her thighs quivered with the strain of having walked for hours. The horses stomped beside them.

The sun had moved slightly in the sky, indicating it was close to dinnertime.

"Hold on a minute," said Dylan.

They stopped beneath a line of spruce trees a hundred yards from the ramshackle cabin. It was roughly sawn, nails visible, square porch weathered by the elements. Neatly done, considering the lack of materials available. The yard, however, was a jumbled mess of stray parts, wooden slats, cast-off iron bits.

They seemed to be inventions of some sort, but roughly detailed, a contrast to the squarely finished house.

Pots stacked in one corner, two straw hats tied together with a bright orange sash, a bathtub stained with mud. Bathtubs were a luxury this far north, for almost everything had to be carried over the mountains by the sweat of someone's back. Paddle wheelers came through in the summer months along the river, but a bathtub, well, was sheer luxury. How could anyone let it seep with filth?

Dylan walked a few steps and picked up a wire brush. He ran his fingers along the bristles.

"Too short and soft to pick a lock."

He picked up a wooden box, stamped Canned Peach Preserves. Its wire lid was too thick to use as a key.

A few more steps brought them to a chicken coop. Oh, Lord, did the occupants have hens? She smiled and braced for the possibility of eating fresh eggs.

Lily looked around the cabin. No sign of poultry. She exhaled with disappointment.

There was, however, a mule grazing in the acre beyond the cabin. It hadn't spotted them. Livestock were a treasured commodity, for many died on the mountainous trails getting here.

Dylan yanked her shackled wrist up to his waist. The wire from the coop's door fit straight into their lock. Hallelujah! He gave it a twist. Metal grated on metal.

"Hurry," she said.

"I'm trying." He kept twisting, looking nervously from the lock to the cabin. She slinked behind Dylan's wide shoulders for cover. Trees blocked them on one side.

"Is it working?" she whispered, her stomach pulling with nerves.

He gave it one strong push and the lock released. She yelped with relief.

He tugged the cuffs off their hands. She rubbed the red welts on her wrist.

"How's your arm?" he asked.

"Sore but happy."

A rifle cocked behind them. Loud and crisp.

A tremble of fear ran through her. She and Dylan slowly turned toward the cabin.

An old-timer with slicked gray hair, gold spectacles, white beard and plaid shirt stood on the porch aiming a barrel straight at them.

They raised their arms.

"We don't mean no harm, mister," said Dylan. "We'll be on our way if you just lower your weapon."

"What are you stealin'?"

"Nothing, sir. We…we got robbed ourselves and know how that—"

"Robbed?" The man lowered his rifle to his waist and scrutinized Lily. She shifted uncomfortably beneath her showy dress. "Where?"

"On the stagecoach coming out of Dawson."

"Son of a bitch. The Maddock gang?"

"Yes, sir."

"You or your wife hurt?"

Dylan paused. His forehead creased with concentration, then, as if making a decision, his dark face lightened.

Was he going to let the old man assume they were married?

The old man squinted. "I said either of you hurt?"

Lily swallowed. Perhaps if she answered, the man would be kind. "No, sir."

"How'd you get away?"

Dylan spoke boldly, much more truthful than she might've been. "Shot two of 'em from the stagecoach. When we stopped, I knocked over the coach and crushed two more. One of the passengers—a smart old guy like yourself—had a pistol and said howdy to the fifth."

The man chuckled real hard. "And the other four bastards?"

He knew a lot about the Maddock brothers. He'd just confirmed there were only four left in the gang. Same ones she and Dylan had seen riding over the crest.

"They got away."

"Goddamn." The man lowered his rifle. "Pardon me, ma'am, for the rough words." He whistled with admiration at Dylan.

"There were two others inside who turned on us, guards hired by the stage company. I don't believe they were part of the gang directly."

"The smart old guy had a pistol, huh?"

"Yup. Pulled it outta nowhere. Just like that old gent Buckley Hicks in—"

"*Stagecoach Outlaw.* I read that son-of-a-bitch book!" He smiled. "Pardon me, ma'am."

She didn't mind his language if it meant he was warming up to them.

He set the rifle down and leaned it against the porch.

She nearly fell over from relief. Or maybe exhaustion.

Sunlight glinted against the left lens of his spectacles but not his right. Something was not right.

"Sorry about the odd welcome," the man said. "But you know firsthand what it's like around here."

Dylan nodded and pulled her closer. He cupped her shoulder protectively. His touch was soothing. She thanked heaven this man, whoever he was now, knew how to handle a gun and pick a lock.

"I reckon you folks must be awful hungry. Caught myself a deer last night. Way too much meat for one man. Care to join me?"

"Mighty kind of you." Dylan hitched their horses to the trees in an area of sweet grazing grass.

She inhaled the fresh breeze and peered over the tumbling field of colors. Wild grasses mixed in a palette of greens—emeralds as rich as gemstones, lighter greens the color of lime, and deep rich ferns. Mountain flowers budded in hues of peach and white. Purple fireweed sprinkled the river's edge where the mule stood, staring at them.

They hopped onto the porch with renewed energy.

The old man extended his hand to Lily. "Otis Forrestor."

"It's Lily."

"Howdy do, Lily."

The men shook.

"Dylan. Dylan Jones."

The surname was a lie but she didn't blink at Dylan's statement. Besides, she was too captivated by what she saw on the older man's face.

Mr. Forrestor wore circular, gold-rimmed spectacles, but his right lens was missing. He must have broken it somehow. The poor man could only see properly through one eye. She took a quick glance at the junk in the yard. That would explain the slipshod workmanship on the inventions. He'd probably still had both lenses while building the carefully hewn house.

Here, months away from civilization, there was no place to buy new specs.

She wondered how he'd lost the lens, but felt it would be too forward to ask. Dylan likely felt the same, for he didn't mention it.

Mr. Forrestor held open the screen door. Lily moved toward it, her blue skirts swishing about her ankles. Dylan glanced down at the rifle.

"Shouldn't you take your gun inside? You never know who else might come calling."

"Nah," said the old gent, waving the air with his hand. "It's got no bullets."

"So how'd you nab a deer with no bullets?" Dylan asked an hour later as he, Lily and Otis—as the old man insisted on being called—finished their meal. It filled Dylan's hollow stomach and he was grateful for the hospitality.

"Patience, my man, simple patience." Otis stretched his legs beneath the hacked pine table. Golden sunlight streamed through the window above his shoulder. "Three hours of sitting in the woods without flinchin'."

"Goodness," whispered Lily, awestruck. She stared at the man with fascination. An inventor by trade, he'd told them.

The inside of his cabin was just as jumbled as the

outside. A bookshelf overflowed with intricate items that Dylan figured were for farming or mechanical use. The place smelled of kerosene and lubricating oil and rusty chains. The smells reminded Dylan of the shack back home beside the stables. It brought him a smile.

Lily placed her fork on her plate. "The venison was delicious. Thank you."

"You like that, little lady?"

Lily nodded. "What are all these things around us?"

Otis picked up a piece of wood looped with a braided cord. "This here's a rope line for drying clothes. For the trail. All you need are two trees, but you can set up seven lines if you follow the tags I've marked here."

"Seven. My." She took the smooth wood from his hands.

"You can have it. Present from me to you," he insisted.

"I'm honored," she said, coaxing another smile from the gent.

"And here's one for you." Otis picked up a hard leather case grooved with a picture of a pipe and passed it to Dylan. Dust from the leather wafted over the table.

Dylan opened it to reveal a pipe. "It's a beaute. But I'm afraid I don't smoke. Not many places to buy tobacco."

"Look a little closer," said Otis.

Dylan picked up the pipe and took a good hard look.

Otis chuckled. "You missed it."

"What?"

"Open the second layer."

Dylan gently lifted one corner. It revealed a glistening hunting knife with serrated edges. He whistled.

"For the road," said Otis. His meaning was clear.

Lily shifted on her chair, rubbing her cheek with nervousness. It was nothing she had to concern herself with, thought Dylan. He would take care of it. "You whittled the pipe and cut the knife?"

"Yes, sir."

Dylan closed the case. "With all your skill, it's a shame you can't craft another lens for your specs."

"Of all the stuff I can do, I can't do that. Say, you wouldn't be carrying any eyeglasses, would you?"

Lily shook her head.

"'Fraid not," said Dylan.

"I broke the lens the day I finished nailing the porch. Up came the hammer, straight through the glass."

Lily winced. "It's a good thing you didn't take out your eye."

"It was bruised for days."

Otis glanced at their tin cups, filled with clear river water. "Care for some stronger stuff?"

"No," said Lily jolting forward. "My…husband's had quite a long day."

"That's when men need it most."

Otis and Dylan shared a smirk.

"Wouldn't mind a taste," said Dylan.

Lily's fingers trailed down her temple. "Don't you think, dear husband, that it may knock the feet out from under you? We've got a long way to go tonight."

"Where exactly are you folks headed?" asked Otis.

"Skagway—" declared Lily.

"Dawson," said Dylan.

Dylan stretched out on his chair, clamped his hands at the back of his head, determined to show no signs of backing down. She gripped her tin cup and sipped her water, even more stubborn.

If she thought he was here to do her bidding…

"I was married once." Otis strummed his fingers on the table. "Same thing. She always said one thing, I said another." He scratched his rough bristles. "Lord, I miss that."

He got up to reach for a flask of golden liquid.

Lily anxiously tapped her foot on the floorboards. What did she have against Dylan taking a drink? He grumbled. She was acting like a wife, all right, wasn't she?

She frowned. "Pardon?"

"I didn't say anything."

"Yes, you did."

"Nah-ha. Not me."

"You said something about me acting like a wife."

He pretended to be interested in the leather case, running a finger along the shiny edge.

She fussed with her skirts and addressed their host. "Did you leave your wife behind when you came north?"

Otis bent over a shelf and pulled out two mismatched shot glasses. "Nah. She up and died on me."

"Oh…I'm so sorry."

"Thanks kindly. It was many years ago, but feels like yesterday. Left me with a son. A good man. We came north together."

"Does he live with you?" Dylan accepted an empty glass and smiled in her direction. He was going to drink with or without her approval.

There went that tapping of her foot again.

Otis shook his head and poured. "No, but he pops in now and again. His business takes him back and forth across the mountains. He visits when he can. Travels a lot to Skagway."

Lily leaned forward. "So you have news of Skagway?"

"Some. Whaddya wanna know?"

Dylan knew what. News about her sister.

Otis finished pouring the whisky.

Lily's disapproval was evident in the stiff angle of her shoulders. Well, at least they were no longer shackled together. He couldn't put up with much more of her in close proximity. This was close enough. In fact, too close.

Otis touched her billowing blue sleeve. "It's not the real stuff, ma'am. Ran outta real whisky three months ago."

Overcome with disappointment, Dylan poised the shot glass in midair. "Then what's this?"

"Strong cold tea. If I drink it from a shot glass and close my eyes, I can almost taste the real goods."

Lily's smile at Dylan felt like a stick to his eye. "Quite an imagination," he said to his host.

"My son says that's why I'm an inventor."

Lily stacked the dirty plates from the table to the counter. She was circling Otis. She wanted something more. "So, sir, what's the news in Alaska then?"

"Last I saw my son was several months ago, so the news from Skagway is old."

"I'd like to hear it anyhow."

"Incoming ships are slowin' down. A lot more stampeders are headed to the new gold fields in northern

Alaska. Most of the land in Dawson's already been claimed, so it's harder for a fella to strike it rich."

"Or gal," Dylan corrected him. He eyed Lily with amusement. She didn't appreciate the insinuation, apparently, for she preferred to be discreet about her wealth. She hadn't identified herself as Klondike Lily to the old man.

"About the businesses, sir," she continued. "How're they doing? Women in particular, how do they manage?"

"Women, eh? There's a lot of gold coming in from Dawson, but nothin' much to buy. More merchandise than there used to be, but as soon as the ships come in from the mainland, they're sold out within hours. It's hard on the women. But they're strong. Some of 'em are opening shops of their own. Can you fathom that? Laundry houses, cafés, that kinda thing."

"The Maddock gang," said Dylan. "Anyone spot them in Alaska?"

Otis swirled his whisky-like tea. "They travel quiet. There's rumors of 'em goin' back and forth to Skagway."

"You said your son carries supplies back and forth. Does he worry about getting robbed?"

"Not since he hired a few men to protect him."

"He must be doing well for himself."

Otis stretched out proudly. "He got his mother's intelligence. My looks."

Well, didn't that make Otis chuckle. Dylan toasted the old guy with his shot glass, then swigged the tea in one smooth gulp. He coughed and sputtered till his eyes watered. It tasted vile.

"I ain't seen anyone down it in one shot."

"Tastes like…like…" Dylan squeaked.

"The rear end of a buffalo?"

Lily rolled her eyes.

Otis closed his and sipped. "Great stuff."

Her skirts swished around their chairs as she tidied. Her bosom swelled as she bent over Dylan's plate. Dammit. He tried to glance away, but she caught him and clutched her neckline as if it was his fault. But she was doing the advertising.

Lily implored the old man. "Have you heard of any women who travel…who travel with the gang?"

What was she getting at? She wavered at the counter. The plates clattered and she jumped at the sound. "I mean, I heard rumors."

"You got a particular interest?" Otis ran a hand along his rough britches. "It strikes me strange that any woman would be willing to go with any one of them. Haven't heard."

Lily cleared the remaining utensils. She wiped her hands on a hanging apron and turned to Dylan. "Time we get going."

Otis looked alarmed. "You're not stayin'?"

"I'm awful tired. By the time we make camp—"

"But I want you to stay here."

Dylan weighed the benefits in his mind.

"You could get a good night's sleep," Otis urged. "I'll rustle up breakfast in the morning. You can stay longer, a few days if you like, but if you insist on leavin' tomorrow, you could get an early start from here. Right from here."

"Sounds good," said Dylan. "We stay."

Lily sputtered. "Shouldn't you discuss this with your wife?"

He and Otis chuckled and dismissed her comment.

She crossed her arms and swirled her tongue against the inside of her cheek, as if holding back an explosion. Did she honestly think she'd have a say? He was on duty! He didn't take orders from her.

Otis rose to show them the bedroom door. "I guess you don't have any bags or blankets. There's a couple you can use in the bedroom."

"Bedroom?" Lily wheeled to the door. Her lips paled.

"Sure." Otis adjusted his broken eyeglasses on the bridge of his nose. "You don't expect me to let you sleep on the floor out here, do ya? You two are welcome to the room. I'll take this spot by the stove."

Dylan rose. He kicked back his chair with enthusiasm. Or was it delight at seeing her squirm? "Let's go, darlin'," he said cheerfully. "I'm tired, too."

Chapter Five

Lily's stomach clenched as she walked through the bedroom door. What on earth was she getting herself into?

She lifted her skirts and petticoats over sacks of flour, between shelves filled with scraps of iron in shapes that made no sense to her, and finally found her footing between the narrow bed and single window.

Light streaked through the windowpane, a pane made of oil-stained paper due to the absence of precious glass.

Dylan closed the door. His height and width filled the doorway. Honestly, he made her feel cramped no matter where they were. Stagecoach. Kitchen. *Bedroom*.

She gripped her moist palms together. What was she doing alone with a man? Granted, he wasn't a complete stranger and he *had* saved her life. But it had been many years since she'd known Dylan, and these were such extreme circumstances.

She struggled to grasp the implications. "Why don't we just tell the man we're not married?"

"It was his mistake to begin with. Why correct him? After tomorrow, we'll never see him again." His white sleeves rippled beneath his suede vest as he surveyed the half-finished inventions on the shelves. "It's better we muddy our trail. If the Maddock gang catches wind that we've stayed in the area, Forrestor saying he put up a married couple will attract less attention. Otherwise, we're a single man and woman spending the night together."

Heat rushed up her face.

Embarrassed, she pivoted to look at something other than his dark, sculpted face. Her hair fell across her shoulder. Annoyed with it, she pushed back the thickness, but then her foot slipped and she toppled backward over a pile of rope. Such a collection of rubbish.

She held out her hand for a boost. He ignored it.

Dylan whistled at the piles. "He sure has some good stuff."

Lily snorted at their difference of opinion.

While she struggled to rise on her own, like a flailing fish on shore, Dylan admired the cords and twine. "Where'd he get all this?"

She tried not to look at the bed, but it pulled her gaze like a nickel to a magnet. It wasn't really a bed. More a sack filled with straw from the fields, with a coarse linen cover that likely scratched the skin. Pillows were yellowed from wear.

"I said, he's got enough flour to bake a hundred loaves."

"Oh." She whirled around to face Dylan, her lips tight. What must he think of her daydreaming while staring at the bed? "Right. Lots of flour."

God bless Otis for offering his bed; she knew it was the best he had. But the wrinkled sheets and pillows would need a good wash before she set her head anywhere near them.

"You can have the bed," she said with a pretend air of truce.

Suspicious of her offer, he anchored a hand on his lean hips. Sunlight caught the bristles on his cheeks, painting them gold. "There's enough room for two."

She gasped, then noticed his sly grin. Such talk to an unmarried woman! Even though she wasn't…even though no one knew…

She tore another blanket off the shelf, one old pillow that she would cover with another sheet to keep her face clean, and nudged her way through the flour sacks to clear a spot on the floor.

He watched her with curiosity. "I don't think that haughty nose of yours could get any higher."

Well!

"Sure you can handle the floor?" His dark velvet eyes glimmered. "You're a rich woman now. I bet you haven't slept on anything so hard in months."

"Ha. Ha."

Scoundrel that he was, he motioned to the bed. "Look, we could squeeze together. You against the wall, me against—"

"Please!"

He gaped at her with mock innocence, spreading a large square hand over his chest. As if he, with the intense expression and mischievous glint, could ever come across as innocent. "The question is…would we lie face-to-face, or face to back?"

She squealed inside. A trickle of perspiration slid beneath her hairline. It was best to deal with a cad as though his seductive words didn't affect her. "My preference would be foot to face. My foot to your face."

"Foot to face?" He put his finger on his chin and stared at the bed, as if imagining the position. Making her nerves twist all the more.

"Yes." She placed a hand over her neckline and her prickling skin, trying to cover any hint of blotchy skin his improper words elicited. "That way I could kick you when needed. And believe me, the need would come."

"Yes, foot to face." He nodded in agreement, shaggy hair thick at his temples. "Just think how our body parts would align—"

He didn't duck in time for the hurling pillow that smacked his head.

Hours later, Lily tossed onto her right side, digging into the blankets. The floor smacked her hip. She rolled onto her stomach with a loud exhale.

"You all right down there?" Straw rustled as Dylan leaned over to stare at her. She tucked the sheet under her chin to conceal that she'd stripped down to her cotton shift. She wore it over her corset. And she was never removing that.

"Couldn't be better," she replied sweetly. She rolled back onto her right side, away from him, and her right breast was nearly strangled by the binding.

"Was that a groan?" he asked.

"Pardon? Are you speaking to me?"

"I thought we were the only two in here."

"I thought we were trying to sleep. Not talk."

"Your groaning is keeping me awake."

"Stuff some of that beautiful rope in your ears."

Silence, then he yammered, "It's a good bed. A little on the soft side. But after all that walking we did, it feels good on my legs. Like a cushion made from a cloud."

"Yes, well, I thought you might need it more than me."

"Kind of you to think of me. It feels good on my backside, too, but don't go dreaming about that. A man has his pride."

She giggled into her sheet. And thought about his backside.

He was sleeping bare-chested. Lord only knew what *he* wasn't wearing down below. She was facing the stacks of flour now, but earlier she was staring at the muscled crevice of his bicep. The angle of his shoulder blades. Smooth, golden skin that went on for inches and inches. Rich sand-colored hair that skimmed his naked shoulder blades.

She squeezed her eyes shut. Sleep. Must get sleep.

"It's not too late," he whispered in the stillness. "You could have the bed."

"Lie back and enjoy. No need for you to feel guilty that you got the good spot and I got the floor."

"Guilty?" He laughed softly. It echoed against the rafters. "No guilt on this end. I'm worried if you don't rest up, you won't be able to keep up to me again."

This time, she tossed her high-heeled boot.

She heard a soft thud.

"Is that a yes?" he asked. "Does the woman follow the boot?"

Exasperated, Lily shoved her shoulder into the bedding.

His laughter was gentle. "Night, darlin'."

Dylan took pleasure in the sound of a woman breathing as she slept.

He rolled onto his back and stared up at the ceiling, listening to the wind lapping at the trees, the call of wolves and the gentle reminder that she was near.

Lily had finally fallen into slumber. The sun was lower in the horizon, but still lit the room softly. The gentle rhythm of her breath lulled him. He hadn't shared a room with a woman in a long time.

He'd shared plenty on his travels, but no woman who could carry a conversation for more than a few hours, not like Lily. The women he'd known had been friendly faces, appreciative of his attention, eager to follow him if he'd wanted that, eager to move on without him if he didn't.

But a woman with grace? With intelligence and dignity?

Never mind, he told himself. He was on a paid mission by the Mounted Police to bring in Bolton Maddock. Being distracted by Lily wouldn't serve anyone's purpose. Least of all, his.

His gut tightened with apprehension. If he ever came face-to-face with that criminal again...would he be able to control the months, the years of rage that was simmering inside of him? Or would he lash out at the man who'd tortured him?

Lily wiggled in her sleep. Her sheet came lose. Perhaps she'd given up trying to hide her body in this warm room. Her body reacted to what it craved. Coolness.

Her shoulders were rounded and creamy, as though they'd never seen the sun. If he had his sketchbook with him, he'd outline the turn of her shoulder. The blades at her neck. The hollows of her throat and swell of her bottom lip. And where the sheet half-draped over her chest, he'd draw the dark and light shadows of the rise of her cleavage struggling to escape the rigid white corset.

She moved again, exposing more. She spilled out of one side of her corset. Her nipple appeared. His body came alive, rushing to match the beat of his heart. She aroused him more now than she ever had as his servant.

And there was nothing he could damn well do about it.

"Rise and shine!" Otis beat his metal spoon against the bottom of what sounded like a cast-iron pot, on the other side of the bedroom door.

Lily jarred awake. Where was she?

It took her a moment to recognize the room, the bed next to her, the sheet around her waist.

"Oh." Embarassed at her visible breast, she snatched the sheet to cover herself, then looked up in Dylan's direction.

He hastily turned away. How much had he witnessed?

He muttered above her head and her pulse subsided. It sounded as though he was just waking himself.

The smell of fresh bread baking in the oven wafted through the room. She moaned with appreciation.

Otis hollered through the door. "How'd you like a frying pan full of bacon and eggs? Some corn hash to go with it and mouth-waterin' flapjacks with syrup piled so high you couldn't finish eatin' till tomorrow?"

"Yes, please." Lily smiled into her pillow.

"Yeah, me, too." Otis chuckled. "But all's I got is more venison and bread."

Dylan laughed softly as Lily sagged with disappointment.

"Rise and shine!" Otis banged his spoon and pot again. "I've got a proposition for the two of you!"

Lily rose on an elbow. "Why does he insist on talking to us as though we're children?"

Dylan, his hair rumpled from sleep, twisted that naked torso of his, making her pulse beat too fast, this early in the morning. "It's his house."

"I feel like my eyes closed only moments ago."

"You slept the whole night through."

How did he know that? She clutched the sheet closer to her chin and debated how to change into her clothing while maintaining her dignity. Not only that, she wondered, from the sheet brushing against her bare nipple, when exactly during the night had she fallen out of her corset? Mortified, she groaned.

Dylan threw back his blankets, revealing a pair of drawers that went midway to his muscled thighs. And a smooth bare torso.

Her ears turned hot. She quickly rolled to her other

side. He hadn't even had the decency to warn her so she could look away.

She heard the rustling of his pants as he yanked them from the crate above her head, then as he tugged into one leg then the other. His boots slid along the floor. She heard what sounded like the buttoning of his shirt. Then the door creaking open.

"The room's all yours."

It took her a few minutes to rise, stretch and don her blue blouse and skirt again. She tried to smooth out the wrinkles, and wondered how long she'd have to wear the same clothing. Surely they'd come upon a place where she could buy something, anything, or barter with a passing stranger. She did, after all, have something of value tucked into her secret spot.

She had no hairbrush, so she clawed her fingers through her hair. When she opened the bedroom door, Otis and Dylan glanced up at her.

She cringed at how unkempt she must look. She'd never exposed herself to company without washing her face. Why must Dylan stare at her?

"Over there," he said, pointing to a washstand with fresh water and towel.

She cleaned up and joined the men for breakfast.

Otis came right to the point. "I'd like to go with you."

She set her warm slice of bread back on her plate. Dylan set down his hot tea—Otis was out of coffee— and leaned back in his chair.

"Very kind of you, sir," said Lily. "But we're really not prepared for...for assisting an elderly gentleman."

"I can hold my own."

"I didn't mean—"

"I can walk twenty miles a day without blinking."

"Certainly, I can see—"

"And I can tell you more about the Maddock gang." He turned to Dylan. "That is, if you plan on looking for 'em."

Dylan stopped chewing. "Go on."

"The way I figure, you must've had somethin' mighty valuable for them to stop you. I figure you might be lookin' for a way to get it back."

"What's in it for you?"

"Little bit a company."

Dylan remained silent. Surely he didn't think they could take the gent, as neighborly as he was, across hundred of miles of bush and mountains.

"Look," said the old man, slapping his britches. "I need bullets. And I need to buy some new eyes. It's hard for me to travel on my own with busted glasses. On the other hand, if I stay here, I'm a sittin' duck. I know this land and know the folks on it. If you want that kind of information, if you need a guide, I'm your man."

Dylan bit into his bread. "Sure. Fine by me."

Lily scowled. Neither man had even bothered to seek her opinion. Again. "Am I invisible to you both?"

Otis nibbled on a piece of bread, as though he was a schoolboy who'd been reprimanded. "What about your wife, here?"

About time! She opened her mouth to voice—

"No need to ask her," said Dylan. "I'm the husband." She nearly spit!

Perhaps Otis sensed the hostility, for he tapped her

hand in a gesture of peace. "Those questions you asked about Skagway. I do recall a place that was being built that a lotta folks were talking about."

Lily leaned in close. "Yes?"

"A bathhouse for women."

"What sort of bathhouse?" Dylan finished his hot tea.

"Not *that* kind. An honest-to-goodness mountain spring and spa. Just for the ladies. Set up by some widow from Norway or Sweden or someplace crazy like that."

Lily smiled. "Mineral springs. I've heard of them in Europe. Some in California."

Otis began packing some of his kitchen utensils as Lily and Dylan rose to get their things.

"My son knows her," said Otis.

Dylan wheeled around, a wall of muscle and sinew. "Your son sure gets around. What's his name?"

"They call him Champagne Charlie. You know him?"

Dylan whistled in amazement as Lily tried to recall the name. "Son of a gun," said Dylan. "Champagne Charlie's father." He shook the elder's hand with new respect. Otis smiled so wide the gap between his bottom teeth doubled.

Light from the window poured into the cabin, taking the chill off the furniture. Otis continued packing, sorting through utensils.

Lily had heard of Charlie, but never met him. He was one of those enterprising men who'd made a fortune in the Klondike. Not by striking gold, but by catering to the ones who had. Supplies were so limited in the north that the men who'd struck it rich were dying to spend their money, but they had nothing to spend it on. Champagne Charlie sold luxury items. He and his bodyguards carried porcelain tubs over the mountains into Dawson City, along with crates and crates of champagne.

Then the very rich and elite soaked in the heated, bubbly alcohol. It was a decadence unheard of in her former life.

That would explain the stray bathtub in Otis's yard. Perhaps he hadn't really wanted it, but it was a gift from his son.

"How's Charlie doing, since his accident?" asked Dylan.

Otis leaned against the counter and rubbed his jaw. "Haven't seen him. Would like to. Two weeks ago, a stranger passed by and told me how…my son broke his leg."

"I saw Ch—" Dylan stumbled, as if he wanted to say something more but changed his mind. "I heard he's got a permanent limp, but at least his leg was saved."

"I'd like to see it for myself, and I believe he's headed to Skagway for more tubs. Another reason I want to go with you. He's such a stubborn man."

Dylan shifted his powerful set of shoulders. "Wonder where he gets that?" Sunlight struck the firm muscle of his cheek.

Otis chuckled.

"He could use the waterways."

"Yep. Yep, he could." The old man slid his gnarled fingers around the handle of a pan. "Might be on his way to see me right now in some canoe." With a change of heart, he plunked down the pan. "Maybe I shouldn't be leavin'."

"A man with broken specs and no bullets," said Dylan, "can't survive long. You said so yourself."

Dylan's quiet manner made the man's eyes sparkle with renewed vigor. The weary shoulders lifted. Lily marveled at Dylan's ability to soothe this gentle spirit.

Otis shooed them out of the kitchen. "Folks, have a look around. Take whatever articles might be useful for the road. By the time I get back, I might be robbed blind anyway."

Lily gasped in delight. It was one offer she'd be mad to dismiss.

She found a bar of soap flakes, tooth powder and an extra toothbrush, a hairbrush, rolls of cotton gauze, a bolt of fabric she might be able to use as a skirt, a sturdy wool blanket, a heavy sweater and an oilslick coat. Otis offered his spare clothes, too, but they were little more than rags, so she declined. She did, however, find a brown felt cowboy hat that would shield her pale skin from the sun.

She didn't see all the things Dylan chose.

Two hours later, they headed out, Lily and Dylan on their horses, Otis on his mule.

Otis had lent them two saddles. They were intended for the mules and were rather short, but would do under the circumstances. Dylan had put soft wool blankets beneath the saddles so they wouldn't rub against the mares.

They followed the tributary to where it joined to the Yukon River. Gushing waters churned in turquoise colors. The rich smell of loam and artic moss rose around them. The golden sun flashed above them in a heavy blue sky.

A cool breeze lifted Lily's hair, which she'd pinned back into a long tail beneath her new cowboy hat. Muscles of the mare shifted beneath her thighs. She patted the bay's neck. The horse snorted and settled.

Lily was comfortable around the big beasts, as she'd spent much of her time away from her duties as housemaid watching the stable hands, and had often sought solace over the sudden death of her parents on a long ride with a gentle mare. She was still terrified of house fires, seeing how a raging fire had robbed her of her parents, but then, there was so little a town could do to fight fire, that most folks were terrified of it.

Horses never asked questions and didn't expect to be treated like royalty, as some families she'd worked for had. Members of the Wayburn household, for instance.

Dylan eased in beside her, a bulk of restrained muscle. Why did he have to be so masculine? Everything about him turned a woman's eye, from the matted forearms to the way he cocked his mouth. "I'd wager you've tried one of Charlie's bathtubs."

"Then you'd lose your money."

He pulled back on the reins of his horse. "That so?"

"I'd never pay five thousand dollars to soak in a tub."

"A drop in the bucket for Klondike Lily."

"I heard most of Charlie's customers are men."

"'Cuz there's so many more of them."

"Then maybe you're the one who's bathed in champagne?"

Dylan reared back his head and laughed. "I'd rather drink it."

"I recall. A champagne flute, filled precisely two-thirds full of the squeezed juice of two oranges, topped with champagne."

He winked. "Only on special occasions."

"Every Saturday morning."

"My brothers enjoyed it more."

She studied the field of grass to their right and the circling hawk above them whose dark expanse of wings sailed beneath the sun.

She twisted in her saddle and dipped her head under a coming branch. "I've already asked about Harrison. How's your other brother? Wilson?"

Dylan's gaze lowered to her open neckline. "Makes his living as a minister."

She spun so quickly her skirts bunched around her knees. "You're fibbing."

"I'd never fib about a man of the cloth. He saw the way of the Lord almost five years ago."

"But you and he…"

"Yeah?"

"All those late nights…the drinking till you could no longer stand…the young women and the dances."

"Not much use for dancing out here."

"You danced around Otis pretty well. Never gave him one straight answer about yourself. Or me."

Dylan laughed again in the same charming way she remembered. It started low in his chest and rumbled up his throat. It had always changed the way every young woman over the age of fifteen felt about him—one of the mighty Wayburn bachelors whose amusement of life and love was intoxicating.

Lily was engulfed by the inflection of his tone, the

delightful sparkle in his eyes and the sheer madness of Dylan Wayburn.

She caught her breath and turned away to the rutted path before them.

They reached a stricture in the road and she fell behind again, allowing him to lead, grateful for the separation.

Otis called out from behind. "The last I heard from Charlie's men, the Maddock gang is staking out in a camp above Skagway. Someplace in the mountains."

Dylan turned in his saddle, the breadth of his shoulders blocking the width of the path. "Which direction then?"

"Take the left fork," Otis hollered. "We're comin' to a wood camp. We can eat and rest for a bit."

Dylan steered his horse to the left, and as they made their way toward the campfire and huts, Lily tried to ignore how much each of the Wayburn brothers had changed, and how far Dylan had fallen from the grace of his family.

His two brothers had made much of their lives. Why was Dylan so different?

Chapter Six

"Did Wilson try to help you sort out your life? Since he became a minister?"

Dylan was surprised by her question. He watched the shadows of the trees move across her face. "How so?"

"I mean," said Lily, astride her horse as they neared the camp, "you…you are down on your luck, it seems, not a coin in your pocket. Making your living chasing reward money from dastardly—" Flustered, she broke off her sentence. "Lord only knows how deep your drinking problem goes."

She stared hard at his profile, making him uncomfortable. What was she looking for? Tremors to his hands? Shakes? Look how damn earnest she was. It was rather amusing, how little she thought of him.

It was none of her affair what he was doing with his life. They were a world apart and would never see eye to eye. He had best remember how easy it'd been for her to turn her back on him, when he could've used a kind word directed to his father.

He turned away and kept his grip steady on the reins.

A hundred yards up river, strangers, two bearded men, stopped chopping wood to stare at the three newcomers. Dylan waved a hand in salute and they did the same.

"Actually," Dylan told her, "I tried to help Wilson sort through his life."

Astonishment caused her to still. The cowboy hat she'd tilted back on her head framed her wide blue eyes and expressive face. Why did he enjoy surprising her? Her lips parted and the flush on her cheeks deepened.

They reached the log cabins—two huts, a supply shed, a roadhouse with its chimney pumping smoke, as well as the aroma of fresh coffee. A wood sign was burnished with the words Steephill Roadhouse, Strangers Welcome.

Every fifty miles along the river, a wood camp sprang up to service the paddle wheelers that navigated the waters. Tons of wood was needed to keep their boilers stoked.

While Dylan and Lily surveyed the camp, Otis dismounted and hitched his mule to a cottonwood ringed with iron hoops just for that purpose. Dylan slid off his horse and did the same.

He made his way 'round to Lily's side, but he'd forgotten how good she was with horses.

With confidence, Lily swung one leg off her saddle, giving him a nice glimpse of her calf. He couldn't turn away from the alluring view.

Back in Vancouver, she'd always ridden in skirts, too, barely finished her hours in the house when she burned for escape on the horses. Now, he watched the slender hands play along the mare's coat. She whispered something into its ear. The mare responded with a gentle nudge and was rewarded with another pat on the nose. Dylan wished Lily would reward him, too.

But how different she was, compared to that fresh young woman she'd once been. What had caused the changes? Was it simply the lure of gold that had caused her to turn her back on her younger sister, caused her to wear such revealing clothes, caused her to speak back so directly to him?

"How could *you* have helped a minister?" she asked.

There it was again, her blunt approach. Didn't she believe him capable?

"He wasn't sure whether to follow his calling."

"And *you* told him how to follow the Lord?"

"No. I listened, night after night till he sorted it out himself."

She lifted her eyebrows.

"How about you?" he asked. "What truly happened between you and Amanda?"

She jerked her head away, as if she'd been caught doing something unworthy and couldn't meet his eye.

Disappointment weaved its way through him. He had no right to feel it, but somehow he'd hoped for more from the beautiful and enchanting Miss Lily Cromwell. More courage, or loyalty to her sister.

One of the men chopping wood hollered, "Howdy!"

"Come for a cup of coffee," Dylan replied.

The man adjusted the broad strap of his overalls. "Cook's inside. Go right in."

The thud of the axes ricocheted off the trees as

Dylan, Lily and Otis sprang up the stairs and into the roadhouse.

The place was dimly lit, warm and smoky. A thick man, as white and sweaty as a strip of half-fried bacon, greeted them. When they settled onto the stools at the bar, he poured their coffee into dented pewter cups.

"Any news to pass along?" His mustache glimmered in the daylight streaking through the windows.

Behind him, their order of canned ham and fried evaporated potatoes sizzled on the griddle.

Otis chomped down on a wad of jerky. "The Maddock gang's around. Keep your guns close."

The cook's hand shook so bad on the pot of coffee he had to set it down. "They get anyone?"

"Robbed these folks here. Took everything."

The cook looked to Lily, who bowed her head over her meal. "Sorry to hear it, ma'am."

She removed her hat and nodded.

"What news can you share?" Dylan lifted his elbows off the counter as the cook slid platters of heaped food at them.

"Not much. Paddle wheelers will be passin' through soon."

"When?"

"Never can predict what day. Sometimes they need a day or two to get out of a batch of mud."

"What direction? Alaska or Dawson?"

"Both."

Lily nudged Dylan's elbow. She whispered, "Don't you dare think about returning to Dawson."

As Otis occupied the cook with questions about the

steamboats, Dylan leaned in to Lily. "What makes you sure your sister's in Alaska?"

"Because it would be just like her to find a job at the women's bathhouse. In Vancouver, she worked as a maid for three years in the upper chambers of the Ladies Society. She's well-skilled."

He waited for more, but that was it. That was all she was going to tell him. He pretended to be satisfied, but it was his right to know more. After all, *he* was helping *her*. She was tagging along on *his* trip.

They finished their meal.

"Much obliged." Dylan lifted his hat to the cook and they left the cabin.

Lily excused herself and used the time to wash up while Dylan and Otis explored the camp. Later, she went in search of Dylan and found him watering the horses. She held out a man's white shirt. It looked clean and unworn.

"What've you got there?"

She beamed a smile. "A new shirt for myself."

"How'd you manage that?"

She stumbled. "Umm…the cook. He had an extra."

There were no such thing as extras in this part of the world. She'd either bartered it or bought it. He doubted she'd trade away any of her own scarce supplies, which meant she'd bought it. Which meant she was holding out on him. She still had money or gold.

Good for her.

Otis snagged his mule's reins but the animal wouldn't budge. "Bessie needs a longer rest than your animals. Go on, take a walk or somethin'. I'll look after your horses. Meet you here after one good stretch of the legs."

"Sure," said Dylan. The old man led his mule a ways down the river as Dylan touched Lily's shoulder. It sent a ripple through her. "They tell me there's a waterfall up ahead. Care to see it?"

She nodded and they made their way through a path of long-needle pines. He tried not to notice the sway of her hips, the slender pinch of her waist, the sweet intake of her breath.

He looked away from her and through the forest. The sound of gushing water thundered beneath his boots.

They turned a sharp corner. Light hit her bottom lip. Beads of moisture formed at her temples. The bounce and wave of her hair framed her shoulders and cascaded down the tip of one breast.

They didn't speak, almost as if they were in a reverent place. He'd always thought there was no place closer to God than in the solitude of the wilderness. At least he did a few years ago, when he still believed in the Almighty.

They turned another corner and the waterfall appeared. It gushed clear glacier water high from the tip of a gray cliff. The dew hit their faces and made Lily laugh.

"Are you wet?" He reached out to wipe her cheek.

She quieted beneath his touch. He let his hand linger, tracing her cheek with his thumb, sliding his hand down along her throat, grazing her soft neck.

He flipped the pins from her hair and let it fall on her shoulders.

She didn't stir as he entwined his fingers into the soft strands. Leaning forward, he inhaled the scent of her hair, her neck, her throat.

Then finally, inches from her mouth, Dylan did what he'd been aching to do since he first saw her.

* * *

When Dylan caressed her cheek and ran his thumb over her bottom lip, Lily's breath swooped. Her senses deepened. The call of the birds grew louder, the scent of the pines stronger. She could almost taste the sweet moisture of the waterfall that misted their faces.

He lowered his head and pressed his lips to hers. Stunned, she allowed him. The gentle pressure of his mouth coaxed her to respond. Softly at first, then more urgently. The heat of their lips slid against each other and warmed every part of her body.

What happened to her resistance?

She wondered about this man, how many women there had been between their first disastrous kiss in Vancouver and this one. There *had* been plenty of other companions; she could tell by his confident reach, in the way he didn't ask but simply took. She wondered what sort of trouble he was in—and why she didn't simply turn away.

More shocking to her was how much she wanted him to just take what he wanted. As hard as she tried to tell herself to resist, it thrilled her when his eager lips sought her submission.

When he wrapped his arm around her shoulder and lowered the other one along her spine, her pulse soared. She stepped closer, rising on tiptoe, pressing her body full against his. Her corset seemed to tighten around her breasts. Her nipples brushed against the whalebone ribbing. Her belly dipped and looped, as though she were on a full-tilt gallop she couldn't control.

When his large hand slid up along her ribs, gripped her waist and inched toward her breast, she gasped and stepped away.

A familiar voice behind them startled her. "Don't let me interrupt," Otis hollered. "Just wanted to say I'm ready to leave."

Lily's cheeks flared with heat. To be caught by this nice old man in the arms of a drifter. She looked to the ground and listened as the old man's footsteps faded.

When she looked up again, Dylan's face was flushed, his brown hair streaked gold by the sunshine. His eyes held hers, deep brown waters of light and dark.

"I don't know you anymore," she whispered. The kiss in Vancouver had been rough and demanding, this one gentler, but demanding in a more subtle manner.

"I apologize." He pressed the back of his hand across his mouth as though he might erase her touch. "It's not what I came here to do."

"Why did you come?"

He made no move to answer, so she did.

"You're a bounty hunter. After my gold, like every other man I've met since striking it."

"You have no gold. Do you?"

His words caused an instant rise in her anger. How dare he speak to her as though it was his business. How dare he assume such intimacy to ask about her finances. It always seemed to come down to how rich a person was, in how well they were treated. Why hadn't he and his family respected her in Vancouver, when she didn't have a dime and it was her word against Harrison's? If she told Dylan anything about her gold, how safe would she be?

"That's none of your bloody business, is it?"

With a swirl of her skirts, Lily turned and left him.

Chapter Seven

Why did her silence bother him so much, Dylan thought nearly two hours later.

It would make his life easier if she never said another word. Then he'd be free to concentrate on his duties without having to tiptoe around a difficult woman who'd lost her gold, that for some stupid reason, he felt obligated to help. He should have left her behind with Otis. She would have been relatively safe.

Maybe there was still time to ditch her.

The kiss had been a mistake.

She pranced around with that eager inflection in her voice, finding pleasure in simple things such as patting her horse or sinking her sights into the pretty view of the rapids as they rode along the river. She didn't know anything about the seedier side of life; the one he fought every day. She wouldn't know anything about men like Bolton Maddock who found satisfaction in torturing the men who tried to stop him.

Perhaps it was better she didn't. Dylan had taken an oath to uphold the law, and it sickened him to see what some men were capable of; perhaps it was best that folks like Lily never knew such cruelty existed.

Dylan pulled his sleeve over the scars on his wrist. God help him, for he was planning to repay Maddock for killing his two friends in Alberta, and everything else Maddock had ever done.

Being distracted by the softness in her would only weaken Dylan. After all, it had once before. It would give Maddock the advantage.

Dylan took a deep breath of pine-scented air and rocked in his saddle as his horse found its footing down a minor slope.

"My wife and I used to argue somethin' bad," Otis said to him.

He sighed. The old man had it all wrong, but it was part of Dylan's duties to work incognito. Most days he never blinked at lying to people, but for some reason, guilt shot through him at deceiving this tender gent.

Otis cleared his throat and blinked several times. "I'm no expert on marriage. But can I give you a word of advice?"

Dylan clenched his jaw. "Why not?"

"Learnin' to apologize when your wife's still around—" there was a soft catch to the old guy's voice "—might give you some comfort when she's not."

Bolton Maddock stood at the four gravesites, dark head bowed in the hot sun. His fingers dug into the brim of the hat clutched at his side as the minister said prayers. The fully loaded guns on Maddock's hips weighed him down. He fancied the heavy feel of them.

They'd waited a day and a half for the holy man to arrive here in the wilderness, but Maddock hadn't wanted it any other way.

While the seven others in the group prayed for salvation, Maddock prayed he'd find the stranger who'd done this.

"And now," said the pale minister, lifting his arms to the endless Yukon sky, "we pray for the souls of Kirk and Sloan Maddock. We ask God that all four men rest in peace."

Fury beat through Maddock's chest. Bile raced up his throat. "Amen."

It was time to bury the dead.

Two others of his men, Big Al and Roper, took up the shovels and threw dirt into the holes. The pine caskets began to disappear beneath the weight of the earth. Maddock felt the weight as if every scoop was hitting the back of his sweaty neck.

Scrape, toss, thud. He was going to kill the bastard.

Scrape, toss, thud. He would squeeze the living air out of him.

Scrape, toss, thud. What would dear Ma say?

He had promised her on her deathbed that he'd take care of his younger brothers. Hadn't he provided? Hadn't he, at the age of twelve, shown his brothers how to survive in the city streets by any means they could? He clenched his teeth and hung his head in shame.

There was no hidin' from his ma now. She'd be greeting Kirk and Sloan in the heavens, and judging him from up above, shaking that terrifying white finger of hers.

He'd find the cruel son of a bitch who'd done this. He'd tear out his heart the way his own had just been ripped out.

Boots trampled the ground around him as his three men drew to his side.

"Sorry, boss. My sympathies." Big Al wheezed. His asthma was working up, due to the digging.

Slick Willie returned his leather hat to his skinny head. "Mighty hard for a brother to lose one of his own."

Wild-haired Roper nervously yanked on the sleeves of his denim jacket while thinking of something to add. "They would've appreciated the minister."

Useless words.

Maddock raised his hand against the sun to shade his eyes. "Did you find out any more?"

They trembled when they answered.

"No one's seen his face 'round these parts before," said Big Al.

"Light brown hair," added Slick Willie. "Built like a gunman. Drifter, someone said."

"And the others with him? The stage drivers? The old couple? Klondike Lily?"

The men shifted their gazes, no one eager to give him the news. "Not—not a trace," Roper finally stammered.

Big Al nodded goodbye to the minister as he was led away by the two homesteaders who'd brought him. Maddock snorted. The minister hadn't had the guts to shake his hand so long. How could the minister be terrified of him, a grieving brother? Some folks were hard to figure out.

Maddock made his way around the trees to the makeshift camp the four men had been sharing for the last two days. In addition to their horses, they'd captured two stray ones from the runaway team and stolen four others from folks on the trail. The beasts would be loaded up in the morning with the gold tied to their backs. At least they'd retrieved that.

Maddock walked to the iron crate of glistening rocks. "What do you figure happened to the red-haired woman?"

"We're not sure, boss. We don't know if Sloan and Kirk managed to tie her up in shackles, or if she rode away alone."

"So she might be with *him?*"

Big Al wheezed and nodded.

"We'll ride out in the morning," Maddock ordered. "I want you to hire nine more guns to join us. Me and a dozen men should be able to track down this animal."

Roper gasped. "Nine more?"

Maddock's glare flew to the straw-haired man he had been kind enough to take care of for the past year. He was weary of the man's constant complaints. "That's right. You know how to count, don't ya?"

"But where in hell are we supposed—"

Maddock's right eye twitched. A slice of cold regret cut through him.

"By tomorrow?" Roper continued to contradict him. "Jesus, I—"

In one smooth grip, Maddock found his gun, aimed

it at the undeserving Judas and blasted a hole through his chest. Big Al's sleeve got splattered. He wheezed so hard his face grew red.

"Make that ten more," said Maddock. "Me and my twelve disciples."

"I'm no expert on marriage, no sirree." Otis squatted by the river's edge and scaled a trout. Lily watched his eyes move from her face to Dylan's. She felt sorry for the old guy, trapped in the middle of a five-year feud he knew nothing about.

Dylan added more branches to the fire, ignoring the ramblings of Champagne Charlie's father in much the same manner she was trying to ignore Dylan. She pushed the thought of his kiss out of her mind. He could keep his lips and his opinions to himself.

"I'm no expert, but what I do know is that you two young-uns need to find yourself a lonely rock in the hot sun."

"Huh?" Lily found some forks in one of the saddle-bags.

"You know," Otis explained. "Warm enough to strip down to the skin. Me and my wife could never have an argument buck naked."

Dylan pretended he hadn't heard.

Lily's eyes popped with embarrassment. She rushed to the saddlebag Otis had lifted off his mule to find a frying pan.

"Of course, she would always try to win the difference of opinion. It's only natural, she *was* a woman." Otis dipped the fillets into the bucket of clear water by his boot. "But with both of us naked, there was always a lot of wigglin' and jigglin' going on. Once that started, I'd cave to anything she asked."

Dylan turned from the fire, unable to keep the grin from his lips. "I could see how that might work." When his eyes narrowed over her blouse and down her skirted thighs, she tossed the frying pan toward his feet. He dropped his sticks and caught the dang thing in midair.

Otis laughed. "Hey, you're a pretty fine catch."

Lily stomped away to find the canteens.

"How can you be mad at this young fella?" Otis's voice called after her. "He saved your behind in the stagecoach. He's gonna cook us up a nice meal. Why, I reckon if you ask him with that pretty smile of yours, he'd do just about anything for his wife."

She waited a few hot moments in the cool forest before re-entering the boxing ring. Dylan's back was turned at the fire. He was placing the fish into the pan, cowboy hat tugged low to block the smoke, crouched with his long legs turned toward the flames.

Thankfully, Otis changed the subject. "Do tell me. What would you folks do if you struck it rich?"

Lily nestled back on a stack of logs. "Why do you ask that?" Had Dylan told him how rich she was?

"It's a form of amusement 'round these parts. Most folks come for the gold. I'm wondering how you'd spend yours."

Dylan slid the pan over the fire. It sizzled immediately and within seconds, the wonderful aroma of frying fish—beloved food—filled the air. They didn't have to worry that their fire would be seen—it was still daylight.

"You first," Dylan told Otis.

"All righty." Otis squatted on a granite rock.

"I'd buy myself a dozen pair of eyeglasses so I'd never run out. Two jars of licorice sticks. And what the hell, a cabin full of whisky."

Lily tucked her skirts beneath her rear end and repositioned her high-heeled boots in the dirt. "I'd buy a kitten."

It was the first thing she'd tried to buy with her gold, but domesticated cats in the Klondike were nearly impossible to find. She'd also wanted to build a cabin of her own, but it would've left her totally unprotected from thieves, so she'd stayed in the local hotel instead. There was a store she wanted to open, and other folks she wanted to help, but her first priority had been to find her sister. Now it seemed she might not have to worry about how to spend her gold, if it was gone.

Dylan looked over from flipping the fillets. His hat shielded the sun's orange rays and cast a shadow on the bridge of his nose and his etched jaw. "A kitten?"

"If I could find one. I mean, I haven't seen one since…since Vancouver."

Otis pushed back on his worn out bowler hat. "A kitten would make good company."

Lily kicked at the pebbles by her feet. "It gets lonely here an awful lot."

Otis splayed his hand over his chest. His shirt was stained from wear. "And you, sir?"

Dylan watched the flames lick the bottom of the pan. "There's nothing I need."

"That's the point," said Otis. "It's not what you

need. You'd be filthy stinking rich," he said to their laughter. "What would your heart desire?"

"I'd like to share a nice meal in a nice restaurant with the woman of my choice."

Otis assumed he meant her, but she knew better.

"You could buy your wife a lotta meals." The old man washed his hands in the river and came back to dry them in the grass. He turned to Lily. "Your hard-shootin' husband's got a soft heart."

Maybe it was the humorous conversation, maybe it was the glacier-fresh air, maybe it was the warm endless sun on her face that made Lily smile and temporarily forget about the problems that plagued her.

"Name something more extravagant, both of you," Otis demanded.

Dylan stood up, keeping an eye on the meal, but coming closer and jamming his hands into his pockets. The guns on his hips swayed. "You like this game, don't you?"

"Played it a lot."

Lily dove in eagerly. "I'd buy a theater hall and hire the best actors and actresses to entertain me. Just for me and my friends, whenever I wanted."

"Wow," said Otis. "I like that. Good-looking women up on stage. Good music. Lots of whisky."

They watched the fire dance, each contemplating the wonderful dream.

"I'd buy canvases," said Dylan. "Charcoal and paper and paint."

Otis scratched his head. "For painting a house?"

"Different kind of painting. I used to sketch a lot. Portraits. Landscape. I miss it." He looked down at his fingers, stretching them out. "Keeps my fingers limber for the trigger. But there's something about capturing the turn of a lovely cheek…or mixing the perfect colors of a stream."

Lily stared at him, dumbfounded.

Otis seemed to sense she didn't know this aspect of her husband. "Ma'am, how long have you two been married?"

"Just a few days." She blurted it before she gave it any thought.

"Lordy! You're newly wed! Land's sake, here I am taggin' along on your honeymoon. No wonder you weren't sure you wanted me along. Don't you worry now, I'll just disappear tonight."

"No, please," she said.

Otis was already leaving with his bedroll. "Make myself comfortable a hundred yards up the river. You two don't have to worry 'bout me."

The gent rambled on as Lily studied the fine turn of Dylan's fingers. She wondered if the branding on his wrist affected his grip on charcoal. She never knew he had the talent of an artist. She'd never seen that part of him. Was he the one who'd drawn the sketch she'd once found while cleaning the library? She'd always thought the magnificent depiction of a runaway herd of wild mustangs had been drawn by his talented uncle, who painted commissions, but now she suspected the bold, clean strokes of the charcoal belonged to this man.

"Night all!" Otis shouted as Dylan's dark eyes settled on hers, making it hard to breathe. "Enjoy the evening!"

If he only knew that Dylan wasn't paying her any attention, let alone anything as intimate as marital relations.

Her dearest wish was to be rid of these confines and to find herself in Skagway. To avoid the hardship of this stewing stranger she didn't seem to have anything in common with.

Chapter Eight

The sleeping arrangements weren't exactly what Dylan had anticipated when they stopped for the night to camp. True to his word, Otis tore off like a lightning bug to another neck of the woods, no matter how much Lily implored him to stay.

"Please, sir, you're not a pest. We'd tell you if you were!"

Trudging through the woods, Otis and his sleeping roll were already obscured in the distance. "I'll make a lotta noise before I bother you in the morning. Sleep well!"

Dylan found the two of them amusing.

Lily, fidgeting like a schoolgirl, turned back to the fire he was building. The flames shot to the level of his waist and warmed the front of his legs and chest.

She unrolled her blankets—another gift from Otis before they'd left his cabin—at the farthest end away from Dylan.

"So then," she said, nervously picking at the lint on

the wool, "you agree the best place for us to head is Skagway."

"Since that's where Maddock makes his camp, yes." He thought his decision was obvious, since that was the direction they'd taken this afternoon. Maybe it was just nervous chatter on her part.

"Thank goodness we finally agree on a destination."

The sun was close to setting. Late August now, the days were no longer perpetual. It was roughly ten o'clock. They'd have golden light till midnight.

She removed her boots and slipped under the gray wool as quickly as she could.

It must be hell, he thought, trying to sleep in a tight corset.

"You could take it off," he said, facing the fire. "I won't look."

"Take what off?"

"Your underthings."

He heard a soft gasp of surprise. When he looked her way again, she used her blanket to cover her face right up to her eyes. And didn't answer him.

"Suit yourself," he mumbled.

When he got the fire roaring to a steady flame and had piled some logs he'd use during the night to stoke it if he awoke, he slid into his own bedroll.

"Aren't you going to take off your boots?" she asked.

"Nope."

His boots were a line of defense. If he had to jump up in a hurry to fight off an animal, or even worse, a thug with a gun, he had to be prepared. His Colts were tucked beside him.

"Suit yourself," she mumbled.

He listened to the popping wood in the flames. The hoot of an owl. Then something wriggled on the ground beyond his head.

Lily bolted up from her bedroll. "Did you hear that?"

"Just an animal."

"Not a snake!"

"They don't come this far north."

"But something *slithered*."

"It's not as big as a bear. You'll be fine. Relax."

"Relax?" She huffed, peering through the woods. Her auburn hair spread heavy over her shoulder, the waves framing her profile. Smooth cheeks glistened in the warm fire's glow. She pursed her mouth.

"Put your head back on your blankets and close your eyes."

"Close my eyes? Are you mad?"

The corner of his mouth lifted as he watched her from his bedroll. "Your movements will attract more attention."

"That's it!" She leaned over, reached for her handbag and pulled out her derringer.

"You're frightening with that thing." But he chuckled softly. With the feminine swoop of her waist, the way her corset lifted her chest, the way her soft hips angled beneath the covers, she looked about as intimidating as a gentle doe.

Sighing, she clutched the derringer and lay her head back on her makeshift pillow. With her weapon clutched next to her face, she gazed at him, just six feet away. They faced the same direction.

"Lily, tell me about your sister. What's she like?"

A quiet came over her. Her mouth stilled. Her eyes shimmered. "That's the first time you've ever asked me about Amanda."

"Maybe I should've asked sooner."

"Hmm."

"When's the last time you saw her?"

"Last year when we came into Skagway. It was not the best voyage. I was seasick all the time, and Amanda…well, she was so young. Just eighteen."

"I know your folks passed away in a fire, but how did it happen? I've never heard the details."

"Ours was a small cabin. I was sleeping in the loft. I took Amanda with me. We liked to pretend we were living on our own."

"Where did it start?"

"The kitchen. The stove, the officials thought."

"You smelled it while you were sleeping?"

"Amanda did. She woke up screaming."

He waited for her to take her time.

"By that time…by that time it was too late to use the stairs. I broke…I broke through the window and we climbed onto the roof…and my parents…they found my father at the bottom of the stairs. My mother was right behind him."

"Trying to get to you."

"If we hadn't slept in the loft, maybe we'd all still be alive."

"Or maybe you'd *all* be gone."

She didn't speak for a minute. Then softly, she said, "I don't know why God took them."

He searched for a way to comfort her. "Maybe that's

not the way to look at it. Maybe it was God's hand that saved you."

Sometimes, he could see God's hand so clearly in the path of others, but not his own.

She nodded softly.

"And when you got off the ship in Skagway, what happened?"

"We had a rip-roaring argument about how long we were going to stay in Alaska. I wanted to keep going as fast as we could to Dawson. She was tired. She lost her will to travel." Lily's voice was almost inaudible above the fire. He strained to hear it. "Amanda left me while I was speaking to the captain about accommodations in Skagway. I never saw her again."

"That must've been hard."

"I searched every hotel. I waited by the docks every chance I got. But the people…the masses and masses of people…"

"And no way to connect with each other. No telegraphs. No railway trains. No horse trails."

"I waited exactly one month and then thought maybe she went on to Dawson City without me."

"Did she?"

"I don't know. I never found her."

"And you struck gold on your own."

"Yes, I did. It's been the saddest time of my life."

He was caught by an unexpected bout of sympathy. The richest woman in the Klondike. If only people knew how her troubles didn't end with wealth.

And look at him. Was he any better?

What did folks see when they appraised him? The drifter and alcoholic didn't bother him, for that was a farce of his own doing. But beneath that, the Mountie in him, what did his colleagues see?

A man eager to track down the man who haunted him, at any cost to his private life? Forsaking everyone he cared about, his family and friends, in pursuit of a vicious criminal, incognito and lying to everyone he came in contact with. For however long it took.

As he peered out in the dimming light, he wondered about the Mountie troops who'd been given the word to help him. Where were they?

And where was God's hand in all of this? Where was God when he was being branded with a heated cattle iron?

The bushes behind them shook.

"Ahhh!" Lily leaped up from her bed, derringer in hand, and aimed it at the bushes. "Get out of there, you damned snake!"

Dylan was already up and beside her. He lowered her weapon as the vermin who'd caused the rustling waddled out from a pile of brush.

"A beaver," said Dylan. "Don't shoot. He's unarmed." His laughter ripped through the air, much to her displeasure.

"Well, he sounded like a snake."

"The nerve. Maybe you *should* shoot him."

She scowled as the beaver made his way along the river, broad tail bobbing behind him. Then as he dipped into the cool waters of the Yukon, she saw the humor here, too. She joined in Dylan's laughter.

She lowered her deadly weapon, tucked herself back into the blankets, and instead of turning away from him, faced him squarely, as though they were friends.

He took pleasure in the outline of her hips, the draping of her silky hair, the dimple in her cheek as she smiled.

Dylan couldn't remember the last time he'd shared a laugh with a woman. Maybe it had been a while since she'd laughed, too.

In the following days, the small gains Lily had made in breaking through Dylan's reserve were lost again as he withdrew into silence.

Otis, true to his word, came barging into their camp every morning as though his britches had caught fire. The gent was amusing in his insistence that he didn't want to interrupt any marital relations. He yelped and hollered and then usually broke out into some crazy song she'd never heard before to announce his coming.

"Don't mind me, folks. Just here to rustle up breakfast."

They usually ate a lean one, then doused the fire, packed the animals and rode for three hours. When they stopped for lunch, Dylan tended to the horses first, making sure they were watered and fed. In the evening, he tended to the campfire while Lily worked the meals. There wasn't much too different she could do with biscuits and jerky, but Otis was awful good at fishing, and Dylan was a genius at snaring rabbits.

They met no one along the wooded trails till the second day. Then two men on a huge raft floated by, headed for Dawson City. They were loaded down with two tons of supplies to sustain them in the wilderness. The Mounties at the border demanded the supplies, because so many stampeders in the early stages of the gold rush had died of starvation.

"Howdy!" Otis hollered across the water.

"How do you fare?"

"Watch out for the rapids a mile downstream," said Dylan.

"Any news of Skagway?" asked Lily.

"Still there!" hollered the older man in overalls. "Soapy Smith was gunned down last month!"

The three of them on shore gasped in shock. Everyone had heard of Jefferson Smith. He was the crook running the town of Skagway by bribery and murder. Or he *had been*.

"Did they catch his whole gang?" asked Dylan.

"There's still sortin' it out!"

"There's a wood camp and roadhouse two days travel down the river," Dylan told them.

"Much obliged."

They were gone.

Another group of six, this one with a married woman on board, floated by later in the day. They stopped to chat on the shore and Lily took out a pebble of gold from her secret supply to buy two tins of coffee.

"Oh, Lordy," said Otis when he saw it.

"How'd you manage that?" Dylan looked her up and down, as though suspecting she was carrying gold or money.

"Friendly persuasion."

"Right," said Dylan, disbelieving. "All you had to do was ask."

She felt a tad guilty but it was *her* gold. None of his concern.

They continued for two more days. The hum of the

insects, the chirping of field birds, the scurrying of rodents kept her distracted most of the hours. It got so her eyes and senses were so attuned to the outdoors that she could spot a circling hawk at two hundred yards, and discern the weight of a passing animal merely by the sound of cracking branches. A heavy thud meant raccoons, a nearly inaudible crunch meant squirrels or mice.

And when everything went silent, when Otis stopped humming and the horses stilled, she knew *he* was in one of his surly moods. Inevitably, she'd turn around to see Dylan in his saddle, rubbing the wrist with the awful marks on it, stretching up to assess the trail and the sky ahead, his dark face reverting into such a tormented silence she could barely look.

There was more to his wanting to track down the Maddock gang than his wanting to find her gold. Whatever reward money he would get, and she'd insure he got a lot, there was a depth to his vengeance that was beginning to terrify her.

On the third evening, Lily couldn't bear his brooding any more. She turned the rabbit on the spit, the heat of the fire singeing her face.

She watched the flames flicker against Dylan, sitting close by.

Shadows of orange painted the stubble on his cheeks. His dark lashes tilted toward the rabbit. His mouth, rigid with concentration, formed a hard line.

She wore the shirt she'd bought at the wood camp, knotted at the front, over her skirts. Her corset strained to contain her bosom. The whalebone ribbing bit into the flesh beneath her arms. She'd like to heave the damn thing across the river. Maybe that, and her annoyance at Dylan's silence caused her to snap.

"You know, a lady likes a bit of conversation now and again."

Otis, coming at them with a full tin cup, pivoted and walked away. "I'll go see how Bessie's doin'!"

"See what you do to him?" she asked when Otis left.

"I'm not doing anything to anyone."

"You're not talking. It's unnatural."

"I'm not here to entertain you."

"You're not here to displease me, either. I'm the one who's going to pay your reward money, remember?"

Dylan snapped his face up so quickly, his hair grazed his shoulders. Her stomach trembled.

"I've—I've come to a decision. Since I'm headed to Skagway for my sister and you're headed there to chase the Maddock gang, I'd like to offer ten percent of my gold as a reward. If you find it."

He blinked. "How 'bout twenty-five?"

"Twenty-five? That's robbery."

His jaw stiffened. "Suit yourself."

"If you say that one more time, I'm going to strangle you. If…if I were to give you twenty-five percent… you'd have to help me locate Amanda, too."

His dark eyes studied her. Emotionless.

She, on the other hand, could barely control the throbbing of her heart. The squeezing of her ribs…or maybe it was the dang bloody corset again. "Is it a deal then?"

"Deal."

"Tell me what's the matter," she said. "You've

met up with the Maddock gang before. You have. I know it."

"They've crossed the line with a lot of folks."

"But what did they do to you?"

No answer.

"Did they rob you? What did they take? Your horse? Your home? Maybe *your* gold? Did you have any?"

"No."

"Then what? What did they take? What? Tell me."

His voice was a deep rasp, the rough emotion in it so overpowering it gripped her heart. "My dignity."

Bolton Maddock devoured the peameal bacon and fried evaporated potatoes as though he hadn't eaten for a week. Beside him, Big Al gulped his coffee. The two of them had ridden into the wood camp alone so as not to raise suspicion. The rest of the gang—and the gold—was a mile behind waiting for his next order.

"Mighty fine grub," Bolton told the unassuming cook behind the counter of Steephill Roadhouse.

"Supplies came in last week from the paddle wheeler."

"When's the next one comin' through?"

"Any day now, going in the other direction. Toward Skagway."

It'd be an easier way to travel, thought Bolton, than horseback. "Those folks who passed through days ago—the young lady with the red hair and her husband. Which way did they head?"

"Why are you so interested?"

"She's my cousin. We lost track of her in Dawson and somehow got split up."

"Ah. There's a lot of those sad stories in these neck of the woods. Business partners break up. Brothers turn on each other. Last week, I heard a woman askin' her husband for a divorce. Can you believe that? A divorce!"

A vein throbbed at Bolton's temple. "Some folks have to learn to control their tempers."

"What's the sense of pinning dreams on a pile of yellow rock if you wind up miserable?"

"Right. And my cousin, Lily?"

"She and her husband and their friend Otis are headin' to Skagway."

Bolton's chest constricted. He missed an intake of air and had to regain his rhythm of breathing. He gulped his coffee. He was close. He could almost smell them.

Chapter Nine

Dylan tried to suppress his worries, but every time he caught sight of Lily, whether she was patting the nose of her bay or leaning over a pan frying trout, fear took hold of him.

He was having dreams—nightmares—that Maddock might show up out of the blue, point a gun and take her. It was what Dylan had been brooding over for two days, and something he couldn't discuss.

It was clear Maddock had wanted her for more than her gold. Over the years, Dylan had worked to solve several murders in his police duties, and if a criminal needed a person dead, they usually were.

In Lily's case, Maddock had ordered her chained instead.

Why?

Dylan almost didn't need to ask. All you had to do was look at her.

Lily straightened from leaning over to wash the supper dishes at the riverbank. Her hair, the color of red wine in the setting sun, danced around her shoulders. She'd removed her corset, Dylan noticed with a blast of surprise. Her breasts were more rounded, softer as she moved. When on earth had she done that?

"Why are you staring at me?"

"I was wondering a few things."

"Anything you want to ask, be my guest."

While she washed, he dried. He took the wet frying pan from her and shook out the water droplets. "Anything?"

Flustered by his intimate tone, she wiped her hands on her apron and anxiously glanced over her shoulder.

Perplexed, Dylan followed her gaze to the woods. There, in a hidden corner, she'd strung up the clothesline Otis had given her, and hung some of her more personal articles.

"Hey, those are private." She pivoted back to the water, knelt and dipped another plate into the river.

Standing behind her, he looked for the shoulder straps beneath her white cotton shirt to understand what she'd replaced her corset with.

"I'll have you please keep your eyes on your work."

He laughed softly. She was sharp. How had she guessed what he was looking at?

"My first question," he said softly.

"Yes?" Her voice echoed over the river's surface.

"What do you miss most about Vancouver?"

Her breath filtered out through her nose, as though she'd been pleasantly surprised by his question.

"The people. Knowing where I belonged."

Her answer touched a soft part of him. "I understand.

When I lived at home, we were all part of the same thing."

The river gurgled past. He inhaled the mossy scent of wet bark and damp flowers. He was drawn to the way her body moved beneath the boxy white shirt she was wearing. Her right shoulder twisted as she dipped, the fabric pulled at her waist as she scrubbed, and when she stood up, all finished with the dishes, her collar gaped to reveal her throat and the smooth expanse of her lower neckline.

The thin straps of her chemise formed a whiter outline at her shoulders. But it couldn't support her bosom the way her corset had. As he took the dishes from her and piled them into a towel, the wind pressed her shirt to the outline of her firm breasts.

Trying to detach himself from the sight, he glanced to the clothesline. "Do you need a hand getting your things?"

"Absolutely not. Don't you dare go near them."

"We're in the middle of the wilderness. It's no time to be shy."

"There are some things between a man and a woman that should always remain proper."

There was nothing proper about the visions of Lily engulfing his thoughts. No corset. *No corset.*

Heaven's idea of tormenting him?

They made their way through the woods toward their far-off camp. Sunlight grew dimmer in the thicker part of the bush. In the distance, fire flecked through the cedar trunks, framing the small shape of Otis as he tended to the night's flames.

Their path dipped into a gully.

"Watch out for those roots," he warned, eyeing a massive cottonwood and its gnarled appendages that jutted from the grass, but it was too late.

Lily stubbed her toe. The clean tin cups she gripped flew out of her hands. One rolled in front of him. He stepped on it and flipped onto his back, flat out like a man in his casket. Their dishes and utensils scattered on the ground.

The fall knocked the bloody wind out of him. He wheezed.

Struggling for air, he stared up at dark clouds as they rolled by. Lily's face appeared in his view. Straight brown eyebrows, tender mouth.

"Are you hurt?"

It took him a few seconds to capture a lungful of air. Nothing was broken. Grass was plush beneath his fingers. "Pride's completely shot."

She smiled and held out her hand.

He took it and, unable to control the Wayburn bachelor in himself, tugged her down with him.

She yelped. Her soft bosom pressed against his chest. He inhaled the soft curve of her cheek, the matted tendrils at the side of her neck.

The current of air between them stilled. She lifted her face so that she was looking down at him, a kiss away. He reached up and stroked the side of her cheek, the edge of her lips.

With a tender hand, he nudged her forward, and she needed no more persuasion to bend her lips to his.

They kissed. Her touch was an invitation. Her mouth glided over his.

She cupped his face, lifted her lips and slanted them

the other way across his. Sheer wonder. A touch from a woman he'd yearned for since first laying eyes on the young servant who'd dutifully brought him coffee and scones and anything else he desired.

He'd desired this. A meeting of two bodies so responsive to each other that neither could let go.

With a groan, he rolled her over, pressing her shoulders to the grass, searching for the perfect way to appreciate this beauty.

She succumbed to his gesture, racing her hands over his shoulders. His gut hardened in that familiar way, his thighs trembled from the anticipation of wanting more.

His fingers slid down her shirt. They caught the bottom hem and hungrily clawed her chemise out of her waistband. Flesh. Deep, warm, soft womanly flesh met his fingertips.

Her stomach quivered beneath his stroke, flat muscles slightly rounded in that pleasing swell that had captivated men since the beginning of time.

When his hand glided upward to stroke the underside of her bare breast, he thought his heart might explode. She gave a rough inhale. Her lips stopped moving on his for a fraction of time. He wondered if she'd stop his hand, and so he waited, torturing himself by stroking just the crease beneath her breast, where the breast met with her ribs.

Such sweet ribs.

Unable to stop himself, he reached for more. His hand slid over the round. The tip felt like pliable velvet beneath his touch.

Lily moaned in pleasure. She released her mouth and pressed it into the crux of his collar, at his throat.

He wanted more.

He slid his hand to her other side, marveling how extraordinary her breasts were. He played with a nipple, feeling it grow tighter and harder, much like himself.

He pressed his thigh onto hers. His meaning was clear. She stopped for a moment, but didn't move away from the firm part of him that pressed along her side.

She kissed lightly along his neck, making him feel as though his entire body and skin were connected to her lips. He responded. Every touch of hers made him harder.

He cupped her breasts together, a finger centered on each nipple. His hands were filled with Lily. She moved closer.

There was something that tied them together, to the past where at one time, each had sensed a belonging.

That part of her drew him now. The feeling of home and warmth and longing.

But how could this be? He had never divulged his true self to her, here in the Yukon. As proud as he was to be an officer of the Mounted Police, and as respectful as she might be of his official position, he wouldn't be proud to tell her he'd lied when it came to his private life. That he'd been dragging her along and pretending he was down on his luck, that he was kissing her now while holding back his very essence.

"You're unnatural," she would say. *"You don't talk. You don't divulge anything about yourself. You use people to get what you want."*

The clarity in his mind made him pull away from Lily. With an awkward cough, he sat up and gave her a moment to compose herself away from his prying eyes.

Then he rose and collected the dishes.

"You go on to camp," he said roughly. "I'll rinse these again." He didn't look back at the woman he'd just disheveled. Dylan strode away into the darkness, wondering how it was possible that he could turn his back on his feelings of warmth and home.

He was not the man she thought he was. Worse, he was not the man *he* once thought he was. He was capable of lying and stealing. And when he met up with Maddock, even killing.

She'd be right. He was unnatural. In chasing Maddock and his ugly gang, Dylan had become a little bit like them. It was a battle he had to finish, and he was ashamed to let Lily see the man he'd become.

Unsettled by his kiss, Lily clawed at the leaves that had tangled in her hair as she made her way back to Otis and the fire.

With one sweep of his dark lashes, Dylan was capable of drawing her into his world, only to confuse her. There was something strong and valid between them. As much as she fought it, she couldn't deny the physical attraction and the eager way she waited for his conversations of home and Vancouver.

Could there be more between them, if she allowed it? How would a courtship with Dylan possibly end?

Happily or miserably?

In her experience with everyone she'd ever loved, things always ended in misery. She knew it didn't always have to, and she worked hard to change the outcome, but for her, life always seemed to take a turn for the worse.

She'd once put a man between herself and her sister on the trail to Dawson. Perhaps until—*if*—she was reunited with Amanda, she should remember that family came first. Men second.

She wanted marriage. Yes, she did. She wanted a family of her own, babies to hold and a man to fuss over. To cook him meals, keep him warm at night, and mostly, to laugh away the pain and sorrows of the day.

But to pin her hopes of companionship on a man who kissed her one moment and pushed her aside the next?

She ducked around a tree. Otis poked at the fire as she approached, then plopped down on a pile of logs to watch him. Dylan had covered the wood earlier with a canvas tarp to prevent bugs from bothering anyone who sat down.

Otis noticed her empty hands. "What happened to the dishes?"

"They're coming."

He stared at the leaves she raked from her hair. "I'm no expert on marriage, but seems to me you could use a little advice."

She wasn't married. She was lying to Otis by not disclosing it. Red-hot humiliation swept up her temples. She was certainly behaving as though she were, giving her body freely.

How could she be an example for her younger sister, if she behaved like one of the paid ladies working in the shacks of Paradise Alley in Dawson?

The fact was, she had gold. Someone had stolen it

from her. Dylan was going to help her get it back. Rather, he was being paid to get it back. There was a big difference between helping because of friendship, and helping because of payment.

Otis removed his spectacles and wiped the single lens with his shirt. He set the specs back on the bridge of his nose.

"Nattering at a man day and night won't get you anyplace."

"I don't do that."

"Not in so many words. But if every look you give him is painted with a brush of disapproval…. Hell, no man can take it for long."

The embarrassment and hurt inside of her lodged into a big lump that sat in her throat. "Is that what your wife did?"

"Nope. My wife and I would always get it out in the open. Never stewed. But my sister drove her husband into the ground twenty years early. She found complaint with everything."

"I'll remember that."

"I don't think you will."

Startled at his bluntness, Lily cupped her throat.

"You say you will, little lady, but you gotta mean it. I don't know what it is between you and Dylan, but go easy on him. He's hurtin' real bad about somethin'."

He was. She knew it in the bottom of her belly, like she knew that horses drank water. But how could she help Dylan if he refused to talk?

Twenty-four hours later, Dylan still wasn't talking, and they were knee-deep in mud.

"The rain! Should we get the horses out of the rain?" Sheets of water came down hard on Lily's cowboy hat as she sought his advice.

The wind lashed at her.

She yanked on her bay's reins, but the mare only moved another inch. Lily's arms ached from the hours she'd spent on lifting branches off the trail that had fallen in the storm, coaxing and pleading with her jittery mare to calm down and trust her voice.

"You're good with her!" Dylan hollered from up ahead. "Keep going! We'll stop soon for the night, I promise!"

It appeared as though he had his own difficulties with his mount. The sleek black muscles of the beast glistened in the downpour. Almost entangled entirely in brush, the dark silhouette of the two together formed an impenetrable mass.

The storm abated. Raindrops fell more gently.

A mellow gust of wind cleared a path through the clouds for the sun to burst through. The scent of berries and rosehips met her nostrils. Mushrooms covered the forest floor.

Thank the heavens, her bay moved forward. Lily almost fell flat on her back from pulling. She eased up and stumbled to get her balance.

Sunshine on her oilskin jacket made her hot. It was as though she were taking one of those Turkish steam-baths she'd often helped Mrs. Wayburn and her female friends visit in Vancouver. They'd never think to invite her in. It had never been her place. In fact, Lily predicted how shocked the gentle old woman would be if she knew her son Dylan thought Lily pleasing.

"I got me a handful!" Otis yelled behind her.

She swung around to see what he was talking about.

He'd removed his hat and had stuffed it with golden mushrooms.

"Be careful they're not poison!"

Otis hooted. "I've been cookin' these things for two years!"

Lily was just removing her jacket when she heard the strangers up ahead.

She spotted Dylan shaking hands with a group of folks who'd stopped their rafts long enough to recover from the rain.

Men. More men. Nothing but men. Some women would find that marvelous. Lily found it odd and against nature.

It made her long for her sister's company— Amanda's humorous method of cooking, always doing things backwards. She threw onions in the pot before heating the lard. She always put the potatoes on to boil first, no matter how long the cut of meat would take.

The eight strangers approached, removing their hats.

"How do you do." Lily shook hands with each of them—bankers, they said they were.

"Lordy," Otis exclaimed. "When you left North Dakota, I reckon you left the entire state without bank tellers."

"There's a few remaining," said one with a chuckle. He stroked his walrus mustache. "Any of you folks run into a man named Marcus Witcheta?"

"No," they replied.

"If you do…please…tell my brother I'm headin' to Dawson City. That I'd like to patch things up."

The sadness in his voice reflected Lily's. Whatever their story, it mimicked so many others. Including a team of college men they bumped into an hour later in the setting sun.

"I dare say, we split up from the rowing team at the base of the mountains in Skagway. We all thought we could do a much better job traveling alone. And now…now we wonder how our college mates are doing. If you see them, you'll tell them we're looking?"

"Yes," Lily promised. And then she asked the question she secretly asked everyone she'd met thus far on the trail. "Have you seen a young woman, long blond hair? Amanda Cromwell?"

Every *no* made Lily's hopes sink a little more.

The rain began again. On went her jacket.

"Here!" Dylan shouted. "Let's make camp here while we can still see."

Lily took her bay to the river for a drink, then hitched her to a tree and allowed her to graze. There wasn't much they could do to keep the downpour off the animals, except protect them beneath the thickest leaves. They seemed content as Lily collected firewood.

Dylan set up a lean-to using canvas tarps and tree branches. He kept it low to the ground so the wind wouldn't take it. Otis insisted on setting his a ways back, as he always did to give them private time.

Lily shivered in the cold. Light had fled. Darkness the color of purple covered the crags and valleys around them.

Dylan threw another log onto the fire. Yards behind them, Otis's fire had reached a nice size to keep him warm.

"Night folks!" he called through the bushes.

Lily's teeth clamped together.

"You're shivering." Dylan felt her hands. "Stone cold. Here, take this spot right here." He led her inside the lean-to. "Sit down."

She was too miserable to resist, and grateful for his help. She shivered uncontrollably, over and over. Even her ears seemed to quake with the frigid air.

"Give me this." Dylan reached below her chin and loosened her hat. He slid it off and propped it by the fire where it could dry.

Lily, seated on the ground on a piece of canvas, kicked off her wet boots and tucked her feet beneath her soggy skirts.

"Got anything else to wear on your lower half?"

"No," she said.

"You've gotta get out of those wet skirts. Even your petticoats are soaked."

He reached into his saddlebag and hauled out a pair of his pants.

"Then what'll you wear?"

"I'm fine like this."

"But you're soaked, too."

"Not shivering like you are."

She understood she could easily succumb to the elements if she didn't take care of herself. So as he walked away, she tugged his loose jeans up her legs and removed her dripping skirts.

He hung the blue skirt and white lace petticoat by her hat, removed his leather jacket and sat down beside her beneath the lean-to.

They sat there for a long time looking at the fire. The

heat seeped through her skin, but she was bone-chilled and still trembling.

In the darkness, Dylan wrapped his arm around her shoulders and drew her to his chest.

"Warm. You're so warm," she murmured into his dry shirt.

"Hmmm."

His long hair dipped around her face. He smelled like rain.

Her severe shivering began to subside. Heat was finally penetrating her core.

She was comfortable in his arms. Safe from the rain and the mud and far from anything or anyone who might harm her.

Her eyes grew heavy. She closed them.

Maybe it was a mistake, for all her other senses seemed to soar with awareness, and perhaps expectation, of Dylan.

He was a gentleman. He didn't take advantage of his position.

She was lulled by his calmness. Then her fingers slowly fell to her side, accidentally touching his.

It was like an instant flare between them.

Gently, he stroked her forefinger with his own. She slid her middle finger onto his. He thumbed the shape of her hand, drew a line into her palm. Every graze brought a surge of warmth. Every gentle circle he drew on her hand raced up her arm, through her chest and straight down her insides.

Yet, they withheld from touching in any other place. Perhaps this amplified how erotic his strokes on her hand were. How incredibly difficult it would be on this journey to resist the charm of Dylan Wayburn.

Mostly, she feared what she was perhaps promising in the unspoken language between them.

Chapter Ten

In the morning, Dylan woke, still holding Lily.

His left shoulder was cramped. Prickles ran up his arm. The weight of his guns shifted around his legs. Blinking, he strained his eyes in the blast of early-morning sunshine.

Lily's head was nestled against his chest. The steady rhythm of her breathing warmed his shirt. Beneath the wool blanket wrapped around them, the parts where their bodies touched were warm and limber—their hips, ribs, thighs.

Her thighs. He imagined them long and curvaceous beneath the cut of his borrowed denim pants.

Lily's hair, rich auburn, draped across his shoulder. It felt damn good to hold her.

Perfectly still, he lifted his gaze off her for a moment to assess their surroundings. The fire was out, but the embers were still red, so it wouldn't take much to ignite them again. Propped beside the smoldering coals, her hat and skirt and petticoat stirred in the wind. They'd dried, too.

All calm. It was just past dawn.

Normally after a large rainfall, the animals would be out. He looked for signs of mother nature—chipmunks, mice, raccoons, anything.

Strange, but he saw none.

A thud in the woods made him turn his head to a sharp right. His throat constricted at what he saw.

Among the trees, two massive black grizzlies thumped across the damp earth. A boar and a sow. They foraged for roots and berries. The boar stood seven feet tall, a thousand pounds, his mate was slightly smaller.

That's why the other animals had taken cover. Fear.

Lily twitched at his side.

"Don't move," he whispered. "Look up, but don't move."

She shifted her head, groggy and likely wondering where she was and what she was doing sitting this close to him. But when her shoulder jolted beneath his, he knew she'd spotted the bears.

"Uh," she murmured.

"They won't attack unless provoked," he whispered. "They're after food. Not us."

"Where's Otis?"

They peered through the wet trees. Otis, God bless him, was already up and cooking over the fire. His words couldn't be heard at this distance, but he looked like he was singing, totally oblivious to the grizzlies.

Terror wrapped itself around Dylan. "Old man," he whispered. "Be quiet."

The grizzlies were already watching him. The faint scent of grilled biscuits wafted over Dylan. Food. They smelled food.

There was no time to wait. Dylan removed his arm from Lily, shoved aside the blanket and slid to his feet.

"Climb the tree," he told her softly. "Your bag's too far away to get your derringer. Here, take one of my guns. Can you climb alone?"

"Yes," she whispered.

He drew his other gun, waited a few seconds till Lily started, then aimed his weapon at the bears.

If he hollered to try and scare them off, they might charge Otis. If Dylan fired his gun, one bullet wouldn't be near enough to down one animal, let alone two. Then what would he have? A raging beast close enough to attack the old man.

Dylan walked toward Otis, swift and silent. If he could distract the bears by tossing them some food, Otis could maybe climb to safety.

Dylan didn't count on the horses, though. Still tethered loosely to a cedar from the night before, the mares spotted the grizzlies, snorted and reared.

Maybe the bears panicked. Maybe Otis did.

However it happened, the boar lowered himself to all fours and charged the old man.

"Ah!" Otis screamed and tried to fling the hot pan in its face. He missed.

Dylan bolted to help, leaping over bushes and roots as fast as he possibly could. Every muscle in his body strained to full power.

"Here! Over here!" he taunted the bears.

He couldn't shoot between the trees for fear of hitting Otis, so he fired in the air. It scared the sow. She turned and ran back into the woods. The gunshot stunned the boar for a second, then incensed him. He charged Otis.

Otis dodged him and circled the fire. He tried to keep the flames between himself and the black beast.

But the bear was faster. Dylan's chest squeezed hard as he watched the inevitable.

The grizzly swiped the air, clawed Otis in the shoulder and tossed him ten feet up, as though he was a ragged doll.

"Oh, no…Otis…no." Dylan took aim and shot. He nicked the grizzly's ribs. The beast roared in rage, but it was only a minor skin wound. Dylan pointed his gun again, but the grizzly looked into the woods at his receding mate. It tore off between the trees, faster than anyone might believe a monster that size could run.

Dylan reached Otis. His eyes were closed, his breath shallow. Blood poured from his torn right shoulder. His glasses had fallen to the ground against a rock.

"Otis, Otis." Dylan gently tapped his cheek. No response. He felt for a pulse in the man's neck. It was rapid, but thankfully, still there.

Lily appeared in a whirl. She hauled her heavy saddlebag behind her as though it weighed but a feather's quill, and was already yanking out a bolt of clean muslin. Behind them, their horses and Bessie had quieted.

Dylan ripped the torn sleeve off Otis's shoulder. A massive sticky mess of blood. A chunk of flesh was missing from the upper muscle. To quell the blood, Dylan clenched the wound tight with a strip of the clean cloth Lily had brought.

"I'll get some water from the river." Lily tore off.

Alone, Dylan soaked away as much blood as he could from the wound, but it was bleeding so fast he had to press firmly. Huge claws had ripped out a lot of muscle. Dirty claws would produce a dirty wound.

"It'll fester without proper care, Otis. We need to get you someplace, fast."

The old man couldn't hear him, but Dylan talked anyway. He tried to control the rawness of his voice, but it was shaky.

"Whitehorse. It's the closest town. We've got to get you to Whitehorse."

They had nothing here in the wilderness. No tonics, no cleansing solutions, no poultices to quell the germs.

Lily bolted back to his side with a pot of clean water. Dylan let go of the wound long enough to swipe it clean, but couldn't see straight from the new blood.

Lily mumbled prayers.

After half an hour of holding and cleansing and holding and cleansing, and hoping like hell Otis was strong enough to survive not only the loss of blood, but the big bump to the back of his head and the terrifying stress to his heart.

When they had done as much as they could, packed and wrapped the wound, Dylan sat back on his heels. Lily leaned forward, and with blood-encrusted fingers, gently lifted Otis's spectacles from the ground. Its remaining lens had popped out beside Otis's head, but hadn't shattered. With loving tenderness, Lily removed her handkerchief from her pocket and wrapped the precious items.

That's when it hit Dylan hardest. His throat tightened and then burst with all the pent-up sentiment he'd been hiding, it seemed, forever. He exhaled in a huge sob.

Lily was worried about Dylan. For now, Otis was safe and surviving, but how would she cope in the middle of a wild territory with two men down?

Dylan was so severely struck by the accident to his friend that he didn't speak for two hours. In between adding more packing to the injury when blood began to soak through again, Dylan would occasionally raise his sleeve and swipe it across his wet cheek.

"You all right?" she kept asking.

"It's not me. It's him."

"Right," she kept saying. But she was well aware that Dylan could easily slip into some sort of traumatic stupor himself. She'd never realized in the years of knowing him, how deep his feelings went for someone he called a friend.

What had caused such a severe reaction in a man she thought incapable of such depth?

Was there something from Dylan's past that surfaced inside him, that made it difficult for him to cope in this life-and-death situation?

She was busy wiping her own tears. She found it almost impossible herself to look at Otis's sad, unconscious face. Her heart quivered every time he flinched in his sleep. She was able to deal with his injury, she supposed, from her past experience. She'd seen worse bleeding in horses, working alongside her father in his employer's stables, tending to wounds that befell the draught horses in the fields.

Lily dabbed a cloth in water and wiped his sweaty brow. His lids remained closed. His lips were pale, but his other limbs were warm to touch, which meant his circulation was working. In the stables, her father had always checked all four limbs even if only one was wounded.

"Bleeding is slowing down," said Lily.

"That's a good sign." Dylan looked to the blue sky. "Rain's gone. I better get moving."

He took their small ax and chopped a slender tree.

Whacking trees? Was he going mad? "Dylan, speak to me. What are you doing?"

"Making a stretcher."

"To carry him?"

"We've got another five or six days before we hit Whitehorse. I can't carry Otis all that way, and he obviously can't ride. But we could fit his mule with a stretcher."

Dylan was lucid. Her spirits soared. "Yes, yes, we could. I'll help."

"We'll need the canvas tarp we were sitting on by the fire. I'll tie it to these two poles."

She rose to her feet in her borrowed pants. Her knees ached from the knelt position she'd been frozen in for two hours.

She dashed away.

"Lily!" he called after her.

She stopped and spun back. "Yeah?"

"I can do it."

She knew what he was implying. That if she was scared of the grizzlies returning, Dylan would collect their things from the other camp and bring them here. She could stay put.

Her fingers shook from her own stifled fears, but she tried to remain rational. "The bears have gone. And I've got my derringer tucked into my pocket."

"It's a firecracker in comparison to their size. But they *are* scared of the noise and the sting."

She raced to do her duties.

Within another hour, the horses were packed, the fires were out, and Otis was snuggled beneath blankets on the stretcher behind Bessie.

Bessie seemed to be accustomed to hauling heavy weight. She fussed when Dylan had tied the poles to her saddle, but settled once they got moving. Dylan took the lead. Bessie and Otis followed, with Lily behind so that she only had to look up to see and assess their injured friend.

Dylan didn't need to tell her why getting to Whitehorse quickly was critical. With every bump in the road, her pulse sped as Otis tossed an inch off his stretcher, moaned in pain, and grew paler.

He might be dead in five or six days.

They discovered the fastest way to travel was to take the time to rest the horses every hour. If they rode for eighteen hours straight, she and Dylan could suffer for hours through the narrow brush and crags, but the horses couldn't keep that pace over all the days necessary.

They knew Otis carried a pocket watch. Dylan removed it and asked her to keep time. Every hour on the hour they stopped for fifteen minutes to rest. Either she or Dylan squirted water into Otis's mouth with a wineskin. He sometimes gagged, but mostly just swallowed unconsciously. If he didn't drink, he'd be gone within twenty-four hours.

Close to sunset, almost ragged from the gnats that bit at her neck, her buttock muscles so stiff from her position in the saddle that her thighs were shaking, Lily pulled out the watch. Just past eleven. Almost midnight.

She clutched the warm, golden orb in her palm and stared at Otis, still unconscious. His breathing was heavier now, as if he was struggling for air.

"Gather your strength," she pleaded. "Keep strong."

They rode till two. At any other time, she would have marveled at the unusual color of the sky, a twilight blue instead of pitch black. Tonight, it hindered their journey. She and Dylan slowed their horses to ensure their footing, and tried to dodge the branches in their path.

The struggle was fierce the following day, as well. They'd no sooner changed Otis's dressing and put their heads on their bedrolls when the morning birds woke them.

She and Dylan got faster at packing and unpacking. Sadly, Otis was still unconscious, but thankfully his breathing didn't seem so forced today.

In the evening, well past dinnertime, after trudging downhill for nearly a mile, they turned past a difficult corner of crags and shrubs where the horses could barely get their footing. The sweet welcoming view of another wood camp appeared. Smoke ballooned from a cluster of shacks, and fresh laundry dangled off a rope.

"We'll stop here for the night," Dylan said. A group of men, about a dozen, nodded from the far end of the camp as they stacked cut logs, racing with the sunset.

Lily slid off her mount and touched Otis. "Dylan, please come here."

In two long strides, he was beside her.

"Does he look…very pale to you?"

"Yeah, he does."

They transferred Otis to a cot in one of the shacks.

"Open your eyes, Otis. Please." It was the only way he'd survive. Sooner or later, he had to eat solid food.

Two of the cooks would remain sleeping in the shack, both promising to keep their eyes on Otis through the night. Judging from her experience, Otis would sleep right through.

"You'll wake us if he rouses?"

"Yes, of course," one of the men promised.

It was close to midnight when dusk finally fell. Unable to fall asleep at their private campfire, Lily straightened her bedroll and turned to face the flames. Dylan's bedroll was unmade and he was nowhere in sight.

She found him crouched by the river. With his dark, lean profile, he looked like a panther ready to leap to protect his territory.

A new thought entered her head, something totally unconnected to the day's events. "Why don't you ever go looking for whisky?"

He rose to his booted feet and swung around, all two hundred muscled pounds of him.

She tried not to be intimidated. "There's whisky here at the camp. Come to think of it, there was at the last one, too. Yet I don't see you going for any."

"I don't drink."

She wrapped the wool blanket she'd brought with her tighter around her shoulders and tilted her head straight up to look at him. "What's the truth, Dylan?"

"I don't drink."

"But you were carrying that flask when I first met you. And you reeked of the stuff."

He shrugged and turned the strong cut of his dark cheek away from her. "For your own good, it's best you know as little as possible."

"Why?"

He didn't answer. He rubbed the back of his neck and shook his head, as though trapped between what he wanted to say and what he *should* say.

"Maybe for my own good, it's best I know everything."

"You'll be in danger."

"Why? Are you a bounty hunter who's being hunted himself?"

"When I get Otis to safety, I want you to stay with him. I'll go on alone."

"I'm afraid," she whispered. "That he's not going to make it to safety."

"It was wrong of me to take Otis on this trip."

"What happened to him is not your fault."

"It was wrong of me to take you this far, too. Look, I—I think I know where we'll meet up with a couple of Mounties. When the time comes, with or without Otis, I'll leave you behind with them."

Her eyes trailed across his face to the rugged appeal of his dark features, the scruff growing on his jawline, the overgrown hair.

A mix of sentiments swirled inside of her. She didn't want to leave him. She felt safer with Dylan, no matter what he was battling.

"What about our agreement?" She spoke softly. "That you'll help me find my sister. And the lost gold."

"I'll live up to our agreement. I'll find your gold and your sister. But I'll do it alone."

Alone.

It's how she'd been for the last year. Without connection to anyone or anything from her past.

She turned to the swirling river. Water gurgled over the stones, past the soft grasses on the bank, and lapped against the treed shoreline further down. A full moon the size of a pumpkin broke through the clouds.

"I don't want to be alone," she murmured. "Tell me what kind of trouble you're in. Explain to me how it's related to that mark on your wrist. Who did that awful thing to you, Dylan? Who?"

As alone as she'd been, she felt connected to him. She wanted to help this man she now considered a friend.

Chapter Eleven

"It's not a story for mixed company." Dylan's voice broke with such sadness, it confirmed her suspicions that he'd been through something horrible.

He was a complex man. Much deeper and passionate than she'd first assumed in Vancouver.

"Don't we all suffer from some painful thing in our past?" Her blanket slipped off one shoulder, revealing her white shirt. Her blue satin skirt, stained forever by the rain and muck of the Yukon, dragged at her ankles.

He was a man who kept to himself, yet the most commanding and capable outdoorsman she'd ever met.

In the darkness, he shifted at her side. "Sometimes it's easier to expose a deep secret to a stranger, isn't it?"

"Is that what we are? Strangers?"

"We've known each other for over nine years, off and on, but I think there's much more to you than you reveal, Lily." He traced an imaginary line at her shoulder. Even through the worn cotton fabric, the heat of his hand seeped into her body. She didn't want the connection to end.

Keep your hand here, she thought. *Keep it here for a moment longer.*

"Lily." He said her name so gently it felt as though he'd strummed the word on a beautiful guitar. "Lily."

"What is it that you'd like to know?"

"I keep telling myself there had to be a reason why you left your sister in Alaska. You talked about her all the time in Vancouver. Her little cat. The dresses you sewed for her. How you taught her to ride."

"I explained. We had a terrible argument. I was seasick on the ship and she couldn't find enough to eat. She was hungry and tired. And young. It wasn't her…the true her…who left me that night."

"That part I understand. The part you're leaving out is what happened on your journey to Dawson."

It was as though he'd raised an arrow and shot it straight through her heart.

"It was awful."

His hand slid lower, between her shoulder blades, coaxing her.

"I did some things I'm ashamed of. I was desperate and couldn't find her…. I turned to the nearest man who paid attention."

She'd found solace for a few nights with a stranger.

"Was he unkind?"

"No, he was very kind. It was awful, nonetheless. There was no feeling behind the action…no feeling at all on my part."

Dylan said nothing, only listened, swirling his fingers round her back.

"I thought getting physically close would draw something out of me that I'd lost. It only made me feel as though I was…"

A woman of easy virtue.

"You are an intelligent, beautiful woman any man would be proud to be with. You were struggling with something painful. The loss of someone you loved."

"She's not lost…. I can't believe that."

"I'll find her, Lily. I will find Amanda."

For the first time in over a year, Lily's heart soared at the possibility. Here was someone—the first person—who'd volunteered to help.

"I may not be able to pay you, if my gold is lost for good. You can back out of the deal if you want. I'll understand."

He took her by the arms. "Listen to me. This has nothing to do with gold. It has everything to do with the fifteen-year-old breakfast maid who walked into my dining room nine years ago. I will find your sister."

Tears stung her eyes. "When I struck gold, I paid a few men to try and locate her. They always took my money but never returned. I don't know if they even tried. You're the only one who's ever said they would help me. The only one."

It was impossible to steady the beat of her heart.

Emotion seemed to grip him with the same strength it did her. His eyes glistened in a stream of golden moonlight. The cut of his cheek quivered, his lips fell open.

"You're a good man, Dylan. I apologize for all the things I've said to you on this trip."

He closed his eyes in empathy, averted his gaze for a

moment while he regained his composure, and then turned back to Lily. He raised an arm and stroked her neck.

"Tell me what's bothering you," she said. "Maybe I can help. Maybe there's something…"

Desperate to know what was tearing him apart, she looked for a way to reach him. His sleeve had pulled up as he caressed her neck, exposing the arches that'd been branded into his wrist. Without thinking, she lowered her head and kissed the mark. It was a gentle kiss, like one she'd often given to her younger sister, when Amanda had been a child and scraped her elbow.

But the reaction in Dylan was stark, vivid surprise. He pulled back, shoulders tight, mouth clamped.

She had dared to kiss his wound.

"It's a part of you, Dylan. You mustn't be ashamed. I suspect it's what's giving you the strength to do what you're doing."

His resolve wavered. Grappling with buried sentiment, he leaned down and kissed her cheek. She adored the contact of his rough bristles against her softness.

"Who did this to your wrist?" she asked.

"Bolton Maddock," he said hoarsely. "It was Maddock."

Suddenly, she understood his pain. She understood it all.

Several minutes later, Lily was still listening quietly as Dylan poured out his story. He was unable to stop himself now even if he tried. He explained how he'd been caught, and how his two friends were shot for trying to stop the cattle ring that Maddock and his brothers had been running from Alberta into Montana. The only thing he left out was that he and his friends were Mounties. She'd be in more danger if she knew, because she might let it slip, and if Maddock found out, he'd want her dead, too.

"They branded you?"

"Maddock's two brothers. Sloan and Kirk."

She flinched. "The ones who robbed me."

Lily looked at his marks with a surge of compassion. Everything about her tonight—the turn of her cheek, the curve of her chin, the flare of her nostrils—told him how affected she was by his gruesome story.

At the end of it, when he was all talked out, she placed her hands on his and simply held them. It quieted the storm that thundered inside his veins, the throbbing of outrage and injustice at the death of his colleagues.

She took the lead, as if knowing he needed direction. She led him back to their campfire on top of the hill, hidden from the other shacks at the wood camp by a line of shrubs and a lean-to with a canvas tarp to protect them from the wind or a further downpour. As it was, he'd chosen the hill because it'd been the driest patch of ground and it had a good view of Otis's cabin.

Dylan turned his head now to look for signs of his recovery, but there was only solitude. "Everyone's asleep."

The fire had almost died, so he placed another log onto it. Kneeling, he blew at the embers till they smoldered and caught, bursting into flames a foot high.

Lily knelt beside him. Her face glowed in the golden sparks, her silhouette captured by the firelight.

"Tell me," she said gently, rocking beside him. "How did you come to be in Alberta?"

Should he tell her? How could he keep it from her? She'd disclosed so much to him. He felt as though the weight of his world had been lifted from his conscience, simply by telling another living soul about the branding—a woman, a civilian—not his commander and not his colleagues who were aware of the inhumanities in the world.

Her strength surprised him. Even more, how much it meant to him.

"You'll be at risk if I tell you."

"What kind of risk? From Maddock? I'm already in danger where he's concerned."

"Not like this."

"Then I'll guess. What kind of risk can I be in by knowing? Are you somehow involved with the gang? Maybe you or your father financed their cattle drive and then discovered they were criminals?"

By her voice, he knew she didn't believe that.

He vowed not to answer, and instead unrolled his blankets.

"We'll sleep head to head. That way, if either of us wakes up during the night, we just have to push the tarp aside to have a look at Otis's cabin."

"Okay, so that's not it." She continued her guessing game, much to his discomfort. "You were on their trail along with your two friends. All three of you were bounty hunters, then?"

On his knees, he kept his face a mask as he straightened out her blankets.

He gave no reaction.

"Not bounty hunters, either." Lily sighed and inched her way toward her bedding. She dropped the blanket from around her, no doubt warmer now due to the fire.

She slipped into her bedroll, keeping her boots on and letting them slide out the other end so as not to dirty her blankets.

"'Night, Lily. Sleep well." Although he longed to reach out, to touch her, he tucked himself inside his own cocoon. And turned his shoulder to the fire.

Suddenly, she leaped out of her makeshift bed to his left side. She rolled his shoulder and his body back to the fire.

Her long copper hair draped over her shoulder, grazing the tip of his. "I can't believe it," she whispered.

"What?"

"You mentioned it earlier."

"The only thing I said was sleep well."

"You said when we meet up with two Mounties, you're going to leave me and Otis behind. Mounties." She dragged herself to her knees. "Have I misjudged you that much, Dylan?"

He tried to steel himself from answering. He braced his arms and clenched his jaw and peered at the fire.

Her fingers reached for his chin and she tugged his face toward hers.

"Dear God, you're a Mountie."

His eyes must have flickered, for he saw the recognition flicker in hers.

She repeated the words with awe. "The North-West Mounted Police. You're an officer of the law."

"I haven't said a word."

"You don't need to. I can see it in your face. That's why you've made yourself look like a drifter and an alcoholic. But you don't drink, you only pretend to. You're chasing them. Oh, Dylan, they'll kill you if they find you."

"Shhh…shhh…." He grabbed her fingers. "No one's killing anyone. No one…"

Resist, he told himself. But he rolled to her side.

Resist touching her. But he reached down and entwined his hand into her soft hair.

Resist the sweet face. But he cupped her cheek. Then the puckered, worried mouth that seemed to ache for his.

Unable to stop, he crushed down on her lips. He responded to the deep yearning inside his gut, the primitive need to be with Lily.

Her lips were soft and pliant beneath his, urging him to kiss deeper, stronger, faster.

He complied with a burning that shocked him. He wanted her. Had always wanted Lily Cromwell.

With a guttural moan, he moved away so quickly she was left breathless. He repositioned himself on the soft grass, a yard away from her and several from the blazing fire.

"What's wrong?" she asked.

"Everything. You. Me. This."

"You don't want me."

"I want you more than you could possibly know. I've wanted you, Lily, since the first day you poured me coffee."

"Then I've turned you away for some reason. I don't kiss well."

"You kiss like an angel."

"It's my manner, then. Too bold."

"I like you the way you are. I wouldn't change a thing."

"Then why do I repel you?"

He moaned again, in frustration. "You attract me like a bolt of lightning to Benjamin Franklin's kite."

She laughed in the soft manner he enjoyed.

She propped her head up on an elbow. Firelight caressed her smooth skin. "Then what is it?"

"You're a keeper, Lily. That's the problem. And I'm in no position to keep anyone by my side. Do you understand?"

She lowered her lashes. They swept her cheeks as she nodded. "I don't know about tomorrow. Or the day after, or the day after that. But I do know about tonight. And tonight, I want to be with you, Dylan."

He stopped himself from reaching, as tortured as he felt. There was nothing more he wanted on the face of the earth than to make love to Lily.

When he didn't go to her, her lips quivered with disappointment and then she went back to her bedroll.

He panted, trying to tell himself to stay away. That they'd both be so much better off if he never knew how her naked body might feel pressed against his.

Straining to control his own desperate disappointment, Dylan tapped the grass.

She turned her back. He watched the fire play on her figure. Her shirt hung freely about her waist. The indented shape of her stomach, the bulge of her hips. One calf visible above her boot.

Wood crackled in his ear. Heat seeped through the

fabric of his shoulder blades. A loon called. In the far distance, the cry of wolves.

And here in front of him, the most beautiful woman he'd ever laid eyes on.

Powerless to control his desire, he moved in behind her, slid the front of his body into the back of hers and ran his hand up and down her curves.

"Lily," he whispered into her ear, nibbling at the dainty flesh, loving how she arched her neck back onto his. "I want to be with you, too. *I want to be with you.*"

Chapter Twelve

Lily turned to face Dylan and watched, fascinated, at the play of warm and cool shadows on his body. The fire behind him flickered well above his broad shoulders and illuminated his handsome face. Even beneath the bristles and the full length of his hair, there was an air of polish about this man. A grace in his quiet manner.

A slow smile slid across his lips. It was like watching the moon tilt down on her—warm and entrancing. When his smile centered on her, her heart beat so fast she swore it was going to pop right out of her ribs.

"How can you do this?" she asked.

"What?"

"Change your mind and expect me to go along with whatever it is that pleases you. As if you're the king and I'm your wench come to do your bidding."

"You are my wench," he said playfully. "You *shall* do my bidding."

His easy charm made her blush. "Now you're joking."

"What on earth makes you think I'm joking?" He kissed her ear, the sound of his breath loud. "Does this feel like I'm insincere?" He kissed her throat. "This?" He ran his hand along her waist and up the side of her ribs. "And this?"

She giggled.

"You think it's funny?"

"Your stubbles are tickling my cheek."

With a swoop, he ran his hand up farther, inching toward her breast. Her stomach was almost heaving, how great his affect was on her. Did he realize she'd removed her underclothes for sleeping? Did he notice the missing whalebone?

"You removed your corset for me."

"It was not for you. I can't sleep in the tight thing."

He breathed against her neck. "I'm just the lucky benefactor."

She giggled again.

"Do you always laugh so much?"

"You're tickling my throat."

With an exclamation of playful ire, he moved his lips lower, down her opened neckline and kissed the top part of her bosom.

"Does this tickle, too?"

"Umm."

He undid the top button. One more and one more.

With each inch exposing more of her soft cotton chemise, she grappled with her breathing until he'd unbuttoned it all and simply stared at her body.

"Through that white undershirt," he said, "I can see the outline of your breasts. The curve of your nipples."

A powerful warmth surged through her. She

shouldn't be doing this. They weren't married. They hadn't even promised anything to each other.

He seemed to sense her hesitation, her embarrassment. Ever so gently, he touched her cheek. "Do you want me to stop?"

"No."

"The way I look at it…" He lowered his head and traced circles around her breast. "Our time together is a gift."

She melted then. "It is a gift. In the midst of strangers, we found each other, Dylan."

He hadn't admitted to her that he was a Mountie, but she knew in her heart he was. As he wandered over the territory, sacrificing his private life to protect people he sometimes didn't even know, she wondered who truly appreciated him.

In a general sense, as a member of the police force, yes, folks admired him and were grateful. But Dylan as an individual, as a man—who cared for him? How many people knew how much he had sacrificed when he was beaten and nearly killed?

She wanted to protect him and love him and hold him all night.

This much she could do.

She reached up and wrapped both arms around his neck. He rolled her on top of him. In a daring move, she sat up on his lap, loving how he looked at her, wearing her see-through cotton. Sparks from the fire popped and hit the dirt a foot away.

He grasped her hand and then in a swift move she didn't expect, he tugged the hem of her chemise free from the waistband of her blue skirt and yanked it up over her head. He tugged the last of it off her hair and admired her.

She'd never let a man see her like this before. Totally naked from the skirt up.

The fire spat again and sparks flew, warming her skin, her breasts, her nipples.

"You are lovely," he whispered. She was enthralled to be so appreciated, when in the past she'd felt nothing but shame.

His bold brown eyes, glossy in the warm lighting, mirrored her image back to her. Was she really here with Dylan? Were they really about to do this?

She shivered with anticipation.

With tenderness, he reached up and stroked her breast. His touch sent an exhilarating sensation through her nipple, down her stomach and between her thighs.

He rose to a sitting position equal to hers, nestling his face against her chest, listening to the beat of her galloping heart.

"It goes so fast."

"It's what you've done to me."

He kissed the underside of her pointed breast. With hands so gentle she could barely feel his touch, he slid his fingers against the pale pink round of her areola.

"So pretty," he murmured. Firelight danced across the broad sweep of his cheek, one side of his forehead, the slant of his eyelids. He smiled slightly and said, "So beautiful."

His tender strokes made her nipples stiffen. Then he took his hands away, sliding them down her ribs and holding her waist.

Dylan seemed to pleasure at the view, almost as

though he was soaking her in. His appreciation was lovely and tender and confusing, as she stood waiting for him to take her.

He took his time, making her wait, making her desire flare into a burning need. She panted softly, bending over to undo his shirt button.

Dylan watched the way her breasts moved. He palmed the rounds and gently gripped her ribs with his long tanned fingers.

She teased *him* then, barely touching his skin as she undid button after button. Her knees sank into the bedding at each side of him. Their bed wasn't plush, it wasn't covered with velvet or brocade like one of his family heirlooms in Vancouver, but it was welcoming and warm and achingly simple next to the fire.

She reached his last button and pulled back his shirt to reveal the smooth curves and angles of his broad chest. His skin was tinted golden by the flames.

She kept moving, lifting him out of the shirt to expose his muscled arms and tight stomach. He worked hard in his profession, riding across the territory, surviving on the trail, and it was evident in his physique.

He swooped up to kiss her, surprising her, catching a laugh in the back of her throat. When he rolled her over and set her onto the blankets, his fingers grabbed one ankle.

It startled her.

"I won't hurt you."

"You surprised me."

His wonderful fingers worked their way up her calf, removing her stocking. He held her foot in his hand, kissing the inside rim, moving up to her knee.

She was shameless with need, unable to control how much she wanted this man.

He tugged off her other stocking, working so painfully slow, she was tantalized beyond control. Finally, off came her bloomers until she was naked beneath her skirt. Just when she thought he would touch her there, he skimmed by as if unaware what part of her body ached for him most.

He smiled at her expression. "Don't worry, I'll be back."

She groaned with embarrassment. Could he see how much she wanted him?

To blazes with propriety. Shucking her hesitation, she wound both arms around his neck and kissed him ravenously. When he responded with a flicker of his tongue, a moan caught in her throat. She moved her tongue to meet with his.

Such bliss, meeting like this, being together beneath the moon, cushioned from view by a circle of shrubbery, listening only to the sounds of crunching embers and the buzzing insects of the night.

Lily had already removed her petticoat for sleeping and she expected him now to remove the last of her clothes, her skirt, but he made no move to. Instead, he slid it above her hips and anchored it around her slender waist.

"Do you want it off?" she breathed.

"It's much more daring this way."

From his hungry tone, she gathered he liked the view. It felt bold and sensual for her, almost naked beneath Dylan, brushing the tips of her nipples against his bare chest. Every sway, every graze made the warmth inside of her grow hotter. She had been ready from the moment he'd touched her shoulder earlier.

How was it possible that he had such an overwhelming affect on her?

She basked in her newfound freedom, running her hands over the contours of his chest, unbuckling his belt—dear heaven—and yanking off his pants.

They came off so quickly she stifled a smile. He was just as eager as she, no matter how hard he was trying to pretend he could take his time.

The knowledge made her feel the power of the moment.

When he was completely naked, he pulled her searching fingers off his body for a moment to gaze with awe at her shape. She hadn't yet looked down to fully appreciate his figure. He tucked a finger beneath her chin, and tilted his head slightly with a smile, as if telling her she could look all she wanted.

Lily's skin was a contrast of light and dark, Dylan thought.

Sharp, vivid images of orange light flowed along the shape of her ample breasts, the swell of her pointed nipples. Then the crisp, black line down the middle of her gorgeous body where the reflection of the flames ended, the line lost in the dark triangle at the apex of her thighs.

She was a stunning work of art Dylan would dearly love to capture on canvas.

"Don't move," he said, touching her hip as she rocked above him. He scanned the area, picked up a jagged stone and sketched her body onto a wet black rock. A piece of granite.

"What are you creating?"

"You'll see for yourself in a moment."

He continued drawing her, the long lines of hair that spilled over the top of her naked breasts, the shape of her hips and legs. Simple, bold lines that captured her essence.

"There."

She dipped toward his face to look. As she stared at the rough drawing, he inhaled the scent of her throat. A hint of soap mingled with the scent of Lily.

"I can't believe what you've done. It's incredible."

"It's you."

He'd drawn what he clearly saw—her beautifully arched back, with her hair reaching over the skirt bunched at her waist, touching the round swell of her hips. The front of her body was a simple outline of breasts pointed toward the sky, an abdomen curved with that womanly flare that was driving him wild.

"You've even got the line of my nose and upper lip. You're remarkable."

"I had a lot of clay to work with."

She laughed gently. "It's so simple. And so fetching."

"Most things worth savoring are."

"I meant your linework."

"I meant you."

"And what now of this rock?"

"The rain'll wash it away."

"Never to be seen again. Such a waste of your talent."

"It's not a waste. I enjoyed drawing it and you enjoyed seeing it. Didn't you?"

"But artwork should be displayed."

He arched an eyebrow. She flushed.

"Well, I don't mean my naked form, but I mean… you shouldn't waste your talent on something that'll be rubbed off. Artwork should be permanent."

"Who says? Artwork is for pleasure. Mine and yours."

She graced him with her lovely smile again, a glimmer of white teeth and full lips.

"You look at things differently than most everyone I know," she said.

"It's usually what gets me into trouble."

She nodded in agreement. "It always has. Even as a young man. Remember that night you took your father's horse and Sunday buggy to the farmer's market? You said they shouldn't only be seen at church. That animals liked a change of pace, too."

"I cleaned that buggy for hours afterward. My father wasn't impressed with the mud I brought home."

"The stallion was, though. He was much too finicky and needed a good coat of mud now and again to remind him he wasn't as superior as everyone treated him. Remember?"

"I remember only you could get close enough to saddle and ride him for more than ten minutes."

This was the kitchen maid he'd dreamed about since first setting eyes on. This was the golden breast he'd dreamed of caressing. These were the lips he'd savored in his sleep on countless nights. Lonely nights that had torn him away from home and the only people he'd cared about in the world.

With a vigorous appetite, Dylan sat up to kiss her.

She was seated on his lap, her nakedness, her private area so close to his own throbbing erection that all he had to do was slip inside of her.

Her lips slid against his own, passionate and yearning.

After several intimate moments, he slid his fingers over her, beneath her skirt and up her soft thighs.

She swayed her hips to meet his fingers. She was moist and ready. He had the luscious Lily Cromwell in his hands.

They'd cherish this night.

Moving his fingers, he pleasured her till she was near the brink. When neither of them could hold back any longer, he pressed her shoulders gently to the blankets, yanked her skirt back up to her waist, and rubbed his shaft along her curls.

She arched one leg and then the other, wrapped them around him. He eased himself inside of her. She parted, ready in anticipation, so tight he could barely breathe.

The fire's glow captured the wonder in her eyes, and the tender turn of her cheek.

"Lily," he murmured, kissing her deeply as he moved in and out of her.

"It's good, Dylan. You feel good."

He pumped faster, knowing he was only torturing himself because he had no intention of reaching his climax before she did hers.

With agonizing determination, he pulled out to place his hand there for her. She understood, pressing onto his grip till he had his fingers and thumb positioned just right. He could tell from the rhythm of her panting that she was close. Almost…almost…

He withdrew his fingers and entered her hard—sweat glistening off his arms, beads of moisture forming at her temples.

Finally, she thrust her hips in pleasure, gripped his arms with such concentration on her face that he wished to remember her like this forever.

"Dylan…"

To hear his name called aloud by Lily sent him over the edge. His muscles clenched, the sweet throbbing gripped him, too, and ecstasy swept over him in waves.

This night with Lily couldn't end. It just couldn't.

Chapter Thirteen

The ping, ping, ping of raindrops hitting canvas woke Dylan. How long had they been sleeping?

Judging by the dark color of the sky and absence of a sunrise, it had only been three or four hours. He turned to Lily who was lying beside him. Her face was pressed into his bedroll. He stroked her downy cheek.

They had both donned their clothing before they fell asleep, lest someone come upon them, or in case he had to fend off intruders.

No one in the camp would think it unusual for him and Lily to be sleeping together for they were supposedly married, but totally naked would be another matter. Perhaps natural, but rather shocking.

He kept one arm beneath her head as he tugged back on the makeshift canvas curtain to look at the shack below. Still quiet. No news of Otis, even when Dylan had checked before going to sleep.

He wasn't a praying type of man, but he said another prayer.

"Is it time to rise?" Lily's lashes fluttered. With a sigh and a stretch, she opened her eyes.

Even rumpled from sleep, she looked inviting. He kissed the blade of her soft jaw.

She murmured and kissed his throat.

Raindrops grew louder on their canvas roof. The droplets instantly broiled as soon as they hit the red-hot coals of the fire.

"Let me toss on another log." He rolled out of the blankets and added several thick branches in a teepee shape. Flames soon licked up against the wood.

He nuzzled back next to her. The sound of the rain beat around them for a solid minute, boring holes into the ground, washing away the sketch of Lily.

She watched the rain hit the heavy granite rock, the drawing, then reached over and twisted a piece off the loose edge.

"What's that for?" he asked.

"To remember our evening." She placed it in the pocket of her skirt.

"You're sentimental."

"Umm-hmm. We may not ever…who knows where…?" She couldn't finish.

"We're together now."

"Just like the artwork you drew last night. You do indeed try to cherish the moment, don't you Dylan?"

"Sometimes that's the only promise we've got. Not the future. But what's happening right this minute."

Perhaps she understood, perhaps she didn't.

She ran her hand along the back of his neck, trailing the soft hairs, setting his skin afire.

He kissed her ear, behind it, along her neck. He unclasped her shirt buttons, revealing her see-through cotton chemise and those tantalizing shapely breasts. She explored his stomach, tickling him with the sweet sensation of her cool fingers.

He pulled himself behind her. Reaching up beneath her skirts, he discovered with pleasant surprise that she wore no underclothes.

"No bloomers?"

"I was waiting till morning."

"Good thing, too."

She giggled into his arm, and he guessed that if he was looking at her face, she'd be blushing again.

He took his time, caressing her calves, her thighs. He stroked the inside of her knees, kissing her neck at the same time. She sent her approval with the touch of her hand and the wiggling of her feet on his legs.

He was the luckiest man on earth.

When he understood that she was ready, he tore off his pants until once again, they were both naked from the waist down.

"Don't we look silly?" she whispered.

"Nothing silly about it. Men and women should always dress like this."

"Shirts on top. Nothing on the bottom." She laughed and he felt such joy that he could please her like this.

They made love again, he from behind, urgent and taking his time to ensure she enjoyed every whisper of sensation. This time as they climaxed, the rain beat down and the fire popped, and he thought—hoped— that maybe all would be right with the world.

* * *

Lily stirred from slumber for the second time that night, realizing that making love with Dylan was nothing like her situation with the other man, a year ago on the trail.

With Dylan, her heart had come alive. All the hopes and feelings she thought she'd lost along with her sister sprang to life. She wasn't sure how long her happiness would last, only that she was feeling it here with him.

When she opened her eyes, though, and watched his sleeping face, the motion of his chest up and down as he breathed, she knew in her soul it couldn't continue like this until they'd both accomplished what they'd set out to do. She to find her sister, he to deal with Bolton Maddock.

What room was there for her in Dylan's life?

Could he make room? Would he?

It made her flesh chill thinking of the torture Dylan had endured. It was his right, his place, to track down the animal responsible.

"Our timing's never good, is it?" Dylan touched her forehead and smoothed her hair. "First there was Harrison. And then when we met again, I thought you'd never come to me."

"Harrison never saved my life on the stagecoach, did he?"

"He might have, if he were there."

"Harrison is a coward."

Dylan closed his eyes and she wondered if she'd gone too far in berating his brother. But she only wished to end Dylan's doubts when he measured himself against Harrison. The older brother had been a coward for kissing her behind closed doors and never owning up the promise of marrying her. And she sensed that perhaps he'd been a coward for letting his younger brother take the blame for many of his flaws.

"Harrison may be a coward—" Dylan's jaw moved back and forth as if he had difficulty saying the words "—but a man like Harrison is a safer choice."

"Safer how?"

"In every way."

"Certainly not physically."

"Yes, even that. He never would have gotten himself—or you—in the position where you would need help on that stagecoach."

She'd never thought of it. "But a man like that is not a safer choice when it comes to protecting my heart."

"No? What have I done to your heart, Lily?"

"You've made it beat stronger."

"If Maddock discovers you mean something to me, he'll destroy you. I have no fort to put you in. I have no army to protect you."

"I knew that last night."

"But I'm saying…until this war is over with Maddock, no one can know about us. I'm ashamed for that, Lily. I most truly am. I want to show you off to the world, and yet I have to cower behind the bushes."

The serious nature of their situation hit her hard.

"You see how I hurt you? I didn't intend it. I didn't think last night would be so powerful. I thought it would be simple to wake up this morning and continue as though we hadn't even touched. I was wrong."

He placed his fingers beneath her chin and lifted her

face. "Wherever you go, I will find you, Lily. When this is over, wherever you are. I will find you."

She placed his palm over her heart, loving the warmth of his hand. "Then I will wait."

"How's Otis?" Anxious to hear about their friend, Dylan asked the question by the river, in the early-morning darkness. He'd checked half an hour ago himself, but she had insisted on taking a peek, too. He splashed water on his face as Lily returned from Otis's cabin. She removed a toothbrush and sprinkled baking soda on it.

With a heaviness to her voice, she said, "Still unconscious. The men with him say he hasn't stirred all night."

"His breathing?"

"Unlabored." Lily sank onto a rock and placed her face in her hands. "Is he going to—"

He touched her shoulder. "Shhh, he'll be fine. We've got to believe that. Look, we're leaving early. We'll make great progress to Whitehorse."

"It's days away," she whispered over the lapping waves. "Days."

"Then we'll have to hurry that much faster. Here, take the cup."

She drew herself together, rose and scooped water from the river. She brushed her teeth as Dylan thought about the best course of action.

Maddock's hiding spot in the mountains above Skagway had been confirmed not only by Otis, but a fellow from the camp here. Dylan was on the run, likely ahead of Maddock and racing to get to Skagway first.

Sooner or later, the bastard would show up at that camp—especially in the free and lawless town of Skagway where the tainted marshal and his deputies turned a blind eye to cutthroats and thieves. At least, the old one had. Hopefully things would change in Alaska with Smith's death, but it would certainly take some time.

Whenever Maddock showed his face, Dylan, and hopefully two other Mounties, according to his plan, would be waiting.

The trouble was…the trouble was Otis. *Wake up, old man.*

Dylan's heart softened with thoughts of the inventor. Otis was harmless, curious, and had taken in Dylan and Lily to his cabin when he could have turned them away. It was Dylan's turn to repay the kindness.

Otis's son, Champagne Charlie, was a man to be respected, as well, helpful in the community and steadfast with his friendships.

But what of Lily?

What should he do about Lily? He was too involved with her and that's why he had such difficulty knowing what to do. What was best for her? For his own selfish reasons, he wanted to keep her by his side. For her own safety, he knew she had to go.

She dipped her bare feet into the river, hitched her skirt up high into her waistband, and scrubbed her face. She shuddered at the cold water.

Courting her went against everything he believed in on this mission. Yes, he'd had other women. In passing moments of loneliness he'd turned to another kind soul, but no one like Lily, who seemed to have changed his world overnight.

Hadn't the Mounties trained their new recruits, training he'd gone through in Regina, that the Mounted Police sacrificed their personal lives, including marriage, to make the territories a safer place?

If a man was preoccupied with a wife and family of his own, it was only natural that he would want to stay behind to protect and provide for them. To build a cabin away from the fort, to chop firewood and hunt and fish for food. To protect his children. No man could give priority to two separate places. It was either choose the law or choose a wife.

There were bylaws prohibiting marriage for the new recruits, the constables, which every man was well aware of before they signed for duty. Officers could marry at their discretion and with their commander's permission. True enough, Dylan was an inspector now, an officer, but he'd sworn allegiance to this mission and that oath had to come first.

Was he simply to wag his finger and expect her to follow, hiding behind boulders and behind the trigger of a gun, waiting for Maddock to appear? A man so despicable, Dylan didn't know if he could stomach seeing his face again.

He filled with shame and frustration at the position he'd placed her in.

He watched her brush her hair, such a feminine sweep of her shoulders. She toweled off her legs and pulled on one stocking, then the other. Could there be a more enticing sight than a gorgeous woman with beautiful legs lifting her skirts?

He had half a mind to—

A sound around the waters stopped him. He stood to attention, drew his guns and jumped to Lily's side.

A lap, lap, lap.

Was it a moose? A big bear? Not the grizzlies again—

A steam engine hooted, then a steamboat chugged around the bend. A paddle wheeler!

Dylan nudged her. "Now isn't that the prettiest little thing you've seen in ages?"

Her smile could warm the sun. They both knew what this meant.

"Otis," she said. "We can take Otis."

"Anywhere this ship's headed, we're going."

"Maybe they have clean bandages on board. We're almost out. And medicines to prevent the wounds from festering."

Firmly rooted to the shoreline in the cloak of darkness, Dylan and Lily watched the steamer come in. Six crew members appeared, some hurling ropes to the shore, others preparing gangplanks. No passengers showed up on deck.

They were likely still sleeping in their cabins, trying to wring another hour from the night.

Out of nowhere, two men from the wood camp appeared. One was buttoning up his sleeves, the other patting down his mass of hair that he hadn't had time to comb.

"Toss 'er here!" they shouted, grabbing the ropes and pulling the steamship closer to the shore.

The captain had to know these waters well, for he'd aimed and positioned the craft expertly along the small dock. Of course, there were cords of wood stacked along the shoreline and a mile of missing trees downstream, for anyone observing—a signal for the captain that the wood camp was approaching.

Paddling down river was one thing—many stampeders did it from Alaska to Dawson City, Yukon, where the gold was. Dylan and Lily were traveling upstream, and it was nearly impossible to paddle a canoe against the tide for the weeks it would take.

Dylan whistled at the paddle wheeler. "Hello, darlin'." It was a stern wheeler to be precise, for the wheel was at the back of the ship.

Lap, lap, lap against the shore.

The wood camp sprang to life. Five muscled lumberjacks helped secure the ship.

The captain of the paddle wheeler, dressed in a white uniform, stood at the bow of the ship named *Lady of the Yukon* and saluted Dylan.

It was the grandest hello, the most welcome one, Dylan had had in weeks.

"Where you headed?" Dylan called.

Before the captain could answer, one of the lumberjacks who was sharing Otis's cabin rushed up to Dylan, breathless. "He's awake. Better go see. Your friend's awake!"

Chapter Fourteen

"Otis?" Lily perched on his bed, trying not to disturb his bandages, although her pulse raced at the possibility of speaking to him.

The sun was rising outside, but a kerosene lantern was needed to light the cabin inside. Otis's face was covered in an overgrowth of white whiskers. His skin had good color and tone.

"Uh," he said.

Dylan knelt at his side. "How're you feeling?"

Otis opened his eyes, trying to orient himself, and moved beneath his blankets. The packing on his shoulder must have shifted, for he groaned with the pain.

"You two," he mumbled, much to their delight. Otis recognized them. *He recognized them.*

"We're still here," said Dylan.

"Where?" Otis blinked at the other two empty cots in the cabin.

"At a wood camp, fifty miles south of where you were mauled by a bear."

"A bear?"

"A grizzly," said Lily. "As tall as a fir tree."

Otis slumped back onto his pillow. "Hell. I remember now," he grumbled. "Pardon my language."

This was one time when she most definitely didn't mind his language one bit. Otis was talking and made sense.

"Water?" she offered.

"Lordy, I feel like my mouth's been suckin' on the back end of a—pardon my language." He guzzled from the wineskin while Dylan sank onto the opposite cot. His long legs touched Otis's bed.

Dylan pressed a hand to Lily's thigh to communicate his happiness at Otis's change of health, and she soared with joy that their friend had pulled through.

"We've got a paddle wheeler waiting outside," said Dylan. "You think you can move?"

Otis gripped the side of his bed and tried to get up. He couldn't do it. With a cry of pain, his face pale and shaken, he collapsed back onto the straw mattress.

"Sorry," he huffed. "Just gimme…a little bit…"

"We won't have you walk," Dylan declared. "We'll use our stretcher. I'll go talk to the captain."

"I'll pack his things," said Lily, rising to his bag. There wasn't much to pack. A soiled shirt that she'd changed him out of this morning, a comb and his precious broken eyeglasses, safely rolled into a flap of suede leather.

"How long have I been out?" Otis asked her when Dylan left.

"Three days."

"I'm starvin'."

"That's a good sign, Otis. A mighty good sign."

Dylan was back within minutes. Two deckhands behind him carried the stretcher they'd been using behind Bessie for days. One of them had a black bag. Another had a sandwich.

Otis looked at the bag and bit into the sandwich. "What are you gonna do to me?"

"They've got opiates for your pain."

"They'll make my head drowsy."

"If you think you can handle these men moving you, you can try and do without."

"That's a good idea," said Lily. "I'm not sure it's wise to give a man who's been unconscious anything that can fog his mind." She turned to one of the crew members. "Is there a doctor on board?"

The young fellow sniffed. "No ma'am. Haven't seen one of those in weeks."

"Then we'll do the best we can. Ready Otis?" she said.

He nodded; they lifted; he stifled a scream. As they shuffled out the door into the breaking dawn and onto the quiet steamship, she leaned against Dylan. "Where's it headed?" Judging from the direction it had come from, she was betting and hoping south.

He nodded with a smile. "Straight to Whitehorse."

Pent-up sentiment and relief stung her eyes. Otis would get medical care soon. And she and Dylan were together, at least for now. She would savor whatever days she had coming, whatever lay ahead.

"We'll need um…" Dylan stared at the captain as they boarded the gangplank and hoped his request didn't seem odd. "Three cabins."

The captain, a stout, red-haired Scotsman, peered at Lily then back at Dylan. "Three?"

"Yes, sir." Dylan knew it must seem strange, he and his "wife" wanting separate cabins, but he wanted to give her privacy—and safety—if he had to take care of any unexpected business.

The steamship towered above, three stories tall, balconies circling each of them. It was a huge monster, an incongruous manmade machine sitting in the midst of nature's greenery and the river's green waters. The rising sun struck the glossy surface of the river and seemed to double the light coming at them.

A few passengers had risen, perhaps sensing in their sleep that the motion of the waters had ceased; perhaps woken by the sunshine. In either case, Dylan was pleased no one was around to ask them questions.

"Don't have three rooms," said the captain. "Only have one unoccupied cabin, and it's very small. The stretcher won't fit."

The Scot rolled back and forth on his polished heels, scratching his red muttonchop beard. "It's right beside the cabin belonging to the kitchen crew, though, and they've got an empty cot. We could put Mr. Forrestor in with the crew and you could take the room. Unless you folks would like to wait for the next steamer?"

"No, sir, that'll do fine."

Lily smiled in gratitude and either didn't notice the curious stares from the deckhands at her soiled skirts and disheveled hair, or pretended not to. Dylan, for his part, didn't give a damn what anyone thought. These were dire circumstances, and Lily was a glittering gem no matter what she wore.

From the steamboat, the shoreline's vegetation looked so thick it was impossible to imagine someone could penetrate it by foot or animal. Wiry fir trees grew in a jungle of purple fireweed. Pine trees, squished by the thickness of growth, grew tall and thin, aiming for the sky and its sunshine rather than growing wide at their base.

They settled Otis into the kitchen crew's quarters. Three bunkbeds were crammed along the walls, with five mattresses occupied. They put Otis on the sixth, near the door where he could reach the knob if needed to call for help off the second-story balcony. The captain ordered his first mate, who handled the limited medical supplies they had on board, to cleanse the wound with special tonics and wrap it in fresh bandages.

"A grizzly?" One of the youngest crew members, James, a freckle-faced adolescent, gazed in admiration at the old man. "Tell us. Tell us all about it."

"Well, he was as big as mountain," Otis muttered.

Otis didn't take well to the change in bandages, but instead of opiates he agreed to whisky. Something, thank God, to help ease his pain.

He continued with his story, embellishing the details to include a possible third and fourth bear, amusing Lily and Dylan. "And then just like that book, *Stagecoach Outlaw*—"

"Buckley Hicks!" the young man shouted.

"That's right." Otis groaned in pain, but continued. "Just like that son-of-a-bitch Buckley Hicks, I took out my rifle and aimed straight for the monster's ice-cold heart."

Smiling at the inaccuracy of Otis's piece of fiction, Lily and Dylan slipped out while he enthralled his audience.

Right next door, Lily and Dylan settled into their cabin with its two single beds crammed on opposite walls, separated by six feet and a wash basin and mirror. A full-length hip-tub, made of tin, was propped in the center for those wishing to bathe, and an armoire sat in the corner. Everything was designed for limited space, ease of cleaning, and anchoring in rough weather.

It was a far cry from the luxury of Dylan's family home in Vancouver.

"It's heaven," Lily whispered. "Absolute heaven."

"I'll go help with our horses," said Dylan. "They might be spooked climbing on board."

"I'm coming."

"Don't you want to rest?"

"Not yet."

He admired her perseverance and tolerance for hard work, and appreciated her help.

On the portside of the steamer, the lumberjacks on shore had created a chute into the hull of the ship, close to the steam engine. The men on shore shot a rapid fire of logs, faster than anything Dylan had ever seen, while the sweaty work crew on board caught and piled the logs inside. All without barely making a sound. Incredible.

As he and Lily made their way down the final set of stairs to the ground level, however, deckhands were pulling up the gangplank.

"Wait!" Dylan shouted. "Our horses!"

"We can't take those onboard, sir," one of the crew told him.

"Why in blazes not?"

"They weigh too much."

"But I've seen it done."

"Afraid we're overloaded already," said the captain behind them.

Dylan wheeled around. "Sir, we need our horses."

"We've already got four in the hull. That's nearly three tons of horse flesh. The ship's not built for horses. It's built for passengers."

Lily burst forward, her soiled skirts ruffling about her legs. "I'll pay you extra."

With what? Dylan wondered. He'd used his few dollars to buy their tickets.

"Sir," she said, desperate now as the crew was untying the ropes from the dock and getting ready to depart. "Sir, I have a bit of gold."

"Save your gold, madam. There's nothing I can do."

The gangplank was up. Deckhands were winding the excess ropes around the winches.

Dylan saw an opening and tore off for the chute the lumberjacks were using.

"Stay put!" he hollered to Lily.

"Come back!"

But he jumped across the wooden trough, balancing between the logs as they were being tossed.

"Look out, man!" A burly lumberjack kept flinging. Dylan ducked the logs and leaped to shore.

He spoke with the eldest man from camp, the one holding their horses.

"Can I sell them to you?"

"Don't have no money, mister."

"Will you take care of them, then? Until I return or send word on what to do with them."

"If you'll let me use 'em in my work, I'll take good care of 'em."

It was all Dylan needed to hear. They shook in agreement and he raced back to the paddle wheeler, jumped on the wooden trough as though he was a tight-rope walker, and plunged back onto the deck in front of a speechless Lily.

"What did you just do?"

"Took care of the horses."

"How will you get around, once we get to White-horse?"

Horses were scarce, it was true. He had little money left to buy one even if he found one. But if he hitched up with the other two Mounties, as planned, they'd likely come up with some feasible plan.

"Can't worry about that now," he said, heart still pumping from his run. "Let's unpack and have break-fast, shall we?"

"I thought you were leaving me," she whispered. "I thought you wanted me to go with Otis to Whitehorse while you took care of…you know."

"When the time comes, Lily, I won't leave like that. I'll tell you and you'll know."

She smiled then, lighter with this bit of knowledge. It made for a wonderful next hour as they unpacked and asked for delivery of coffee and biscuits to their cabin.

"Mrs. Jones," said the freckled young man from the kitchen crew as he delivered the tray. "Here you are."

"Yes, lad. Set it here." Dylan opened the door wide.

Lily beamed. "If you could send the word…I'd dearly love to bathe."

The young man blushed and looked at his boots. "Yes, ma'am. I'll have them heat the cauldrons."

"Please send us two trays of breakfast immediately. One for our friend next door. One for us."

"Yes, sir."

When he closed the door, Dylan moved in from behind, wrapped his arms around her waist and kissed her throat.

The ship rocked. They were moving. She stiffened.

"You all right?"

"Feel a bit queasy."

"Maybe you need someone to scrub that delicious back of yours."

She slapped his hand playfully. "Shhh. They'll hear us next door."

"Perfectly acceptable."

"I can't Dylan. Sooner or later, Otis will discover we're not truly married, and I—I can't let him think that we actually…"

"Your entire body is blushing."

"It is not."

"It is."

She shook her head and stabilized her wobbly legs. "The seasickness is not too bad. The river's smooth. Not like the huge waves on the ocean."

"Feeling better?"

She nodded.

"Then back to our discussion about your blushing. There's only one way to prove me right." He eyed her blouse with mischief.

"Don't you dare!" She clasped her gaping neckline and scooted to one of the beds. "I'll take this one."

"Separate beds this soon?"

"You tease me so readily."

"I don't wish to. I wish to enjoy your company."

"My company or my body?"

"Must I choose?"

She wheeled around as he approached and accidentally smacked his ribs with her elbow. It stung.

"Ow!"

"Oh, I'm sorry." She rushed to assist. "Did I—" She must have seen the gleam in his eye, for she cuffed his shoulder. "I thought I'd wounded you."

"You have. You refused my invitation."

"Shhh."

"Good Lord. I married a prude."

At that, she giggled. She pressed her face into his shoulder. Perhaps it was relief that made her jubilant. The days they'd been through, the rainstorm and the mud and the fear of losing Otis, all that relief, had lifted her spirits. Whatever the reason, Dylan appreciated seeing her like this.

A rap at the door brought him to attention.

He opened it a crack. Young James.

"Sir, since it's close to breakfast time for the rest of the ship, the captain has requested that you dine with him."

"No breakfast in our cabin?"

"We can't spare the deckhands, sir, going back and forth to the rooms when meals are provided on deck."

Their food supplies were limited on board, Dylan surmised, and having a deckhand tend to one of the third-class passengers would likely make them short in the kitchen. First-class passengers might have things different, though.

"I see, thank you. We'll be there shortly."

"Dining hall is on the top level, sir. Toward the stern. Shall I have them hold the hot water for the tub till after you've eaten?"

"Yes, thank you."

It didn't take Lily long to prepare. She didn't seem so disappointed to be leaving their cabin. At least, not like he was. He'd prefer having her to himself, alone with her for as many moments as he could.

They checked on Otis. He was resting, almost asleep.

"Would you like us to bring you something to eat?" Lily asked.

"A platter of bacon and eggs," he teased.

"And flapjacks piled so high it'd take you an entire day to finish them?" asked Dylan.

"Maybe all they have is venison," Lily finished.

Otis grumbled in his sleep. He almost smiled, but then the pain must have hit, and he flinched.

Twenty minutes later, feeling refreshed in a change of clothes, Lily and Dylan made their way down the covered aisle of the ship.

Lily misplaced her step and grasped the railing, and thus he grabbed her elbow. "How's your stomach?"

"Not quite stabilized, but not too bad. I mean, I don't feel as though I'll be sick."

"Good to hear." He kept his grip firm on her waist, nonetheless.

It seemed as though the passengers had all awakened while Lily and Dylan had been unpacking.

The deck was populated with early-morning strollers making their way up the tight stairs to the dining hall.

"Howdy," said Dylan to an older couple.

"Nice morning," said the old gent in the black hat.

They heard the sound of another steam engine. Upriver, another paddle wheeler approached. Dylan smiled at the pretty sight and tipped his cowboy hat at some of the waving passengers on the other side.

"That one's headed to Dawson," said Lily.

"Yup."

It disappeared behind a bend in the river.

When they turned the corner and approached the breakfast hall, Dylan stopped suddenly. The bristles at the back of his neck stood on end.

It couldn't be.

With a rapid fire to his pulse, he wheeled around, grabbing Lily with him and ducked behind the shoulders of oncoming men.

"What is it?" asked Lily. She peered ahead, looking through the dozens of people forming a line.

Dylan's skin turned cold. He swallowed hard. "It's him."

She bobbed in place to look over the heads.

He clamped down on her movements so she wouldn't attract attention, and started nudging her back through the crowd from where they'd come. She turned with a frown.

"He's here," Dylan whispered through dry lips. "I can't believe he's here."

"Who?" Lily glanced over her shoulder, but he kept dragging her, racing for freedom, for escape.

Finally, Dylan lowered his face and whispered gruffly in her ear. "It's Bolton Maddock. He's here."

Chapter Fifteen

Horrified, Lily spun around to lean over the deck railing, following Dylan's lead to escape the vicious eyes of Bolton Maddock. Her heart pounded in her throat, threatening to suffocate her.

"I saw them," Dylan whispered. His face paled. "The two bodyguards on the stagecoach."

"The ones I hired?"

"One still has his wrist bandaged, but I guess he's recovered enough to be of service." Dylan reached between her shoulder blades and yanked her shawl over her head. "Hide your hair."

With trembling fingers, she caught and tied the shawl's dangling ends beneath her chin.

Dylan kept his hands close to his guns. She breathed against his broad chest, feeling safer the closer she stood to him.

But how could she remain calm, pretending to look over the railing and enjoy the pretty view of sunshine hitting the tiny white rapids down below, when what she wanted to do was scream and run?

Passengers jostled behind them, bumping elbows and shoulders as they made their way to the dining room.

Dylan stared over the churning river. "I thought we were safe. I thought you were safe. What have I done?"

When they saw a clearing on the stairs, he gripped her wrist and pushed against the crowd. Both were careful to turn their faces away from the direction of the dining hall.

At any moment, she felt as though hands as cold as steel might snatch her away, might stab her or throw her overboard.

Reeling from the fright of unknown terrors, Lily panted down the stairs. A blast of sunshine hit her face, although nothing could penetrate the cool chill that had snaked up her spine.

"Nice and slow," Dylan murmured at her side. "Easy now."

They passed an older couple dressed in faded country clothes.

Dylan nodded. "Mornin' folks."

"Is breakfast being served?"

"Yes, sir. Filling up fast."

The couple increased their pace in the opposite direction, toward the food, while Dylan and Lily kept outwardly calm as they turned the last corner on the deck.

Otis's door was shut.

Dylan shoved his key into theirs. He swung it wide open, she scooted in and he bolted it behind her.

"What are we going to do?" The urgency of the situation made her temples throb. Her sense of hearing magnified—footsteps on the deck outside seemed to be coming straight for them. They passed, but then a stranger's whistling grew louder and louder till she braced for a kick at the door.

It didn't come, either.

Dylan wrapped his large arms around her and drew her to his chest. "They didn't see us. Don't worry."

She listened to his heart roar behind his shirt. "You can't be sure."

"I'm sure. Maddock would have given orders to attack."

"Maybe he did."

She jumped onto her bed and dug her derringer out of her handbag. Slats in the transom above the door let in horizontal ribbons of sunshine. They fell upon Dylan in an eerie manner, slicing his thick body in shades of black and white.

"Do you think they're coming?" she whispered.

"I don't believe they know we're on board. We docked in darkness and came on after they did. You think Maddock would be waiting in a lineup for breakfast if he knew?"

He fell onto his cot. The quiet sounds of the steamboat chugging, the strange silence of everyone having disappeared for breakfast accentuated how alone they were…and how much they had to lose.

"We could jump," she said hastily.

"They'd notice us for sure," said Dylan. "Jump to where? We have no horses even if we got to shore. What about Otis? We couldn't leave him behind."

"They don't know he's with us."

"They might find out if we left."

"We could sit tight inside our cabin for two days till we reach Whitehorse."

"We don't have much of a choice. That seems the most logical option."

Logical, she thought. How could they deal in logic when there were madmen out there willing to kill?

"Do you think my gold's on board?"

"Might be. Steamboat is the fastest way to get it the hell out of the Yukon."

Lily stared at the wrinkled fabric of her clothes. Someone had filled the water basin with fresh water while they were gone, and left another filled pail. Her mind raced with a mad mixture of hope and despair.

His boots scuffed the floor. "Lily…the captain said we couldn't take our horses on board, remember?"

She nodded, unsure what he was getting at.

"We couldn't take our horses because the ship was already overloaded. He wasn't concerned about horse-flesh after all."

"He was talking about my gold," she whispered.

"It's not unusual for Maddock to be seen carrying it with him. Most of the gold leaving the Klondike leaves on ships like this."

"So my gold's here, but we've got no one to help us retrieve it."

"The captain's in no position to help. He's not a lawman. And no other Mounties till we get to White-horse."

Her lashes flashed up at him. It was the first time he more-or-less admitted he was one. But just one man against what seemed like an army? "How many men does Maddock have with him?"

"He was talking to a very heavy man with a holster, as well as the two bodyguards. I didn't have a chance to look for more."

"Would they all recognize you?"

Dylan grit his teeth. "I came face-to-face with Maddock only once. Three years ago. It was brief and at night. My hair's longer now and I've got a month's growth of beard. He wouldn't recognize me."

"The two bodyguards would know us both."

"Your red hair is visible a mile away. Can you braid it or put it up? Maybe tuck it beneath a bonnet?"

"I don't have a bonnet. Just the cowboy hat Otis gave me."

"Dammit. You'll attract more attention wearing that than if you looked like every other woman…but cover up your hair best you can."

She raced to her bag. Nausea hit her hard. Not from seasickness, but from the thought of someone pulling her hair out by its roots. She swallowed past the sick feeling and searched for ties she could use to fasten it.

She braced herself for the question she had to ask in order to protect herself. "What does he look like, Dylan? The man who'd see you dead."

He clenched his jaw and came to stand at her side. With his broad hands, he held open her bag so she could rummage inside of it.

"Maddock's tall. Brown shirt, tan Stetson. Mustache. Has a tooth missing on the upper left side. Pocked skin."

She found what she needed in her bag and walked to the oval wall mirror. With a quick brush of her hair, she divided it into three strands. She worked quickly, her fingers weaving the loops in and out.

"I saw him, then. Walks like he thinks all eyes are on him. A well-dressed, evil snake."

The whisky slid down Maddock's throat. The big gulp seemed to overstretch his throat, as though he were swallowing live prey, then came the wicked burn of liquor.

Nightfall had come slowly on board *Lady of the Yukon*. The day had begun with a boring breakfast where he was seated next to a boring captain who found his own stories of life back in Scotland more amusing than anyone else's. Maddock had had half a mind to blast the old geezer straight through the breakfast rolls, but it would be too big of a complication to run the steamboat without him. And a waste of damn fine rolls.

Three hours till lunch, another boring meal. And finally dinnertime, where the stewards had served them in this fine suite. The best that gold could buy.

He chuckled.

Moonlight shone through the slats above their door, onto the card table and the four men who were playing. Kerosene lamplight hanging off the wall illuminated the grit of sweaty faces. Big Al, Slick Willie, and the two brothers—bodyguards—Cliff and Dick Hanson, one with a bandaged wrist.

Maddock was sittin' this one out. He preferred to keep his eyes sharp, and he needed the time to think. So far, there'd been no luck in trailing Klondike Lily and her drifter. Maddock would leave that to the four men he'd ordered to stay behind. He was getting on with the more pleasant task of tending to his newfound wealth.

Peering through the opened door that led to one of the private bedrooms, he spotted the lower half of a woman—faded brown skirts and high-ankled boots—on the edge of the mattress. Was she still sleeping? How long could a danged female sleep?

Everyone, it seemed, was troubled by the death of his brothers.

The thought of his brothers made his eyes sting.

Dammit, he hated getting soft. He poured himself another whisky and guzzled it. The steamboat rocked beneath his feet. He heard deckhands calling outside. They'd likely arrived at another wood camp, the one the captain had told him about, the last wood camp before they would hit Whitehorse tomorrow night.

Spotting something he didn't take kindly to at the card table, Maddock pulled out his gun and aimed it at Big Al. "I said no gamblin'."

Big Al wheezed, pushed the sack of gold dust back into his pocket. "What the hell else are we supposed to do on board this floating church? Hell, a man could starve of entertainment."

"They'll be plenty of entertainment when we get to Whitehorse. You can gamble all you want once we know the gold is on its way to where it's goin'."

Aching to move his muscles, feeling constrained in the limited quarters, Maddock rose and took his whisky outside.

He leaned against the rail, facing the dock. They'd come to a stop and he spotted three passengers getting off. Old men dressed in faded mining gear. No one he recognized. They had no heavy sacks with them. Obviously hadn't struck gold. He grinned. Unlucky bastards.

Crew members hustled to carry bags and unload precious supplies of rope and shovels.

On the deck, he stopped one of the passing crew members, a freckle-faced boy no older than Maddock was when he shot his first man.

"Hey there."

The young man stopped. "James at your service. What can I do for you, sir?" He glanced at the shot glass. "More whisky?"

"Never mind the drink. Tell me something. Is anyone getting on here? Any new passengers?"

"Not that I'm aware of, sir."

Maddock had a strange feeling in his gut. "Did anyone board in the last day or two? In the middle of the night, maybe?"

"No one since dawn."

"Dawn? I didn't realize we'd made any stops."

"It was a quick one. Most passengers were sleeping. I reckon you were, too. Picked up a man who'd been mauled by a grizzly."

"You don't say."

"He might lose his arm still."

Maddock wasn't interested in idiots. "Some men don't know when to leave well enough alone."

"Sir?"

"He was probably askin' for it. They always do."

The ship heaved again. Maddock steadied himself against the rail. The crew untied the ropes at the dock and the steamboat once again chugged away. "Anyone else get on with the grizzly fella?"

He scratched the freckles on his nose. "A married couple, sir. They appear newly wed. Haven't seen too much of 'em." He snickered. "They haven't left their cabin all day."

"What does she look like?"

"Maybe I shouldn't—"

"What color's her hair?"

"That's an odd thing to ask."

"What color?"

"Red, sir. Vivid red."

It snapped him in the gut. His breathing tripled. "Where's she at?"

The boy seemed to panic. His eyes darted around the deck, then over the dark rip of the waves. Was he sorry he disclosed something? "They...they just disembarked."

Maddock wasn't sure whether to believe it. He'd just witnessed three miners getting off, no one else, but then again, he hadn't been watching the gangplank from the beginning. He narrowed his eyes at the boy. "That so?"

James nodded nervously, bowed and scampered away like a scared squirrel.

Maddock took another swig of firewater and tossed the glass into the black swirling waters below. The ship was moving fast already.

He returned to the suite and ordered the two brothers. "Take two other men with you from the other room. I want you all on horses. *Right now.*"

"Horses? But boss—"

"Do as I say!"

Dylan bolted the door as the steamboat took off from the dock. Still panting, with his pulse racing as it had been most of the day while they'd hidden themselves in the cabin, he turned to face Lily in the moonlight.

She looked soft and hopeful, and he wished he could protect her forever.

"I told them we were leaving. I gave young James our bags."

They'd saved their clothes and essentials, however, and had stuffed their outgoing bags with sheets. To the casual observer, it would appear they'd left.

She whispered. "What if someone comes knocking on our door?"

"So far, no one has. I didn't see anyone boarding, so there's no need for anyone else to use our cabins."

There was nothing he could do except wait it out till Whitehorse. Getting off here wouldn't serve a purpose. If Maddock spotted them, he and Lily wouldn't get far on foot in the woods. Their chances were better staying put.

Dylan sighed. They were trapped on board, he in the most vulnerable position he could imagine—with a weak and injured old man and a woman who barely reached Maddock's chin.

What had he done?

"Did you slip Otis the note?" Dylan asked her.

"I didn't want to write it down in case the note got to someone else. While you were talking to James, I snuck in and spoke to Otis directly."

"Anyone see you?"

She shook her head, her braids tightly wrapped around her neck and hidden beneath her hat.

"You sure?"

"You didn't see me, did you?"

"True enough," said Dylan. "You were sly."

"I brought some food back with me, too. Otis has a steady stream of it coming in from the kitchen crew."

Lily tore the pillowcase from her bed and shoved in her clothes. He did the same with his necessities—she glanced at his extra bullets, and the leather case containing the pipe and blade Otis had given him.

"We'll be in Whitehorse tomorrow evening," he told her.

Lily slumped onto his cot. She ran her fingers along the leather case. Her expression was overcome with sudden remorse. She reached over to his hand, brought it up to her lips and kissed it. "There's something I need to tell you."

He opened her fingers and kissed her palm. "I'm listening."

Her blue eyes glistened. "It's about Amanda."

"Yeah?"

"She—"

Loud noises interrupted them. People were whistling outside their door. Hollering and splashing.

His heart thudded. His neck infused with heat. What now?

Dylan drew his gun and slowly turned the doorknob. She peered beside him, pressing her warm arm against his chest. Two crew members were hanging off the deck, watching the waters churn below.

She couldn't seem to see past their uniforms. "What is it?" she whispered into Dylan's shoulder.

"I don't believe it," he gasped. "Four of Maddock's men just jumped off the ship. On horseback."

He gently closed and bolted the door.

She struggled to grasp the meaning. "All four on horseback?"

Nodding, he slumped against the wall and tilted back his Stetson. Worry creased his brow.

"You know what this means?" she said.

His lips thinned with strain. "They're chasing us. They think we got off at that camp. They do want to kill us."

"But that's good, then, isn't it? Oh, Dylan, we're safe aren't we? We're safe here for a while longer."

Lily listened to the yelling of passengers and crew, the excitement and fear in the voices outside, and tried to convince herself the temporary commotion didn't matter. What mattered was that Dylan's plan had worked. Maddock thought they were gone.

Dylan's voice was a rasp. "It was Maddock's two bodyguards and two others I didn't recognize. Maddock gave the command."

She closed her eyes. The command to kill. He was onto them, and it was difficult to override her terror.

Chapter Sixteen

"But they think we're gone," Dylan finally said, soothing her again. "We do have a little cushion of time."

Their diversion with the luggage appeared to have worked.

"Why didn't they all leave?"

"Hedging their bets, maybe, that we're still on board. Or maybe they'd prefer to stay with the gold. Whichever case it is, keep your gun with you at all times."

She eyed her handbag on the stand. "I need to tell you something, Dylan."

"We need to figure out what to do. Otis is pretending that we left him behind, right?"

"Right."

"So no one will be looking for him outright. But we can't be seen talking to him again. It'll put him in danger. James must've told Maddock we left the ship. I gave him our bags, but made sure two of his crewmates overheard me. So it could've been any one of the three."

"Dylan," she implored. "It's about Amanda."

He tore his concentration from the door. Things had settled outside. Her pulse subsided, the flush left his face. She pulled him to the cots and sat him down.

"What is it?"

She fingered her palm. "It's not easy to say."

He tossed her denim pants and shirt to the other side of her pillowcase and placed his hands on either side of her, enveloping her with his strength.

"I'll…I'll change into the pants and shirt when we get closer to Whitehorse," she mumbled. "Easier to get around in clothes that don't bunch at your knees."

"Never mind the clothes. What is it?"

"I haven't told you everything. For that, I apologize. But I couldn't bear the thought that my sister…that Amanda was so in need of help she turned to the wrong people."

"What people?"

She unlaced the many laces of her spiked boots. He reached for her hands and stilled them.

"There was a rumor I'd heard when I first got to Dawson. Someone told me there was a young woman in Alaska who looked an awful lot like me…that she'd…she'd been sighted with…"

Dylan's face drained of color. His dark eyes flashed. "The Maddock gang."

Lily buried her face in her hands. "It was two boot-makers who told me. They were robbed at gunpoint in Skagway. Amanda was apparently…staying in the house where the Maddock men were last seen."

"Were the thieves caught?"

She shook her head. "They got away."

"What makes you think it was your sister?"

"The bootmakers said her name was Amanda."

"Amanda what?"

Lily's throat squeezed. She could barely say it. "Amanda Maddock."

He was stunned. After a moment, he spoke. "Might've been a different Amanda."

"Long blond hair. A small mole beneath her left eye."

Dylan stood up in the cramped space, yanked her up by her hands and wrapped himself around her. It was a loving gesture, full of compassion for how she was feeling—the sorrow in her heart for a younger sister who'd turned to the wrong people for safety and security.

After a solid few minutes of holding her, Dylan said the words she feared most, that made her heart tremble. "I wonder which one she married. Bolton, or one of his two dead brothers."

The following afternoon, after a restless night of little sleep, the sway of the ship lulled Lily into a trance as she lay beside Dylan. He'd slid into her bed, trying to give her comfort.

The afternoon sun had made its way around to blaze across their side of the ship and it was stifling hot, keeping her awake. It beat through the overhead slats, casting stripes across their bed. But today, the shadows of black and white didn't look as frightening as they had yesterday when she'd gotten news of Maddock.

Or was she simply exhausted from running scared? Drained of energy?

Having discussed her sister with Dylan, Lily didn't feel any more hopeful about Amanda.

Dylan cupped her waist gently from behind. She lifted the hemline of her skirt to expose her bare feet, welcoming any coolness that came her way.

"It must've been agony for you, wondering where she was."

"She was left to my care. I disappointed my parents terribly. If they're looking down from heaven, they must be sick about the way I handled everything."

"Amanda has a will of her own."

"But she was young and I should've—"

"You were young, too. You were fifteen when you were left to look after her. She was eighteen when she left you in Skagway. You see…you were younger than her when you were left to take over the motherly duties."

His words were comforting. Surprising. "I'd never thought of it like that before."

"If you forgive her for what she's done in her youth, then you must forgive yourself."

"It's easy to say. Much harder to do."

Lily stiffened at the approaching footsteps outside.

"They'll pass," Dylan whispered. His lips were at her ear. "They don't need this cabin for anyone else. No sense cleaning it till they get to Whitehorse. It's easier to swab the decks all at one time."

The footsteps faded away, as he'd promised, and Lily eased back onto the mattress. He stroked her hair from behind. Then her neck.

"How do you forgive yourself, Dylan?"

"What do you mean?"

"How do you forgive yourself for the things you did in your past?"

He said nothing.

"You see…it's easy to say these things about someone else's life…more difficult to do in your own."

"You're wise."

She didn't feel wise. They were trapped on board. How could they persevere under these circumstances? On the other hand, no one had come knocking on their door. Maddock had bought the story that they'd disembarked at the last stop. It was the only feasible explanation. The weight began to lift from her temples. Energy returned.

He swung his long legs out of the bed. "Are you going to change out of these clothes?" he coaxed. "Into your pants like you said?"

"Is it time?"

"We still have two or three hours, but it's best to be prepared."

She lifted herself out of bed and reached for the stack of clothing she'd piled on the dresser.

He was fully dressed in his white shirt and denim pants. He'd unbuttoned the top few due to the heat, and had rolled up his sleeves, and she enjoyed seeing the parts of him that were usually hidden—the top of his muscled chest and his sinewy forearms.

Although she and Dylan had been intimate by the fire two nights ago, they'd kept their distance since. She couldn't look at him now for shyness, and wondered how to do this without exposing herself.

She eyed the door. Bolted tight. Chair propped beneath the doorknob in case of trouble. Guns at Dylan's side. Hers in the handbag beside her.

Instead of turning away from her to allow her privacy, he kicked back on his bed, leaned against the wall, folded one arm behind his neck to prop it up for the view, and the other over his chest. "Go ahead. Entertain me."

"You've got mischief in your eyes."

"That's what my mother used to say."

Something in his voice resonated. "Used to?"

By the sad glimmer in his eyes, he confirmed her passing.

"Oh, Dylan."

"Four years ago. Died in her sleep from a fever. It wasn't a bad way to go. She didn't suffer."

Sadness wove around Lily. "She was always a kind woman. She knew her mind when it came to the hired help, but she was decent. Your father?"

"Still around. Uses a cane due to a fall on the ice last winter, but seems like nothing can stop him."

They were silent for a few minutes while she gathered her soap and towel and brushed her hair. He seemed to have recovered from his mother's passing, but she wanted to say something nonetheless.

"I've been selfish, asking about your brothers and no one else. Telling you my problems but not listening to yours. I'm sorry."

"Apology accepted," he said. His gaze lingered on her skirt as she pulled out the tail of her blouse. "Feel free to finish what you've started."

She laughed softly. "How can you turn your sentiments around so quickly?"

"Because I'm staring at a beautiful woman."

She turned her back to him and walked to the wash-basin.

Behind her, she heard him slide something off the floor. "Even your boots are a pleasure to look at."

Undoing her blouse buttons, she let the fabric slip to the floor. Her bloomers followed.

She untied the stays of her corset. The cloth opened. Her breasts parted through the fabric, soft raspberry nipples. She accidentally brushed her arm against one and the sensation rippled down to her thighs. She slipped the corset off her shoulders, then her chemise, until she stood there naked. It felt wonderfully cooler.

She heard him inhale sharply.

Unrolling a washcloth, she dipped it into the lukewarm water, then lifted it to her face. When that was scrubbed, she took the cloth to the underside of her arms, and her belly. She'd missed the opportunity for a full bath in the hip-tub, but was already feeling re-freshed from this scrub.

She knew the entire time she was being watched. It thrilled her. With tendrils of hair moist around her face, she gently lifted her gaze to the mirror propped in front of her, and found his eyes.

They were a mesmerizing shade of brown, sparkling with depths and desires and unspoken feelings.

The ship swayed gently. How could she feel such exuberance and fear at the same time? The thrill of being alive.

She was terrified they'd be caught, or that she'd lose Amanda, or Otis, or even her gold, and yet somehow safe as long as she was with Dylan.

His adoring gaze ran down her shoulders, down the back of her spine, over her backside and down her legs to her feet. She basked in the simple pleasure of being a woman. She saw his admiration in the way his lips tilted, the pull of his cheek, the firmness in his chin as he watched her body move. And when his gaze came back to her in the mirror, she felt the wonder of being here with this man, so full of life.

Finally, he spoke to her in the mirror. "We can't do much about what's going to happen three hours from now," he murmured above the hiss of the steam engine, "but we can enjoy this moment, Lily."

The anticipation between them was almost unbearable.

"Turn around," he begged.

She did, turning gently in the shadows of light and dark.

"Slower."

She did as commanded, conscious that he was staring at her naked hips and legs. Her bare feet lapped on the cool boards.

"Come here."

He stood up and welcomed her.

"You sure like to order people around," she whispered against his mouth when she reached him.

"I think you like my orders."

She did. She loved to please him.

Her breasts felt heavy and she yearned for him to caress them. He avoided them instead, frustrating her, but when he stroked one thigh, working his way up to her hip, she felt so womanly she didn't want him to stop. He caressed her buttocks, placed both hands on her naked behind and rolled her to the bed on top of him.

Still he didn't touch her breasts. He kissed her neck and throat and teased her with his fingers on her arm next to her bosom, then trailed a blaze from her bellybutton over her stomach.

It tickled and she gasped a kiss onto his cheek. He circled her bellybutton. The tickling sensation stopped, giving way to a heavenly rippling of muscles.

"Hmm," she said, savoring his strokes and the delightful effect he had on her body. "You've got magic fingers."

He was lost in kissing her throat and cleavage. She clawed off his shirt and ran her hands over his smooth shoulders. He kissed her feverishly on the mouth, prolonging the sensation by dipping his tongue. She traced his tongue with her own, marveling that no other man had ever kissed her like this.

They rolled over so he was on the bottom. She watched sunlight play on his chest. Long intermittent shadows accentuated the curve of muscles, the dip at his breastbone, tanned skin, and the trail of golden hair that led downward beneath his belt.

No one could have prepared her for the intensity of this moment with Dylan. A moment to savor, to cling to hope.

He kissed her deeply, scooped his hand upward and captured her breast. She rocked with sensation. She enjoyed the joining of their mouths as much as their interwoven bodies.

"I like looking at you," he whispered.

She pulled back and he ran his hands over her hips,

up her bare stomach. His eyes settled on her dangling breasts.

With an eagerness she found endearing, he rose to his feet, ripped off his belt and got out of his jeans till he was splendidly naked, too. Such perfect form. Erect and ready.

"You're a beautiful example of the male species," she remarked with stifled humor.

"Yes, professor."

Surprising her, he pushed her down on the bed, planted his hands firmly on either side of her and touched her only with his mouth. A spiral of kisses engulfed her shoulder, the soft bulge beneath her arm, the bend of her elbow. He trailed his lips to her stomach, then nuzzled the tip of each awaiting breast. Waves of pleasure rippled through her.

When his mouth slid lower, she stiffened in surprise. He clasped her hand to assure her and kept moving, spreading kisses dangerously lower. And lower and lower.

When he kissed her *there,* she was unsure how to react. It felt so blissfully sensual, every whisper of his mouth caressing the sacred place she'd never imagined a man would want to go. Yet it felt so right with Dylan. She succumbed to the pleasure and allowed him to give what she intensely wanted.

She relaxed on the bed, wove her legs around his shoulders and just when she thought it would culminate into a glorious explosion, he moved away from her center and kissed her thigh, her knee, her calf.

"Now," he said, with those captivating brown eyes, "I think you're ready for me now."

He was fully erect and she adored watching him. How odd that men had such parts of their bodies that could rapidly swell to such heights.

"You're smiling," he said.

"At your charm." She knelt at his knees and kissed him there.

His groan was indication that he enjoyed it as much as she. She kissed a path upward along the silky shaft and licked the tip. He was rock-hard.

He stroked her neck and lifted her to face him. She kissed his mouth with such passion, winding her arms around his neck, that her bare bosom pressed against his nakedness.

He tilted her over on the bed, her hips away from him.

"Dylan?" She wondered about the position.

"Some angles will please you more."

Trusting him, she lay on her side and he slipped in from the back. A snug fit in a moist place. She filled with Dylan.

She was unprepared for the intensity of her reaction, physically and sentimentally. Her body rocked with his. He was a gentle but firm lover, intent on waiting for her to climax, insisting that she was his priority. She was unsure of her body and how she might appear to him, vulnerable and contorted.

He reassured her. "Trust me, Lily. I want to please you. This is the most natural thing between a man and woman."

He gripped her shoulder. Her breathing grew louder and erratic, the heat of the room engulfed her, and she peaked. Contraction after contraction squeezed around his shaft, filling her with the splendor of making love with Dylan. He let out a soft moan and climaxed partway through hers; as though the vision of seeing her in such throes of bliss was what pushed him into his.

Their breathing subsided, their hearts slowed. He pulled out of her and crumpled onto the bed, kissing her shoulder blade with tenderness.

"You weaken me, woman. I won't be able to walk."

She laughed into the bed sheet, totally swept away and spent herself. "You started this."

"I did not," he teased. "You had to change, remember? And how could any man resist a view like that?"

Thrilled that she'd pleased him, she rolled over in the cool sheet. A sheen of perspiration covered his broad chest. They cleaned up quickly, then started for their clothes.

The ship tilted. They swayed. A rising tide of voices filtered from the deck. The paddle wheeler bumped into something and it jarred them.

Lily gasped. "We can't be there already."

Dylan had already donned his pants. His words sent another chill through her, a new fear she hadn't thought of. "It just occurred to me. Could your sister be on board with Maddock?"

Chapter Seventeen

Lily tried not to panic. She tugged her denim pants up her legs so fast, she lifted her feet right off the cool boards. "Oh, no…she can't be."

Dylan raced to button his shirt, long arms twisting, broad shoulders tugging against the fabric. "It is possible that Maddock's traveling with a wife."

The word *wife* stabbed at her heart. Not her Amanda.

But another part of Lily, the part that hungered to see her younger sister again at any cost, was already desperately praying it *was* her.

"Is it in Amanda's nature?" he asked. "Is she the kind of young lady who'd ride with men like these?"

Lily shook her head. The tight pins in her braided hair pinched her scalp. She swallowed a tide of remorse. "Not like her at all."

Finished dressing into his suede vest and a clean blue shirt, Dylan turned the knob and peered out. Within a few seconds, he closed the door with a look of relief. He shared the good news. "We hit a sandbank. I can see the docks of Whitehorse up ahead."

"We're that close?"

He pushed back the dark hair at his ears. "Must've made better time than the captain anticipated."

Lily took a look out the door, slowly peering through the crack. No crewmen on their deck.

The men were all down below, focused on the sandy shore and what they could do to disengage the steamer, stuck in mud. They were hoisting ropes and pulleys. Several deckhands jumped into the river, knee-deep in water to help from the bottom position.

"When should we get off?" she whispered.

He reached around her with a muscled arm and pressed the door closed. His face was inches away. He didn't have to touch her for her to feel him—his tender look alone caressed her. "I'd like to search the boat for your sister."

Lily staggered back against the door. "Not *now.*"

"Now's good. Everyone's occupied with the sandbank. Maddock and his men are likely watching the entertainment, too."

"You don't know how many men he's got with him."

"Quite a few, if he could afford to send four after us on horseback."

"You see? It pains me to say don't search for her…but you'd be jeopardizing your life and maybe hers. Wouldn't it be safer to check for her once we dock and we're on solid ground? How many Mounties are waiting for you in Whitehorse?"

"There are usually two or three on duty."

She was appalled. "You haven't spoken with them directly about this gang?"

He rubbed his jaw and paced the floor. "Word was sent."

"Oh, Dylan." It wasn't as secure as she'd imagined. In her mind, she'd concocted an entire troop of Mounted Police, with guns and horses, ready to help.

Pressing his big boots into the floor, he spoke bluntly. "If you weren't with me, if Otis wasn't next door, I'd hunt them down one by one. Right this bloody minute."

Misery broke in her voice. "My gold…my sister… I've put everyone in jeopardy with this hunt. The people I treasure most."

His bulk filled the cabin. "That's always the way it is with these type of people. They count on your soft spots to get away with how much they do."

He found her handbag on the dresser and handed it to her. "Take out your gun and tuck it beneath your belt." He watched her do it, then pressed his fingers beneath her chin and lifted her face to his.

Defiance was etched in his expression, and a softness behind his eyes when he spoke.

"If I don't come back in twenty minutes, wait till the steamboat docks in Whitehorse, then disembark on your own. Wait till everyone else leaves the ship and then you go. Find the Mounted Police tent and tell them everything that's happened. Will you promise?"

"Yes," She fought hard to retain her composure. "Where are you going? I thought you agreed to leave Amanda—"

"Not Amanda. Otis. I'm not leaving him behind. I'll

take him overboard on the other side of the ship. Now's my best chance to get him to safety. Unnoticed."

Despite her misgivings, she knew he was right.

"I'll come back for you as soon as I get him to shore. But if I don't—" he clutched her waist and brought her close "—you know what to do."

"I'll do it, Dylan."

They kissed softly. She stood on tiptoe and draped her arms around his neck, never wanting to let go.

With a sadness that tore at both of them, he opened the door, slid his cowboy hat low over his brow and strode out.

Once again, he was putting himself in danger to tend to someone else—an old man with a wounded shoulder who couldn't move on his own. She prayed for their safety and worried at this unexpected turn of events.

Maddock kicked her dangling legs. The waif rose off the bed and rubbed her eyes.

"Mrs. Maddock," he said with a smirk, "we've landed."

She didn't look near old enough to be a missus, but her plump curves turned every male head she passed. He liked that—he had something they didn't.

"Best get ready."

She said nothing.

She'd slept for three solid hours, yet still looked drowsy. A ring of dark circles glossed the thin skin beneath her blue eyes. There was strain in her brow, and all the tension of the last week on her tight little shoulders.

The death of his brothers had affected her deeply. He wondered what she was thinking as she whisked her shawl over her arms, brushed her long blond hair and took a sip of water.

Of course, she never told him. No matter how close they'd become this past year, she kept her mouth shut and her eyes lowered.

Her silence didn't bother Maddock. No sirree, not at all. In fact, he liked his women scared.

It made his arteries pump and a fever burn beneath his skin.

Dylan didn't return in twenty minutes. Not in thirty. Not in thirty-five. Lily's ribs squeezed beneath her corset. She feared the worst.

She couldn't understand why it was so quiet outside. If he'd been caught with Otis, there would have been noises. Shouting and accusations and an attempt to flee. Maybe, heaven forbid, even gunshots.

Gripping her derringer, Lily pressed her ear against the cabin door and strained to listen past the call of the gulls and the shuffling of feet. No one stopped at her door. She kept it unbolted for Dylan's return, but a good chunk of time had passed and he was no where.

The steamboat hadn't budged beneath her boots, either. They were still stuck.

The minutes passed. An hour went by. She moved from the door to the bed to the remaining food and water, gathering her strength and worried sick about Dylan. She glanced at Otis's pocket watch and tucked it into her handbag.

Dylan's pillowcase, stuffed with his clothes and essentials, lay on his bed. He hadn't been able to take it with him since he was carrying Otis. Now what?

She opened the flaps and took what she thought was the most important thing inside—the leather pipe case with its hidden compartment and knife.

Trembling at what she had to do, what she knew she must, Lily straightened her white shirt, hoisted her pillowcase to her side, leaving Dylan's behind, and slowly turned the knob.

The deck was empty, but the hum of people ricocheted off the gangplanks below. The boat was still grounded, but the captain had apparently decided to let everyone disembark from here.

Perhaps he thought it easier to get the boat unglued with lighter weight. Or maybe the crowds were too anxious to wait, within sight of Whitehorse but unable to reach it.

Rays of the setting sun washed over the balcony. Flies buzzed past her head as she lifted her black shawl and encased her face. Her hair was still braided and pinned to the back of her head, as hidden as she could manage with what she had. Her cowboy hat was strung around her neck and dangled against her back. She strode casually to the railing and peered at the throngs below.

They marched in groups of two or three, hollering to others on shore. Some hauled suitcases so heavy they could barely lift them. Gold. They were carrying gold, tucked inside their carpetbags and leather trunks. Gold weighted down the pockets of more than one man she witnessed. Others had shiny teeth capped with the yellow mineral, some tossed nuggets from one end of the line to the other as though its worth was meaningless. Most everyone who carried gold carried a gun.

The folks who'd struck it were a mix of society, ranging from men in tattered tophats to politicians to farmers, to sailors from overseas who spoke in Finnish and Norwegian. Some men were black Americans freed from slavery and finding their fortune in the Klondike, returning to civilization to tell the world about their luck. Others were of Spanish descent, or Russian or British.

She wondered where her gold was. No sign of Maddock. The further they traveled from the spot where they'd been ambushed, into the density of a more populated place, the more likely the gold would be dispersed.

She cursed Bolton Maddock for all he'd done.

Rising on tiptoe, she peered over the edge at the farthest gangplank near the stern, the one apparently reserved for deckhands and crew. No sign of Dylan. No sign of a kind old gent who'd been mauled by a grizzly.

Anxiety made her stomach churn. She had to find the Mountie tent. Her spirits flared with hope; Dylan would look for her there.

Waiting a few more minutes for the crowds to thin, she pressed her chest against the rail and leaned way over to get a glimpse of the tented town of Whitehorse.

Throngs of folks made their way down the docks that were lined with small shacks.

She read the hand-painted canvas signs: Guides for Rent, Martha's Best Restaurant, Fresh Seafood, Klondike Outfits Supplied Here. There was merchandise to buy for both the people arriving to the gold fields, and for those leaving whose pockets were either filled with gold or empty.

What a strange relationship men had with gold, here in the Klondike. At least there was more to buy in Whitehorse than there had been in Dawson. In Dawson, in the middle of the wooded rivers, there was little of anything. Initially, men and women who'd struck it rich found themselves with piles of yellow rock that was almost useless, for there were no restaurants, no shops, little trade and little food to buy.

They owned a mountain of gold that meant virtually nothing, till they brought it back to wherever they'd come from.

Her heart began to pump a stronger beat. She was ready to make her move.

Few people remained on board. Two men, dressed in old wool suits that looked as though they'd been worn straight through the spring and summer, hopped off the gangplank. Lily didn't wish to take a chance of being seen by other passengers, fearing Maddock and his men, and thus turned right and made her way down the stairs the crew used.

Two young deckhands, buckets and mops in hand, nodded as she passed.

James came screeching around the corner, nearing knocking her over.

"Beg your pardon, ma'am. Captain ordered me to the deck."

"That's fine, James, goodbye."

He adjusted his cap and narrowed his eyes. "But weren't you...didn't you leave a few hours ago?"

She pulled her shawl tighter, pretending she never heard, and kept going.

As she turned the final set of stairs, almost free to board the crew's gangplank, she spotted Dylan in the crowds below.

A tide of welcome relief washed over her. She hadn't realized how much strain she was under until she spotted his familiar face.

He was wearing a white sailor's hat and dark Norwegian uniform. Otis was slung over his shoulder as if the man weighed nothing more than a sack of corn.

Dylan hadn't spotted her yet, but she came to full alert, speeding her pace, winding through the crew on deck to catch up with her men.

Dylan flung Otis onto a folding canvas chair by a hut marked Ships for Sale. He scouted the wharf, tucking himself and Otis beneath a tree under the shade of the hut. Land's sake, they were safe.

She wondered if there were any hospitals now in Whitehorse, tented ones or perhaps a log house. Last year, when she'd passed through the town, it had seemed ten times smaller in size and had no proper hospital.

"Pardon me," she whispered to a crewman as she squeezed past. He carried a wicker basket of empty cooking jars.

A hundred yards away, Dylan finally looked up from his hidden spot. Across the water, his gaze met hers on board, and all the world seemed right again. They'd get through this together.

Around the final stretch of decking, as Lily slowly and surely made her way, she was suddenly confronted with two hardened men wearing holsters and a man with black, slicked-back hair. Bolton Maddock.

She nearly wretched her last meal. She caught her breath, pressed her shoulders to the wall and halted on the deck.

They didn't notice her. The men with the guns reached the crew's gangplank first and waited for their boss.

"Take care of her," Maddock ordered as he pushed his way through.

Her? Terror careened through Lily. She looked for a place to run.

But it wasn't Lily that Maddock was referring to. A younger woman turned the corner of the deck behind him. She was dressed in a faded brown skirt and brown blouse, a white shawl pulled around her. Blond hair cascaded over her shoulders. As she made her way to the gangplank behind Maddock and his vicious men, her sorrowful eyes moved up from the river to look straight at Lily.

For ten pulsing beats of her heart, Lily stared at her younger sister.

Chapter Eighteen

Amanda was alive. Lily's breathing came in a torrent.

Her sister, though, looked like a stranger. Her face had aged, but her body was still as slender. She stiffened with wide-eyed fear at the same time she held her head high with dignity. Such conflicting sentiments in the body of a nineteen-year-old woman.

Lily gripped her skirt pockets, still shadowed by the wall of the boat, desperately wanting to go to her, but stuck in a moment of suspension.

Fading sunlight flickered in Amanda's pale blue eyes while she stared back at Lily. Her mouth dropped open, about to speak, then she dared a glance at the men waiting for her. She blinked several times, tilted back her head and then steadied herself, nostrils slightly flaring as though she'd made a decision. She clamped her lips together, swirled away from Lily and strode down the gangplank.

Who was this young woman who stared back at Lily? Why didn't she breathe a word of hello?

Lily's mind reeled as two crewmembers barreled past her with an empty keg of ale.

"Excuse us, ma'am."

With her eyes on her sister's receding back, her unspoken words trapped in her throat, Lily stepped out of the way as two more men came through with a sack of dirty linens.

She and her sister were both in danger. That's what Amanda understood. It had to be why she left so abruptly. She was sparing Lily's life. Perhaps instinctively knowing that alerting Maddock to the fact she had an older sister would cause nothing but harm.

Not one touch of her sister's hand. Not one gentle kiss on the cheek. Not one loving word.

The impetuous girl who used to bubble with laughter, who rarely stopped talking, had said nothing.

Shaking in the fading sun, Lily wrapped her shawl around her face and faded into the crowd of men stepping off the ship.

Dylan, it appeared, had seen everything. His widened eyes and expressive dark features showed great compassion for Lily, but he motioned with a simple nod for her to keep her distance from Amanda as well as himself.

He put his arm around Otis.

Somehow, he'd managed to either hire or persuade another man to help him. The young man, dressed in fisherman's boots and hat, stepped to Otis's other side.

Anchored between the two healthy men, Otis stood up, grimaced, and was more or less carried between them as they faded into the stream of people at the dock.

Lily dragged her pillowcase of clothing and took her time behind the men. No one thought her odd for her pillowcase, for this town, this country with its gold rush, had attracted the oddest set of characters she'd ever met. Folks, from the poorest unemployed to the richest landowner, all wanting to try their hand at lady luck.

Lily craned her neck in the opposite direction to locate the blond head. There it was. Her sister was following Maddock through the crowd, with a gunman on either side of her.

When Maddock tapped her on the shoulder and leaned in to say something against her cheek, nausea welled inside of Lily. She kept her eyes riveted on the sickening sight and wondered if her sister was married to the worst criminal in the territory. The very one who'd ordered Dylan tortured.

Surely Amanda didn't know of Maddock's cruelty. Lily couldn't imagine that the young woman who'd taken extraordinary care of household cats and dogs for her employers would stand beside this man if she did.

When Amanda got a chance, she glanced behind her and scanned the crowds. Her eyes settled on Lily and for a brief moment, ever so lightly, Amanda smiled.

Oh.

Then Maddock snatched her by her arm.

"Watch your step, ma'am." A stranger pushed Lily from behind, spinning her in a new direction.

Snapping out of her quiet storm, Lily came to her senses. She gulped the fresh air that blew off the river and inhaled the scent of cedars. The clear sky above seemed to twinkle with a deepening, vivid blue, as the orange ball to the west touched the edge of the darkening mountains.

Where was Dylan? Where did he go?

Panicked, she spun to her right. Hagglers argued over the cost of flour and baking goods. No Dylan.

She pivoted to the left. Men with livestock, goats and two mules bargained for them on the spot.

Lily bolted further up the dock, ignoring a group of men settling on a price for canoes.

A tall blond man in a wide sombrero, holding a walking stick carved with the head of a magnificent lion, boasted the canoes' benefits. "They've been planed and greased by two locals."

"What makes you think I want two? I said one."

The seller gave the man a pat on the back. "Because William, you've got a young boy. He'll want his own."

The buyer chuckled. "You do have a point."

Weaving and bobbing, Lily fought the panic taking hold. Where was Dylan?

Almost when she was on the brink of screaming, she spotted the sailor's hat making its way down the far side of the docks, the old man with a bandaged shoulder, and a fisherman on the other side of him.

Lowering her head, Lily squeezed through the sweaty bodies, dodging baskets of fresh fish, jugs of kerosene, and the leers of men who hadn't seen a woman in months.

Come on, Lily, thought Dylan, *show your face. Let me know you made it.*

Dylan hoisted Otis into the fisherman's shack, set

him down on a greasy bed and paid the fisherman a few bills. "Thanks, mister."

"Just be sure you're out by tomorrow. My partner's comin' back from an expedition and he don't take kindly to strangers."

"Understood."

The man left, and Dylan let the door stay ajar.

Reddish sunlight, from a sunrise that seemed to take forever to set here in the north, gave the items inside a warm glow. There was a table hacked from pine, two equally rough chairs, two narrow cots with moth-eaten gray blankets, and a newspaper from Chicago dated six months previous.

Propped on the bed, Otis leaned against the roughly sawn lumber wall. He groaned, nursing his bad arm. "Sorry to be such a thorn in your plans."

"You're no such thing. I'm glad the bleeding's finally stopped."

"It's not feelin' any better."

Which meant, Dylan, knew, that it must hurt like hell. "I'll go scout for a doctor."

"Good luck," Otis said sarcastically. "I'll be beholden if you just come back with fresh bandages."

Lily slid into the cabin so smoothly Dylan never heard her footsteps till she was beside him.

The shadow from his heart lifted.

She smiled with absolute elation. "Thank God. I thought I'd lost you."

"Your husband's takin' good care of me." Otis grinned in approval. "I'm much obliged to you both."

"Yes, my…my husband has a way of doing that." Lily's features lit with curiosity at Dylan.

He was conscious of Otis's stare as he asked her, "How'd it go back there?" He was referring to her sister. "Are you all right?"

Lily bowed her head and removed the shawl from her face. Her fingers trembled, and she was pale.

"What happened back there?" Otis eyed her, but without his spectacles, his focus was a bit off.

Dylan waited for her to disclose what she wished about Amanda. Otis didn't know the story.

"I saw my sister," she told the old man.

"Your sister?" It registered slowly in the man's face. Then he looked 'round her shoulders. "Where is she? Did you bring her?"

"Afraid not, Otis. She's with…she's with Maddock."

"Maddock?"

Dylan stepped back. He pulled out a chair for her and one for himself. They sat down. He put a hand on her shoulder to comfort her in any way he could.

"Explain it, so an old man like me can understand."

"You need to be careful, Otis," she whispered. "If something should happen to either one of us, you need to be careful. They might come after you."

How could the old man look after himself, worried Dylan, when he couldn't see straight?

"Listen, nothin's gonna happen to either one of you," said Otis. "Now what's this about Maddock and your sister?"

"I left Dawson City nearly two weeks ago to look for my sister. She's in trouble. She's young and made some mistakes and I made some mistakes and…Lord knows I deserve to be punished…but not her…"

Lily stopped talking, unable to go on.

Dylan took over. "We think she married one of the Maddock brothers."

"Holy hell," snapped Otis. "Pardon my language."

"It's my fault for leaving her," said Lily.

"How old is she?"

"Nineteen."

"How old do you reckon a person has to be," said Otis, "to take the blame for their own actions?"

"You both keep saying that, but…but what if they forced her? What if they kidnapped her and forced her into marriage?"

"Did she see you just now?" asked Otis.

Lily nodded.

"Then she could have come with you. Here to safety."

"She was saving me. I know it. She didn't want Maddock to see us together."

The two men didn't have a reply. They sat and thought.

"I'm hungry," Otis declared.

Lily frowned. "How can you think of—"

"I imagine the both of you are, too," Otis ploughed on. "My wife and I would never stew over a problem on an empty stomach. Always made the problem bigger somehow. Now, why don't you two rustle up somethin' for us to eat?"

Dylan understood what the old man was doing. In a roundabout manner, he was bringing the focus back to their problems, giving them sustenance and endurance for the battle they were about to fight.

Although Dylan was the experienced Mountie, used to leading troops of men into danger, he wondered if in this case it was an old man whose shoulder had been ripped open by a bear, who was leading them.

Simplicity was key, thought Dylan.

Whenever his heart was bruised, or his mind needed rest, or he was battling something, the simple things in life were always a balm. Looking over at Lily as she tended to Otis, supporting his shoulder with a pillow, Dylan wondered what would be simplest for her.

What would keep her safest?

His mind told him that he should leave her in order to chase down Maddock, that that would be the simplest and easiest solution, but his heart whispered, *never*.

"Okay, so you know the plan?" Dylan clasped Lily's hands an hour later when they'd finished the biscuits, smoked salmon and raisins he'd bought from a dock vendor.

"Yes." Lily wished he'd leave his hand on hers for just a moment longer. But Dylan withdrew and looked to Otis for his answer.

"Yup," Otis declared. "And remember, keep your eyes open for my son."

"What's he look like?" she asked.

"Tall fella. Light hair. Wears a big Mexican hat. He's got a bad limp, I hear."

Otis struggled to rise. Dylan helped him up and handed him one of his guns. It left Dylan with one.

Lily didn't like the feel of a cold metal pistol inside her pants belt, but understood the need for arms.

"Fare well, my friends," said Otis as they slipped through the opened door, leaving him behind. "Godspeed."

Lily didn't think she'd feel such confidence, but as she strode behind Dylan five paces to avoid being seen together, her muscles felt tight and sturdy and ready for action. Perhaps it was the food, as Otis had said. Perhaps it was the knowledge they had a plan, a good one, and were *doing* something rather than waiting. This was just the first step. Or perhaps it was simply knowing her sister was alive and Dylan and his Mounted Police would be on their side.

It was half-dark now, past eleven o'clock. The sun had sunk below the top rim of the mountains, but would take another hour or two to sink lower. Therefore the night sky would remain an unusual pretty purple.

Due to the long summer days, some vendors kept their shops open twenty-four hours. They simply opened the flaps to their canvas tents and nodded off in-between customers.

Some vendors along the wharf lit kerosene lanterns to display their wares, but others, more practical ones, refused to waste the precious oil.

She walked by one stall that smelled a little different. Whale oil, likely. Two young men displayed timepieces in all shapes and colors. Hour glasses, shelf clocks, pocket watches—each one scratched and used, but a godsend in a country where every comfort from home might mean the difference between survival or death.

"No, thank you," she replied to their waving of hands.

It took her and Dylan a while to find what they were looking for. She was beginning to lose hope they would at all.

Finally, thirty minutes later along one of the last aisles, they passed several tents, some marked as eateries, one a sleeping tent, another used clothing, until Dylan looked over at Lily and nodded that he'd found something.

He pretended he didn't know her, and left to talk to an older woman rocking beside a tent marked Laundry Done Here.

Lily inched her way along the display tables. When she at last came upon the desired table, she smiled in wonder at the dozen or so spectacles displayed.

"Somethin' I can help you with?"

A man in a spotless plaid suit exited his tent. How on earth did he keep himself this clean? An optometrist, for certain.

"Dr. Sturgeon," he said.

"Howdy." She omitted giving her name.

Gently, she removed the broken spectacles tucked inside her handbag. She unraveled the suede cloth and held it out. "My…my father…" She stopped for a moment, blinking at her choice of words. Yes, Otis truly felt like a father. He reminded her of the one she'd lost in the fire many years ago, who had always been available for advice and comforting words.

"My father broke his specs."

"Let's have a look."

Her eyes stung. It wasn't from exhaustion, but due to the overwhelming desire and need to help Otis with his vision.

"I'm afraid not," the gent said, blasting her hopes to smithereens. "Don't have replacement lens for these wires and don't have any supplies left to grind some."

She sighed and fingered the tablecloth. "Then could you kindly fix the lens that popped out? It's better he can see from one eye than none."

The man remarked tenderly, "Life's hard on some folks, isn't it?"

Yes, it was, but some kept going.

He took a cloth, placed the lens inside it and popped it back into position, just as simple as sunshine. Lily and Dylan hadn't dare try it themselves for fear of shattering the glass.

"Thank you kindly. How much do I owe?"

He flagged his palm in the air. "No charge. Tell your father I've got a new shipment coming in next month."

Next month seemed a lifetime away when talking about one's ability to see. But some hope was certainly better than none. She smiled and stepped away.

"Hang on a minute," he hollered after her. "There is one thing. Hang on!

Dr. Sturgeon disappeared into his crisp tent. Uncomfortable at standing out in the open, an easy target for Maddock or his men should he happen by, Lily caught Dylan's eye across the way.

He was seated next to the laundry lady in his own rocker. Lily couldn't help but smile at his charm. It seemed to affect women of all ages.

He signaled to her and she responded with a look indicating no luck with Otis's spectacles.

"Here we go." Dr. Sturgeon returned to the table. He opened a black case. It contained a slender set of narrow specs.

Twenty minutes later, breathless with excitement, Lily followed five paces behind Dylan back to the cabin. Dylan carried a surprise of his own in a sack strung over his broad shoulder. Her Norwegian sailor, she thought to herself.

Otis took one look at his new spectacles and

bellowed, "Lady's spectacles? You brought me lady's specs? Jesus Christ, whaddo I look like?"

Exasperated, Dylan stood up in the tiny cabin. "You look like a bruised old man who's as blind as he is vain. Now put the damn things on and use them."

"You look lovely this evening, madam." Two hours later, Dylan teased Otis as he pulled some clothes from the sack he'd brought from the laundry woman.

It was clever of Dylan, thought Lily, to bring them back a change of clothes. He was keeping his sailor's uniform—white cap and dusty navy jacket—but he divided the remaining articles between Lily and Otis in the darkened cabin.

"Why don't you button that wisecracking mouth of yours." Otis snarled beneath his petite frames.

"Would you two quit arguing?" She arranged the calico kerchief over her pinned-up hair, without benefit of mirror, and tugged on a large, flat miner's hat. The laundry woman had neatly repaired missing buttons on the miner's shirt and had mended tiny rips on the pant legs. The clothes smelled heavenly clean.

Dylan had also brought back clean linen gauze, and they'd rewrapped the old man's shoulder. It was so stiff he could barely move it, but it wasn't inflamed and wasn't oozing anything nasty.

The laundry woman had told Dylan the bad news— there were no hospitals in town.

Otis kept up the heated banter with Dylan, and she couldn't fathom why men liked to prod each other so.

"Did you bring me back an apron and heeled shoes?" the gent asked.

"You know your legs are too heavy for delicate heels."

Otis glared at Lily. "Well, she's dressin' up as a man. Figured you wanted me as a woman."

Dylan stopped for a moment to appraise her. She flushed at the slow manner of his stare, up her woolen pant legs, over her shirt and suspenders. "She could never pass as a man."

Lily tried to keep her frantic thoughts at the task on hand. "I'm not fooling anyone in this get-up."

Dylan yanked on the brim of her hat. "No, you're not. Not up close. But in the dark and at a distance, you won't be noticeable."

It was dark. The clouds added blackness to the night. And all they had to do was get to the top of the second hill at the edge of town.

"Are you ready, Otis?" she asked.

The old man muttered. "I don't even need these bullshit eyeglasses. It's dark out. Can't see a thing anyway."

"Pardon your language," Lily prompted him. "You keep forgetting."

He scowled.

"If you don't need them, toss them." said Dylan. "Go ahead. Toss them."

With an exaggerated sigh, Otis let them be on the bridge of his nose. He rose from bed, a bit steadier than he was earlier, likely due to the proper meal and drink.

"Can you walk between us?" Lily asked. "Are you sure?"

"You brought me this walkin' stick to lean on, and I reckon I can get myself to the Mountie tent."

"It's at the top of the second hill."

"I'm aware. How far to the hospital?"

Dylan's gaze met Lily's.

Her stomach swirled in sympathy. "There isn't one here, Otis," she said as gently as she could. "No doctors, either. We asked everyone."

The potential ramifications of the situation reflected in the soft turn of his saggy cheeks. Gangrene? Amputation? She shuddered and pushed the possibilities out of her mind.

"What about the optometrist you were talking to?" Dylan asked. "Dr. Sturgeon."

"I didn't see him with any medical supplies."

"But he *is* a doctor."

"Not a medical doctor. He knows eyes and how to grind lenses."

"Better than nothin'," said Otis.

"True. We'll ask the Mounties about him."

Dylan peered out the cabin. A full moon bore down on his thick shoulders and the cut of his navy lapels. The long hair looked misplaced on a sailor, but folks here knew that all types of men walked the Klondike.

"We'll aim for the Mountie tent first," said Dylan, "and go from there. They're liable to have clean bandages and…maybe a poultice…perhaps trained in medical aid."

"We've got to rinse his wound soon," said Lily. "With some sort of cleansing solution. And more opiates," she whispered. Now that Otis had proven his mind clear after his concussion, there was no danger of giving him something strong to ease his pain.

Dylan agreed. "Top priority."

"Thank you," said Otis, forgetting his irritation at his

lady's eyeglasses for the moment. He grimaced as he put his weight to the walking stick. The three of them slid out of the cabin into the cover of a star-filled Yukon night.

Just another few minutes to blessed help, thought Lily. Twenty minutes to the comforting protection of the North-West Mounted Police.

Chapter Nineteen

Maddock clasped his arm around the waif. "Pretty moon, isn't it?"

She yanked his hand off her shoulder so fast, you'd think he was a bloodsucking leech. Her reaction made his gut churn.

"That's not very ladylike."

She spit. The slime hit his boot.

He clenched his fist. "Now see here—"

"Boss?" Big Al interrupted them beneath the cluster of trees.

"What the hell is it?"

"Some word."

"Better be good. It better be good."

Big Al hesitated. He looked to Slick Willy, who was making his way slowly to join them. Both avoided Maddock's eyes, but they watched his hands as they lowered to his guns. Maddock was itchin' to blast something. He hated chicken-hearted men.

"Well? *Well?*" he hollered. "Don't tell me you couldn't bloody well find anyone!"

Big Al whimpered. His asthma got the better of him and he wheezed. "Sir…we hired eight more to take the gold over the mountains. Eight, like you said. But…they can't start till the morning on account a gettin' enough horses."

Was that all? Waiting overnight before they started out might be wiser, anyway. The men would be rested and ready.

"Mornin' it is, then. For us, too. Matter of fact, why don't we go celebrate in that fancy restaurant up on the hill? Tell the others."

Likely relieved that he hadn't blasted a hole through their guts, the two men turned and dashed away.

Maddock's head throbbed. The pounding was sometimes unbearable. Strong enough that he couldn't sleep.

And here was this young thing gazing up at him as though he was a monster. If his head wasn't throbbing so hard, he'd give Mrs. Maddock a pounding that would make her remember what ladies did for gentlemen.

"One more thing!" Maddock hollered after his men.

Slick returned.

"Leave a message behind for the others. When they find that red-haired woman and her no-good drifter, I want their throats slit."

With an unexpected cry, the waif took a few steps back, turned beneath the tree and vomited.

"Dammit." Maddock turned away in disgust. "Go clean yourself up, will ya? We're headed to one of the finest restaurants in Whitehorse."

The beast was made for Dylan to hunt. If he didn't stop Maddock, no one would. Dylan believed it in his soul.

"Maddock's traveling with four other men." Dylan crept through the vendors along the dock as they made their way toward the Mountie hill. Some vendors were asleep, some drunk from the liquor they'd consumed at the local saloons.

"How do you know it's four?" Lily stayed close to his side. If it were any other time, any other place, he'd pull her in his arms and say, *Run away with me. I don't care where we go. Let's leave this behind.*

He rubbed the scars on his wrist. But he couldn't do it. He and Maddock were entwined at gut level. Lily had her sister to find and her gold to recover.

And Dylan had a beast to kill.

Lily would be sickened to hear him think like this, but she didn't know what Dylan was capable of when it came to righting a wrong.

"When Maddock was getting off the boat," Dylan said calmly, "I watched him with some of the other passengers. They didn't stick together so it was hard to know they were a part of the same group, but they nodded at each other and signaled with their eyes."

"Five altogether." Otis puffed, out of breath. "How can we compete with five gunslingers?"

"*We* don't," said Dylan. "*I* do. When we reach the Mountie tent, that's as far as we go together. You'll be fine with the officers there. They'll hide you."

Otis looked puzzled. Of course he did, because he was unaware Dylan was a member of the force.

"You know 'em? The Mounties?" Otis asked.

"They're good men."

Lily was silent. It took a moment for him to gain the courage to look at her.

Her eyes glistened in the pale moonlight. The glow from the sky flooded her hat, spilled over her shoulders and suspenders, and outlined the gentle curves she so valiantly tried to hide.

Her upper lip trembled, the dimple in her cheek flickered, and she turned away, perhaps unable to show him the sorrow in her expression.

He saw it anyway. A deep humbling of her spirit.

"Otis, excuse us for a moment, please." The old gent was only too happy to stop for a rest. Dylan settled him against a tree, then pulled Lily to a private area behind one of the vendor's shacks.

"This isn't easy to say," he began.

Her eyes flicked with regret.

"When I said to Otis that the Mountie tent's as far as we go together, I meant us, too."

She dropped her chin to her chest. Her mouth parted and she breathed through her nose, trying not to show what was in both of their hearts.

"I promised once that I'd tell you when we had to part. When it was time for me to disappear. This is it, Lily," he said gruffly. "I'm sorry. This is it."

"But you'll come back to look for me," she whispered.

"I said that once...but I'm not sure what..." It was difficult to keep his voice on an even keel. "I want you to go on without me."

It was as though he'd struck her, how deep was her reaction. She stepped away from him, shaking her head. It had to be this way, he thought. If he never came back, if the beast got him, then he wanted her to feel free to go on. But he would do everything to find her.

Otis called, "I see it! I see it!"

Startled by the old man's calls, Dylan did what he had to—pressed a hand to Lily's shoulder blade and guided her back to the tree.

Otis was already shuffling up the hillside. It was covered with lanterns and tents and log cabins. The old man pointed to the army tent that stood on the peak overlooking the Yukon River valley, the wharf and inhabitants.

"The tent! It's there!"

As desperate as Dylan felt in having to leave Lily behind when they reached the summit, he was overjoyed to see evidence of police presence.

Lily and Otis would be safe, and that was all that mattered.

They passed a saloon, one of several. Piano music drifted from its doors. Voices inside carried in the wind—laughter, the call of someone for a horse.

The café twenty feet further up was quieter, serving men dressed in suits. Their jackets were dusty and grimy, but one could see that, once upon a time, they came from wealth back home, wherever home might be.

He ached for home now.

"Fancy digs," Otis declared. "Look at that one."

The old man stumbled with his walking stick and Dylan grabbed his shoulder. He steadied.

Lily turned her flat miner's hat toward the tented restaurant Otis had pointed to. Its patrons were lost in the shadows. There were cloth-covered tables, wine goblets—filled with imported flavors, no doubt—lit candles and small sculptures made of wrought iron sitting as decoration.

"The folks who strike gold eat there," said Otis.

"You'll eat there soon," Dylan whispered to Lily.

She didn't seem to hear him.

They were almost past it when a party of six—cussing, it sounded to Dylan—caught his eye. A waiter appeared in fancy duds, white shirt and black satin vest. The group was annoyed with something he carried on his tray. They flagged him back to the kitchen and he cowered as though he feared for more than his job.

"Hurry," said Dylan, not liking the looks of things. He stepped between Otis and Lily. "Faster."

One man at the rowdy table leaned forward for another to light his cigar. A woman appeared in shadow, seated behind him. A woman?

An ominous feeling flashed through Dylan. He clutched Lily by the underarm and Otis by the shoulder and pulled and pushed them. He and Lily could run, but Otis needed more time.

With a quiver in the pit of his stomach, Dylan turned his head once more to the fancy restaurant. The table of men were turned and staring across the hill. Then one head wearing a dark hat, turned in their direction.

Dylan's blood turned cold.

"Run!" He heaved Lily up the hill. "Run as fast as you can!"

With a stumble, she turned back to look at him, then seeming to understand, tore off for the Mountie tent.

Otis was caught unawares. He tried to muster strength, but was winded. With a swoop, Dylan hoisted the old man over his shoulder and raced like a lunatic behind Lily.

Gunshots fired in the air. The thunder resonated down Dylan's spine. He lunged faster and screamed with the weight of Otis. "Yah!"

More gunshots. Why weren't the Mounties coming out of their tent?

Unable to reach for his guns, Dylan clenched his teeth and bore down. His thighs seemed to rip with the weight, his arms shook. Still he carried on with Otis.

Maddock and his men be damned!

Lily reached the tent. She raced inside. Dylan leaped in behind her. He dropped Otis to his feet.

Otis stumbled back and fell.

The place was empty.

Empty!

"Out the back door!" Dylan shouted, rushing to help Lily and Otis past the two desks, the racks of food supplies and tins.

A gun fired past his ear.

Then a knife stabbed into his back. No, not a knife. A bullet.

Pain seared through him. He fell to the hard dirt.

"Dylan!" Lily's voice was eerie, almost mystical. Lights swirled through his head.

Then the sight of the young woman from the restaurant. Walls of blond hair. A face like Lily's, only plumper and younger. Sobbing.

Maddock's pointed black boots entered Dylan's frame of vision, upside-down in a haze.

Maddock had a gun on Lily. She raised her arms slowly, clinging tight to the old man at her side who could barely stand.

Dylan shouted at the top of his lungs but no one heard him. Or maybe he was *trying* to shout….

The gun cocked. Then the younger woman stepped in front of her older sister and took the blast.

It was all Dylan saw before everything went black. And the screaming. Everyone was screaming.

"Sister," Lily whispered, bending over Amanda two hours later in a loud careening wagon, so overwhelmed she might lose the frail young Amanda that she raced to do everything she could. The bullet had passed through the upper right part of her sister's chest and through the collarbone.

Beneath the glow of the moon, they were on the run. Maddock and his men had dragged them out of the Mountie tent, whisked them away by boat, then horse-back, then brought them here in this wagon. She and Amanda were alone in the back, with two of Maddock's men sitting in the front.

What did Lily know of medicine? Nothing. She was learning much too fast on this journey.

Maddock, galloping behind them with two other men, apparently didn't know they were sisters. He was watching closely, though; his cold dark eyes bored into Lily.

Amanda's bleeding slowed. The bandages no longer seeped a vivid red. One of Maddock's men—the one who wheezed so heavily when he breathed—had done the initial bandaging on Maddock's orders, but for reasons unknown to them, Lily was so eager to help them, that he gladly let her take over.

Sweat covered Lily's brow as she dabbed her sister's cheeks, trying to ease her agony.

Amanda moaned in stupor.

When the flow of red finally ebbed, Lily sat back on her heels. Her arms shook, her legs wobbled.

Dazed by the unexpected trauma of what she'd witnessed, and burning with sorrow at the sister she might lose before they'd even spoken, she stared at Amanda's still face. The small nose, the childlike pink lips.

Lord only knew how Otis and Dylan had fared.

Lily sobbed.

Amanda's eyes flickered open at the sound. "Lily," she whispered. She was barely audible above the clomp of horses.

Lily leaned forward. "Yes, Amanda, I'm here at your side."

"I didn't know who they were…when I first met them…I didn't know…"

Lily understood she was referring to Maddock and his men.

"It's all right," Lily whispered into her temple. "Don't worry now. You've got to pull through. You've been shot."

"Lily…I'm sorry. For leaving you…for the problems I caused on the ship. You don't know…how many times I've gone over it…"

"I'm sorry, too. It's behind us, all right? Behind us." Lily rinsed the dried blood off her sister's neck and tried to smile. "You've got to get better and we've got a shop to run, remember?"

"Did you get a shop, Lily?"

"No."

At one time, she had the gold to buy any shop she wanted, but now she had nothing. The tiny nuggets in her purse were nearly gone. "We'll get one together. Just get better."

"I'm sorry for everything…most of all…for Maddock."

Lily trembled and asked the question she most feared. "Is he your husband?"

"Kirk was…"

The horrid life her sister must have led weighed upon Lily's soul. "Was he awful to you?"

Lily needed to hear the truth. She needed to allow her sister to tell someone what she'd gone through, even if that life had been horrid.

"He was sickly in that way…he couldn't…was unable to…no one knew."

Lily bowed her head and thanked the Lord.

Amanda's voice was a groggy rasp. "I'm afraid of Bolton. He wants me as his wife."

"He's not in the wagon. You can rest for a moment. You saved my life, Amanda. You stepped in front of the bullet."

"What's this?" Maddock galloped closer to the wagon, and his unexpected voice beside Lily caused her to jump in fear.

"She comin' to?"

Lily nodded with nervous exaggeration.

"How come she took your bullet?"

Head bowed over her sister's pale face, Lily didn't know how to answer. *Because she's my sister. Because she would rather die than live with you.*

"I asked you a question!"

Terror ripped down her spine. She was saved from answering, however, when the trail wound down a narrow ledge of rock and Maddock was forced to recede.

Lily bent lower to Amanda's face. "When he comes around, pretend you don't hear him. Close your eyes and pretend you're unwell."

Amanda struggled to smile, so gentle, so familiar. "We used to pretend a lot, didn't we?" She drifted off again, lost in pain.

Lily shifted forward on her knees, careful to conceal the derringer still tucked inside her belt. "Whisky," she begged the wheezing man in the front. "Do you have any whisky?"

He must have felt sorry for Amanda, for after an initial hesitation, he removed a flask from his pocket and passed it back.

Lily poured some into Amanda's mouth. She cringed but took it.

How could they escape this?

Lily had a gun, but didn't dare make a move until she figured a way to get her sister and herself to safety. And nestled in the corner of the wagon was Lily's pillowcase of clothes, with a leather pipe case and its hidden knife.

When the trail widened again, Maddock didn't approach. He slowed his horse and stared at the two women beneath the moonlight.

Something venomous quivered in his eyes as he looked from Lily's face to Amanda's, then back to Lily's.

Scared of what he saw, Lily looked away and scratched her nose to obstruct his view.

An hour later, as they neared a hideaway cabin in the middle of nowhere, she pleaded, "Please…could you tell me what happened to the men who were with me?"

Maddock snarled. "What do you care about a no-good drifter and a useless old man?"

"Did they…were they…"

He spat on the ground. "They're both dead."

She slumped hard against the back of the wagon. *No.*

Chapter Twenty

It was obvious why Maddock wanted the two women alive. Every leer in her direction sickened Lily.

Two days passed. He and his men took Lily and Amanda and headed south through the mountains. They still had their horses and the wagon for part of the journey, traveling through the crags and wooded slopes of the Yukon. Headed for Alaska, Lily was sure.

On the third day, Lily took a saddle and rode her own horse. She welcomed the change in position, while still careful to observe her sleeping sister.

Lily prayed for her recovery, but Amanda never came to after that first night. It was likely the horror of waking up to Maddock that kept her eyes closed.

Lily was on her own. Hadn't she always been alone? Is this how she was meant to live her life?

At first, she refused to believe Maddock had murdered both Otis and Dylan, for the monster was a liar.

But as the hours and days wore on with no word, no

help, and no indication to believe otherwise, Lily began to pray for their souls.

Lily removed the tiny granite chip from her pocket and stroked its black surface. Dylan had produced something of such beauty it pained her to think he might be gone forever.

And now it seemed, she may lose her sister.

She lifted her face to the blazing sun. *Why bother to go on?*

She wiped her damp cheek with the back of her sleeve. Because, as Dr. Sturgeon had said, life was hard on some folks. Yet they chose to survive.

It was a choice, and as the sun beat down on her shoulders, Lily filled with vibrancy and renewed determination. She pressed on.

Her mind worked through the people who might help her. Where were the other Mounties? They would help. Maybe folks they met in passing, on the road. There was always Alaska, and the promise of lawmen there.

Where was her gold?

She'd been studying Maddock's men and their horses for days. Maddock's saddlebags were weighted down with something awful heavy, but no one else's. There was no chest full of the precious metal and no talk of where it had disappeared to.

It hardly made a difference anymore.

Her mare snorted. Lily gave her a pat and with that pat, it was as though the mare was sharing something kind.

"Wake up, Amanda," she whispered in the saddle. "If you wake up, I'll get us out of this. I promise."

The mare snorted again. It was a sign. Perhaps of hope. Perhaps telling her she wasn't alone. She had her animal and animals didn't take sides in good and evil.

The mare's presence gave her great comfort.

Dylan didn't remember the hands that lifted him. He didn't remember the kindness in the voices of the strangers, the soothing touch of healing hands, nor the frightened concern when they lifted Otis.

Dylan awoke some time later, unable to pinpoint where he was exactly and who he was with.

He blinked in the cool light. He was in a cabin, in a room alone. Men's voices carried in from the propped door, and outside his window, the tops of two Stetsons appeared as two other men talked in muffled voices.

His guns. Where were they? He spun in the bed to look, and nearly crumpled from the throbbing in his ribs. Heavily bandaged, he was well-secured around his middle. The bandages were clean and tight. How had…?

A gunshot. The memory flooded through him. Pain and grief and horror. And Lily…he closed his eyes…Lily.

Footsteps thudded in the hall. His eyes flashed open and he fisted his hands, ready to fight.

A stranger entered. A man in his thirties, moustache, clean-shaven, with a large belly. "You awake, mister?"

Was he friend or enemy?

A taller man, one with long blond hair, needing a cane, limped in. "Dylan."

Should he know the man? Dylan's vision blurred. The man made his way to a chair beneath the window, the cane thumping beside him. "You remember me?'

Dylan said nothing. An ache trembled through his torso. He studied the cane, carved from deep rich cedar. It was topped with a carving of a lion's head.

The man introduced himself. "Champagne Charlie. Thank you for saving my father."

Friend. Charlie was a friend. The memory rushed over Dylan. Of course he knew Charlie. They'd met twice before on the trail coming to Dawson City. Charlie knew he was a Mountie. It didn't matter anymore, though, who knew.

Dylan parted his dry lips. "Otis made it, then?"

"Yeah. His shoulder will take a while to heal. Mostly 'cuz he's old, doctor says."

"Doctor?"

"Dr. Sturgeon. He's the opt—"

"Optometrist," Dylan finished.

"He's had a look at you, too. Three of your ribs are busted. You're lucky."

"How long have I been out?"

"Four days."

Dylan mumbled regret.

"Doctor thinks you'll be fine with another week or two of rest."

Dylan winced, gritted his teeth and heaved himself out of bed. His bare feet hit the cool floor and the pain sliced him in two. "I don't have a week or two."

"Now just a minute. Hold on. You helped my father and I'm gonna see to it you heal completely before you go—"

"Where's Lily?"

Charlie turned his head and stared at a spider web in the corner. "They took her."

"Alive?"

"Yeah."

"Her sister?"

"We don't know. She left behind a lot of blood."

Dylan cursed beneath his breath. He was dizzy with weakness and his mouth was parched. "Where'd they go?"

"South. Likely to Alaska. From there, the ships to the mainland. Freedom."

"Did the Mounties go after them?"

"Dylan...there *are* no other Mounties in the district right now. Two of 'em headed off to chase some gunslinger at the border. And two others are investigating a ring of robberies fifty miles north."

Hell.

Dylan reached for his pants on the chair and tugged into them. He stopped for a moment to sip some water from the nearby glass. "Then I'll go it alone."

"I've got some men I can lend you. I've been waiting for them to come back from a delivery of tubs. They rode in this morning."

Dylan rose on shaky feet. His arms felt light with the weakness of not eating for days. He had to sit down again. Then he held out his hand and the two men shook. "Thanks, Charlie. Where'd you put my guns?"

"A Mountie, huh?" Three hours later, Otis stared in awe as Dylan pulled himself up onto the horse. He was still weak but feeling better after a full meal. "You're good at lyin'."

The old man meant it as a compliment, but Dylan wasn't proud of his skill.

Lying to himself. Lying to Lily about how he felt and what he wanted from life. Lying to the whole goddamn world about who he was and what he needed.

Champagne Charlie came over and shook his father's hand. "You know I've gotta go."

Otis's mouth trembled with pride, and then fear for where his son was headed. "You wouldn't be the man I raised if you stayed behind."

With great emotion, they patted each other on the back, and the group of six left Whitehorse.

It wasn't easy.

On their first day, they rode through brush so thick it scraped their face and intimidated his horses. Dylan's ribs pounded with misery.

The second day was no better for they were riding fifteen hours a day, and on the third, Dylan's wound reopened and bled.

He tried to tend to it on his own, but Charlie must've noticed something wrong, for at midnight when they made camp, he brought a roll of bandages and insisted on having a look.

Charlie winced for looking at it. "You should rest. We'll take one day—tomorrow—to rest."

"Like hell we will."

Dylan ground his jaws together and mustered every ounce of strength he possessed.

The next day, exhausted and still with no noticeable trace of the Maddock gang, Dylan dismounted at the riverbank to water his horse.

He stated the thing no one wanted to say aloud, but

that was grating on everyone's mind. "They're not carrying any gold."

"I know," said Charlie.

"We would have seen deep tracks, grooves in the trail from the weight."

"I know," said Charlie.

"What did they do with it?"

"I don't know," said Charlie. "But Maddock can hire a lotta men with that gold to haul it out of here. The gold's going one way, he's going the other."

Dylan clenched his jaw. He blamed himself for missing it.

"Nothin' you could've done," Charlie assured him. "You were guarding Lily and my old man. How could you've chased the gold, too?"

Charlie was right. Faced with the same choice today, whether to follow the gold or protect his companions, he'd choose them.

The following evening, Dylan noticed a buried campfire hidden to one side of a tree. And footsteps. Lots of footsteps.

"Over here!" he hollered.

"What do you figure?" Charlie asked after studying the prints.

"The huge boots belong to men. But look at these smaller ones. And these." Dylan pointed to two feminine sets. "This set of female feet are all over the place."

"A woman who can walk."

"But these ones are barely there. Just a couple of sets, like she was sitting in one place for a long time."

"Someone convalescing?"

"God, I hope so."

"Then Amanda's alive."

Dylan's heart soared.

Two days later, after a heavy rainfall, they found more footsteps in a damp area.

"Two women again. The second one's moving around more."

Charlie nodded. "She's getting stronger."

Dylan looked into the wind. "Hold on, ladies." Dylan and Charlie were riding as fast as they could, sunup to sundown. They were making better time than Maddock.

Lord, I haven't asked you for much in the last few years, but I'm asking you this. Keep them safe till I get there.

It was a week after they first left Whitehorse that the sky finally opened up with glorious possibility. His prayer was answered.

With a pounding eagerness, Dylan spun around and signaled Charlie and his men to halt.

The scent of the waterfall in the misty woods drew him. In the setting sunlight, Dylan dismounted and walked toward it. Then came the thunder of rushing water, the braying of a horse, a flicker of flames among the tree trunks.

Life.

Finally, they'd caught up to the Maddock gang.

Two of Maddock's men sat on boulders across from the waterfall, perched fifty feet high, guarding the canyon entrance. It would be difficult to get past them.

So, nature's beauty drew even the ugliest of men. They weren't able to resist making camp at the crux of fresh water and air scented with willows and ferns. They were so pompous and arrogant in their belief that they could get away with murder that they'd built a huge fire for anyone to see. Skinned hares were propped above the flames, several fish, and a tin pot brewing coffee.

The aroma of the crushed, percolating beans drifted over Dylan. Lily loved coffee. He focused on trying to locate skirts. Where were the skirts?

With no sign of them, his breath hastened.

He walked his horse back to Charlie and the men where they'd taken cover in a gully a hundred yards away. The gully had its own stream that muffled some sounds.

"I don't see Lily," said Dylan.

"She's there," Charlie assured him.

Dylan hitched his horse to one of trees, as the others had done, and stared at the two moving dots on top of the cliffs. "You see those two men?"

Charlie pushed back his sombrero. "Yeah."

"One of them is awfully interested in something going on to his far right."

Charlie chuckled. "You got that figured."

Hope found its way to Dylan's lips. "The women."

"I'll cover you if you want to have a look."

Charlie murmured orders for two of his men to explore the left side of the canyon, while he and Dylan pressed forward to their right.

Dylan's boots barely scuffed the ground on the bottom of the forest floor. The heartbeat pounding through his ears grew louder with every step. His nostrils flared as he sucked in cool, moist air.

He drew his Colts. Keeping his eye on the man closest to him on the cliff, Dylan took cover in the woods.

If the outlaw peering down from the canyon wall spotted Dylan, Charlie had given orders for his men to shoot. But it came with dire consequence: a gunshot would alert every person in the camp. War would rage. The women would be trapped in the middle.

How in blazes could Dylan get to them?

Two horses grazed beneath a faraway tree. And then Dylan saw skirts. Heavenly skirts.

The welcome sight of blue satin and red hair warmed his heart as if he'd been away from her forever.

It had been forever.

He'd thought he'd lost Lily and didn't understand until this moment, as a galvanizing relief gripped him, how much more he'd feared for Lily's life than his own.

Taking a deep breath, he turned to the cliffs. The two watch guards were distracted by the food and hollered for their portion.

"Toss us somethin', will ya?"

"Give me the hind quarter of one hare!"

The horses near Lily shifted in their stance, and Dylan peered over one animal's neck to look at her. She wore the flat miner's hat still, and a yellow oilskin jacket in the cooling air. Even at this distance, the sharp lines of her straight eyebrows and stoic chin seemed unrelenting. She seemed to be hanging laundry—men's clothing—on the line of ropes Otis had once given her.

Amanda appeared in view, standing up to hand Lily three heavy canteens.

The younger sister was thin and pale, but obviously well enough to haul water with one arm. Her other arm was wrapped in a sling. That meant the gunshot had either passed through her arm or her collarbone. If it was the collarbone, the sling was protecting movement of the arm, which would otherwise yank the muscles out of place as it was healing.

And then she did something strange. She lifted the hand that was in the sling to screw the cap onto a canteen. As if there was nothing wrong with her arm at all. Were they faking her weakness?

Two scruffy men hollered something at the ladies. Amanda quickly shoved her hand back into her sling. Dylan steeled himself from responding to the men. He could easily pull the trigger, but he'd only get one man down, maybe both, before the shots were heard. Who knew where Maddock was standing? Lily and Amanda would be in worse jeopardy if he fired.

Then the beast himself showed his face.

Dylan's gut twisted, his skin grew cold. Maddock, dark, oily and deliberate, shoved Amanda aside as he hauled two heavy saddlebags off his mare, then reached for a shirt drying on the ropes. Lily clasped her sister's side to avoid her falling over, and with heads bowed, they cleared the way for Maddock.

With an icy grip, Dylan brought one Colt up to his line of vision, centered Maddock in his sights and fondled the trigger.

His finger didn't budge.

Sweat broke at his temples.

Maddock's grin made Dylan sick.

The man who'd ordered him bound and branded.

Who'd given the sharp command to his brothers to burn Dylan's wrist.

Dylan's finger trembled. His vision blurred.

"Hey."

"Hey," the voice said again.

It was Charlie standing beside him. Dylan blinked. "You all right?"

Dylan cleared his throat. "I can't decide what method to kill him by."

"You don't have to, just yet."

Dylan slid his guns back into his holster and tried to control the urge to strangle the devil right here and now before he had a chance to harm another soul.

By the strain in Maddock's arms when he carried his saddlebags toward the campfire, Dylan guessed. "Gold?"

"Sure looks like it. What's that? The red-haired one is passing something to her sister. Some sorta case."

Dylan whirled around. It was the case that contained the pipe Otis had carved, along with the hidden drawer.

"She's got a blade in there," said Dylan, growing tense.

"Then we better make our move. Those two ladies try anything surrounded by all these men, and they're dead."

Hearing Charlie say it aloud ground the cold fear of hell into Dylan. "I've got a plan. It might not make much sense to you, but hear me out."

Chapter Twenty-One

Lily wished Maddock would keep his poisonous eyes off her. For the past week and a half, she had barely been able to make a move in camp without turning to see him gawking at her. Initially, he had needed her to nurse her sister back to health, but now that Amanda was stronger, Lily feared for them both.

Five days ago, Lily had stopped looking behind her for signs of hope. No one knew where they were. She and her sister were on their own.

She had almost grown accustomed to the sob that'd been clinging to her throat for all these days, and realized she'd likely have it for the rest of her life. But whatever sorrow she felt for losing Dylan would have to wait. Now, she was looking ahead for signs of promise. She had a sister to help.

Maddock sucked back on the smoking pipe he'd snatched from her, while the others finished eating. The smell of tobacco made her nostrils flare. He'd been so greedy in taking the pipe when she'd presented it to him—as she hoped he would—he hadn't noticed the hidden blade.

So greedy that he slept here at the campfire with his two saddlebags. She knew what was in them.

Lily whispered to Amanda. "Don't make a move until we get him alone."

Amanda nodded.

"Put your hand over your skirt," Lily warned her. "I can see the bulge when you twist."

Amanda's arm slipped over her pocket to conceal the knife she'd removed from Otis's case.

Maddock's voice made her jump. "What are you two so serious about?"

Lily looked down at her plate and scooped another mouthful of fish. She forced herself to eat for the power it would provide.

"It's my nature, I suppose."

Maddock stared from one woman to another. "I want you to tell me somethin'. How come you two ladies look so much alike?"

Four pairs of male eyes turned in their direction.

Amanda infused with color. The less Maddock knew, the less he could use against them.

"It's our hair," said Lily, pushing back her braid. "We wear it in the same fashion."

"That so?"

"Perhaps you haven't seen very many women."

The men snickered. Maddock growled.

"Maybe we should remedy that. Come closer so I can see you both."

Amanda groaned. Lily slid her teeth together. The derringer tucked inside her skirt waistband, concealed by her jacket, bit into her side. She hadn't wanted to use it while Amanda was recovering, but her sister was strong enough now that she could make a run for the horses once Lily did the deed.

Maddock inhaled his tobacco again, two of the men rose to scrape the bones off their plates, and Lily leaned in to Amanda. "Did you untie our mares?"

"Everything's ready," Amanda whispered.

The fire blazed six feet high. Branches cracked in the darkness, in the woods. Must be one of the watch guards coming down to change positions with someone else.

Lily saw the tall figure coming toward her. She blinked. Smoke from the fire must've gotten into her eyes. She blinked again.

Her eyes widened, her pulse reeled, her gut slammed.

Dylan. Alive!

He walked his horse toward them. His eyes found Lily's and for two brief seconds, he held her heart in his palm.

What was he doing? Dear God, what was he doing?

Maddock saw him, too, and jumped to his feet. He looked around for help, but his men had temporarily left his side.

"How the hell did you get past my lookouts?"

"They're not very good."

Amanda and Lily clawed their way up the logs to stand up. Did Amanda recognize Dylan from the Mountie tent, just before he'd been shot? Did she realize he was a good man, on their side? Amanda's blue eyes sparkled in her direction. *Yes.*

Dylan looked all right. Thinner. He pressed one arm close to his right side, as if he was protecting his ribs. Shot in the ribcage?

Maddock spat, "We left you for dead."

"Wasn't the first time."

"What?" Maddock strained to understand.

"But it'll be the last."

Maddock peered at Dylan as if he was trying to place the face. "We met before?"

Maddock was cocky, waiting and asking questions because he knew he had his men. They lined up behind him.

Dylan nodded slightly to Lily to indicate she should run soon. She understood. Then he called out to Maddock. "You and your men are under arrest."

For a brief moment, fear flickered across Maddock's thick nose and sweaty cheeks. He nervously glanced at his saddlebags, then slowly grinned. "You brought the law with you? I don't believe it." Maddock chuckled as he looked around. His men followed suit. No one else was there.

Lily was horrified that Dylan may have come alone. Surely, he had help. Why had he just walked alone into the center of this lynch mob?

Dylan gave her the signal. This was it. She grabbed her sister by the hand and leaped flat down to the grass.

Gunshots fired above their heads from above the canyon—must've been the lookouts—and the rest of Maddock's men went wild.

"Run!" Lily hollered to her sister. "Run for the horses!"

She and Amanda tore off and never looked back. By

the sound of the gun blasts, Dylan had brought backup. But who had better aim?

Frantic, the women reached the horses. Lily pushed Amanda up to her saddle and slapped the horse to go. The mare tore off.

With her heart speeding, Lily grabbed her saddle horn and was about to yank herself up when she dared a glance back. Two of Maddock's men lay lifeless on the ground. High on the canyon walls, Dylan was chasing Maddock.

What now? Should she leave?

Lily tore the clothesline off the tree, jumped on her horse and followed behind her sister. Branches beat around her head as they whipped through the trail. Up ahead, two men, friendly voices, stopped to help her sister.

"Don't be scared! We're with Champagne Charlie and Inspector Wayburn!"

Here was Lily's chance to help Dylan. She dug her heels into the side of her mare and pulled on the reins. Up she climbed on her horse, fighting a steep slope of moss and boulders to the top of the cliffs.

"Wait!" shouted Dylan's men behind her, but she kept going, dragging her rope, her derringer jabbing her waist.

She followed the river that led to the waterfall above the cliffs. Spotting them, her pulse surged with terror.

Maddock had Dylan's head pressed beneath the water with his heavy saddlebag, grinding his boot on top of the gold, on top of Dylan. With a chill running through her bones, she charged her horse and fired a bullet into the air.

Maddock paused, and in that brief moment of hesitation, Dylan leaped up from the water as if resurrected from the dead.

Their guns were gone, so they fought with their fists. Dylan pummeled Maddock. The criminal panted like a trapped animal, clawing at his saddlebags, getting away on the boulders, but Dylan grabbed him by the scruff of his collar and yanked him to his feet. They both wobbled from the fight, struggling for air and balance. Maddock tried to break away.

Lily took out her pistol and lifted it to the monster.

"Who the hell are you?" Maddock shouted at Dylan.

Dylan slid his hand inside his vest and pulled out a badge.

Maddock reared back. His face paled. He gasped, "Mountie?"

"You're under arrest. For the murder of Constable Hank Pitcher. Corporal Dirk Bittleman. And God knows how many others."

Dylan's sleeve had tugged up as he flashed his badge, revealing his branded wrist.

Maddock noticed it. With a yelp of alarm, he kicked Dylan in the gut, heaved his saddlebag over his thick shoulders and raced toward the top of the cliffs.

Dylan crashed to the ground from the kick, then leaped back to his feet and followed.

Panting, Lily aimed her derringer at the moving target, but even if she got him in range and fired, the small pistol likely couldn't reach the distance.

"Dying's too easy for you," Dylan shouted, facing the beast on the ledge. "It's taken me three years to realize the worst thing I could do to you is put you in a cage."

Maddock's face flashed in terror. With a sneer, he

opened his arms, screamed, and raced head-on toward Dylan.

"No!" Frantic, Lily took aim and pressed her trigger.

But a more powerful gunshot blasted from behind her. It ripped past Lily's ears, missed Maddock, but hit one of his saddlebags. Instead of letting go, he clutched the bags tighter. They weighed down on his shoulders and, perhaps realizing too late that he should've released his grip, he gasped in horror and toppled over the cliff into the canyon, following his precious gold straight down to the rocks.

Breathless, Lily turned around in her saddle.

Amanda, pale and uneven on her horse, clutched the smoldering gun.

The next few minutes whirled around Lily so fast she could hardly comprehend the events. She raced to her sister's side. "Amanda?"

Two of Charlie's men dashed up from the gully where the women had left them. "She took my gun! She took it right out of my holster!"

Trembling, Amanda slid off the horse. "Is he dead?"

Lily spun around to look at Dylan. He teetered at the top of the gray basalt cliff, the river rushing by his feet and fading sunlight striking his powerful silhouette. Peering into the canyon below where Maddock had fallen, Dylan placed his hands on his hips. With a slow deliberate sweep, he turned to their direction and, as Amanda, Lily and the two men waited for word, he lifted his muscled arm and signaled.

Maddock was dead.

Amanda crumpled into Lily's arms.

Lily stroked her head. "It's all right. It's all over now. We're safe, no one can harm us."

It took a few moments for Amanda to recover from her shock. In the meantime, Dylan and his men deliberated how to handle things.

Then Charlie himself, with his cane no less, reached the summit. "Three dead down below. Two apprehended."

He limped his way to Dylan on the rim of the rocks. They conversed while another man helped Lily with her sister. Amanda clung to the gun. Finally gaining hold of herself, she pulled out of Lily's embrace, placed a hand over her eyes to shield them from the blistering sunset, and gazed at Lily.

"You're a godsend," Amanda whispered.

Lily's throat tightened. She blinked back tears of relief. "You'll never be able to get rid of me now. Wherever you go, I'm coming."

"I wouldn't have it any other way." Amanda's wet lashes clumped together. She peered to the men standing on the ridge. "But I think you have someone else to talk to."

Dylan kept looking over. In between his conversations with Charlie and the others, he'd swagger back and lift his dark head in Lily's direction.

Lily's heart turned a thousand times in response.

She nodded at her sister. Amanda returned the revolver to the man she'd taken it from and accepted his help in climbing down the cliffs with the horses.

With a steady beat of her heart, Lily made her way along the boulders, over the gushing river. Water drenched the bottom of her tattered blue skirts. She didn't care. The remaining half of the sinking red sun blazed into her eyes.

Dylan stepped away from Charlie. Dylan's Stetson shielded his face from the sun's rays.

How long had she prayed for this moment? With arms wide open, he rushed to grab hold of her.

They met and he whirled her off the ground, soaking skirts and all. They held onto each other, bodies molded.

"You'll hurt your ribs," she said.

"I don't care. I'm never going to let you go." He pressed his soft lips against her cool throat and kissed her flesh. "Never."

"Where did you come from?" she whispered into the bristly side of his neck, loving the scent of his rough skin. "How did you know where to find us?"

"We've been tracking you for a week. I thought I might never…" He couldn't seem to say the awful words.

She loosened her hold, and they faced each other. All her answers were written on his face.

His eyes shone a glossy brown, his rough cheeks pulled into a tender line, his lips tugged with raw emotion.

Lily whispered, "I'll never give up hope like that again."

He leaned down and kissed her. She closed her eyes, and his hands tucked inside her oilskin jacket around her waist, squeezing and drawing her so close she thought she might not breathe. His kiss was full of promises, tender whispers and memories of the two nights they'd shared together as lovers.

It lasted only a moment, though, interrupted when duty called again.

Charlie hollered. "We best leave this ledge before the sun disappears. Dylan...Dylan...we need to take care of things down below!"

Chapter Twenty-Two

It was well past midnight when they buried the dead. Dylan could barely see in the moonless night. Clouds blocked the stars. No men were wounded on Dylan's side, thank the Lord, but three of Maddock's men were dead, plus Maddock himself.

Three years it had taken Dylan to reach this point. Three years of nightmares, chasing live monsters across the prairies and territories. It was over. His arms ached from shoveling. It was finally over.

He thanked Charlie and his men for their help, all the while keeping his eye on Lily and her sister.

The women were exhausted; bedraggled in worn-out clothes they'd washed and worn and washed again on the trail. Lily never left her younger sister's side, always ready with a handkerchief, a murmur of encouragement, an arm held open to lean against.

He'd barely had time to tell her about Otis, to let her know the old man was all right, when he was called away again on another matter.

At the gravesites, the sisters swayed on their feet from lack of sleep, but insisted on being present when a prayer was uttered for the wasted lives of these men.

It was behind them, Dylan vowed. From now on, he'd look to the months ahead. He wanted to get Lily alone to speak to her about their future, but had to take care of the pressing matters first.

Two of Maddock's men had surrendered to Charlie, and were tied up by the ropes Lily had supplied. Otis's clothesline, it seemed, was not only long enough to hang seven lines of laundry, but long enough to tie as many as seven men.

The prisoners refused to give away much about themselves. One was a big fella whose lungs rattled when he breathed, more from fear, thought Dylan, than his asthma. The other man was skinny and only thing he'd admit to was his name, Jeremiah Roper.

When Charlie's men were settled for rest, when Charlie disappeared to unroll his blankets by his campfire, Dylan finally turned to look for Lily. It was past three in the morning, he figured.

She and her sister had settled by a second campfire, one he'd ordered the men make especially for the women. Later, Dylan would spend the night 'round it, too, for their sense of protection, but right now he was staring at the empty wool blankets Lily should be in.

Amanda was sound asleep, he noticed with a softness to his heart, and he had no intention of waking her with questions about her sister's whereabouts.

Stepping through the brushes of the gully and making his way to the rippling waters, he found Lily at the river's edge.

Her oilskin jacket hung loosely over her shoulders. Her hair had fallen out of its braiding, and fell like silken ivy around her. In the darkness, he couldn't see its auburn color, but imagined the fiery nature in his mind. Her face was tilted toward the junction of the waterfall where it met with the river. Pleasant sounds of the gurgle and spray held her attention.

It was calming here.

Surprising her, he sat down beside her on a stone, still warm from when the sun had baked it earlier. She swung her boots over the crest of the riverbank.

"Mighty late," he said.

"Couldn't sleep. Are the others settled?"

"Amanda's snoring."

Lily smiled gently. "First time she's slept so well in two weeks."

"She's got you to thank for that."

"And you."

He draped his foot across the rocks, lounging as if he had all the time in the world, as if it wasn't just a few hours before morning. "It's good to see you at ease, Lily."

"Oh, Dylan…" Her voice was soft and appealing. "We did it, didn't we?" She tapped her high-heeled boot on a mound of grass. "They robbed our stagecoach. They chained us together. They shot at you and Amanda, and yet, we made it."

Something still nagged at him. He braced his hand on the warm stone. "We've questioned the other two men. There's no gold. Not here."

"I know."

"Maddock had some in his saddlebags, a small

portion, but he's stolen from so many people, we can't be sure who it belongs to. We'll likely have to divide it evenly."

"I understand," she said gently, no remorse, no accusations.

He spoke with apology. "I said I'd help you find your sister and the gold, but I didn't manage—"

"You managed just fine."

He nodded. His eyes flicked over the shape of her body in the shadows—the boxy lines of her jacket, the wild curls of her long hair. "You're an understanding woman, but the gold—"

"Please stop talking about that." Her face was turned fully to him now, the river gurgling past her shoulders. Her voice was firm, but he needed to finish what was on his mind.

"When we get back to Whitehorse, we'll enlist the aid of the other Mounties. They'll help us track your gold."

Exasperated, she rose from her boulder, chest drawn tight as she wheeled around and headed for the campfire.

"What is it?"

"You men are so obtuse." She trudged along the river. "I'll talk to you in the morning. Get some sleep."

He leaped toward her, his pulse pounding that steady beat, the rhythm that only she could evoke in him, the wild surge of lust and love.

"What did I do wrong, pray tell? I'm discussing your future."

"Land's sake, I don't care about that part." She yanked free of his hold and wove along the river's trail, back to the faraway flames.

With a swoop, he pulled her from behind. Her jacket fell off her shoulders. He wrapped her waist with a firm grip.

"In all my born days, I'll never understand women."

"We're simple. All we want is your full attention now and again."

"You have my full attention."

"On my bloody gold. I don't care about that right now. I don't care!"

"How can you not care? It's what this whole situation's been about!"

"It's not about the gold at all!"

"You know what you do to me, Lily?" He growled his frustrations.

"What?" Her hair spilled about her shoulders. He must have tugged her blouse out from her skirt, for it sat disheveled on her hips.

His senses hammered, the rush of heat, the exhilaration of chasing Lily.

When he didn't answer, she sighed in frustration and kept walking.

"Marry me," he shouted. "Marry me, Lily Cromwell!"

She stopped and turned around. Breathless at first, then with eyes glistening. "Not while we're discussing gold."

"No more talk of gold, okay? Not tonight."

He was done being polite. With a pull on her hips, he tugged her so that she fell right up against him. Then he backed up and pinned her to the nearest tree.

"That's not fair," she said, squirming against the bark. "You're taking advantage."

With her wrists locked beneath his fingers, he kissed her neck.

"You know I'm a gentleman and would never harm a lady."

She clamped her mouth, so stubborn. He kissed behind her ear.

"And besides, you know you have full advantage here…because I love you, Lily." The words caught in his throat.

Her lashes lowered. He kissed her temple.

"I love you, Lily. I have always loved you."

She seemed unable to speak, and they both seemed to realize she was still pinned against the tree. To her surprise, he tightened his grip rather than loosened it. Her lashes flew up and he gazed down into sparkling blue eyes.

"Tell me what I want to hear," he said, "and I'll let you go."

"That's bribery."

He smiled. What the hell…he released her simply because he had to gain a better hold. With his palms on either side of her face, he watched the moon's glow ripple on her lips.

Emotions stormed through him, needs and wants and desires so raw they rocked him.

"If you keep looking at me like that," he murmured, "I won't be responsible for what I do."

She uttered a faint exclamation.

He besieged her with kisses, pressing his mouth against hers, his beloved Lily.

"What's your answer, sweetheart?"

He stopped his lips from touching her throat. She

nibbled at his, sending a flood of heat through his chest, making his belly tighten with need.

"I'll admit," she whispered into his ear, her voice trembling, "I want you, too."

His eyes drifted open and he found hers, intense, longing, loving.

She laughed gently, the same throaty laughter he remembered from the first time she ever poured him coffee as a breakfast maid. He had struggled to find something charming to say to her that day, and instead, had complimented her on her apron.

Now he cupped the graceful curve of her soft cheek.

"You've earned the respect of everyone here, Dylan. Including me."

He lowered his face, how touched he was by her words.

She ran her fingers up his sleeve and touched his scars. "He's dead now. Will you be all right?"

He inhaled a deep breath of chilled, Yukon air. Blood coursed through his veins and tingled through his skin. He'd never felt more alive, more hopeful.

"I looked into his eyes, Lily, and I didn't see myself. Do you know how good that felt? I thought a part of me had become just like him, but when I looked into his eyes, I knew it wasn't true."

"Oh, no…you were never like him."

"You were always sure of that."

"When you believe in someone, you see the truth." She buried her face into his neck and gripped him so hard he thought his ribs would crack. "I love you, Dylan. I'd be honored to be your wife."

With a swoop, he kissed her throat and felt the throb

of her pulse on his lips. "Can you wait till we reach Whitehorse? We'll find a minister. Or a priest. Or a justice of the peace. *Somebody.*"

But she was laughing again, kissing his neck and hugging his waist and whispering words of endearment, not concentrating at all on the arrangements they had to make.

Chapter Twenty-Three

Much to Dylan's frustration, when they reached Whitehorse there was no minister, no priest, no justice of the peace.

There were, however, several dozen sea captains all willing to do the honors.

Captain Macduff from *Lady of the Yukon* was their choice, and an appropriate one at that, thought Dylan as he strode along the crowded docks to get ready for tomorrow's momentous day. Otis huffed beside him, shoulder raw from the healing wound, but mending and getting stronger.

The midday sun hit Dylan's Stetson. It cast a shadow in front of his big boots as he walked. He was a head taller than most of the customers and dock workers who bustled to display their fish, canned preserves, and the stacks of gold-mining pans that would likely rust and never hit pay dirt.

It had taken them a week and a half to travel from the canyon back to Whitehorse. Lily had stuck close to her sister the entire time, and it seemed to him that once they'd agreed on marriage, Lily had turned into a blushing woman.

She kept her distance, always with the excuse about her sister needing her, while Dylan rolled in his bedding, night after night, alone.

Alone! How much longer? Now that he'd found the woman who charmed him beyond reason, he wanted to hold her tight every evening, whisper silly things into her ear, and dammit, make love to his bride.

The Mounties had arrived in Whitehorse early this morning, and he rushed to find Lily to tell her the news.

"Stop runnin' so fast," said Otis, shuffling beneath an awning. "Give a fella a chance to breathe."

"I don't know how she's going to take my new haircut." Dylan rubbed his clean-shaven jaw. Running a hand through his temples, he was taken by surprise again by the short length of his hair. The barber in town had done a fair job, but Dylan wondered what Lily would think of his changed appearance.

"You're as jittery as a mountain lion circlin' his prey. She'll take it just fine. She's not a child." Otis stopped among the canvas tents. He eyed the crowded hill. "Dr. Sturgeon's up there. Maybe his new shipment of specs came in. Why don't you tell Lily I said howdy? I'll see her tomorrow at the do."

"Sure thing." Dylan wove through the customers.

"Dylan!" Otis shouted.

Dylan whirled around and hitched his hand into his pocket. His holster, weighted down by his Colts, shifted around his hips. "Yeah?"

"I'm no expert on marriage, but if you spend some time—"

"I know, I know. Women are simple. All they want is our full attention now and then!"

Otis chuckled and planted his gnarled hand in the air goodbye. "By golly, I think you learned somethin' on this trip!"

Dylan grinned and raced to the far cabin by a small shack marked Mercantile. When he knocked, Amanda let him in.

She was still on the skinny side, but her color had improved remarkably. Her sling was gone, her collarbone almost healed. She did still cradle that arm, holding it gingerly at her side.

"Howdy," he said.

Amanda smiled and slipped out of the cabin so he could go in. "She's inside."

He removed his Stetson and entered. "Lily."

In a fresh set of clothes, cream-colored blouse and matching skirt, she turned to face him in a stream of light. She flushed when she saw him, taking her time to assess the bold new cut of his hair and brand-spanking-new blue shirt.

Teasing him, she ran a finger down his smooth jaw, setting his skin on fire. A smile lifted the corner of her mouth in that sweet, seductive way she had of making his heart drum.

"I approve." She kissed his cheek. "But now you've got me thinking I'm about to marry a tall, dark stranger."

"It's still me, darlin'." He pulled her by the hand, sat her down on the table, and leaned in to kiss her. The bristles at the back of his neck rose in heated response.

One kiss was all she gave him, then squirmed out of his grasp. He removed his hat and tapped it against his thigh in frustration. "I do declare, you are the most exasperating female."

She pleaded as he admired the fine cheekbones, the grace of her fingers. "It's not proper till we get married."

"What sort of illogical female thinking—" He stopped when he realized she was serious.

"Please, let's wait till the steamship tomorrow. After we're married, believe me, you'll need plenty of rest on the ship's voyage back to Dawson."

She stood there, so entrancing beneath the Victorian cut of her lace blouse, the rounded hips beneath the flowing fabric of her skirts.

His voice was gruff. "I think it's you who'll need the rest."

She smiled, slow and charming and seductive, and ran her fingers nervously over her collar.

Laughter found him. "I'm here for something different, Lily. The Mounties came back from their search."

"And?"

He planted his Stetson on the table. "Your gold, and the men hauling it, disappeared."

Frowning, she lowered her eyes, making it difficult to read her.

"There was some word," he said. "Apparently when they reached Alaska, the team of men got wind that Maddock was dead. They fought over the gold. Two of them were killed, the gold disbursed. Some say it disappeared on the trails, others claim to have seen the others taking it on board a ship headed to London."

She rocked back on her heels, thinking. Then went back to packing her things into her luggage

She'd pinned up her auburn hair, and when she turned away from him, he watched the slender curve of her neck. Her face was scrubbed clean of dirt and all trace of the trail they'd left behind.

"Lily…I don't have much. Not like my folks had. Not like what you're accustomed—"

Her eyes misted in the light from the open doorway. "I'm not accustomed to anything. Don't you see, Dylan? When I struck gold in Dawson City, I thought the world was doing me a favor. I thought, oh, now it's my turn…let's see how much and what I can accomplish."

He listened.

"Men came after me. For no other reason than because I had gold and they didn't."

"It wasn't easy, was it?"

She folded a clean blouse into squares. "I would rather have the gold than not," she admitted. "But you see, I always thought…I always thought you and your family lorded it over our heads, how much you had. When in fact, I believe it was me who had a grudge against you. I was the snob, believing you were high and mighty, when you were only going about your business."

"Gold has no feeling. It has no sense of self-worth or dignity. Those are things we assume people of wealth have in abundance."

"Forgive me," she whispered.

"I wish I had better news to bring. I wish I had your gold."

"Dylan, I am more wealthy today than I've ever been in my life. I've got my sister…and I've got you."

He moved toward her, kissing her fingers, rolling his thumb across the soft arches. She raised on tiptoe, reached high and wove her arms around his neck. She kissed his neck and murmured with such joy it filled his heart with longing.

"What would you like to do, Lily? We're headed to Dawson City, but I could ask the commander for a transfer to Alberta. Or I could sign with the regular police force in Vancouver."

"I've talked with Amanda. She'd like to see Dawson and where I struck it rich. We'd always had hopes of opening up a shop of our own. It's not a shop I have in mind…but there is something Amanda and I would like to do with our lives. It won't be easy, but with or without the gold, I decided months ago to do this on my own."

"What is it?"

"We'd like to set up a visitor's lodge. A place where separated folks could come together. Leave messages. Stay a day or two."

"You're remarkable. And that's a wonderful idea."

A knock on the cabin door interrupted their privacy again.

"Special delivery for Miss Lily Cromwell!"

Dylan would have to wait till tomorrow to hold his bride.

It was a beautiful September day on board *Lady of the Yukon*. To Lily, the cool crisp air smelled like fresh glaciers. Sunshine bore down from a stunning blue sky. Layers of scant clouds, thousands of feet high, formed a pretty canopy.

When she heard the organ play, Lily followed her sister, who was dressed in a fine burgundy blouse and skirt, out of the first-class cabin on the main deck to join their men.

The breeze lifted Lily's veil and rustled against the twelve-foot train of her wedding gown. She'd spent her last gold nugget on buying the gown from the laundry woman, Mrs. Tremlain—the special package that had arrived yesterday at Lily's door. Of course, the gown wasn't brand new, but it was laundered and pressed to perfection, and the most beautiful thing Lily had ever worn.

When she joined Dylan, standing by the captain, she could see by the dampened look in his dark eyes that he appreciated how she looked.

His tenderness made her feel loved. His breath, warm and fast, beat at her throat as he dipped his lean, tanned face and whispered, "You're lovely."

Her eyelashes flicked with moisture as she stared up at her Mountie. He wore no uniform, for his was back in Dawson City, but the sharp cut of his gentleman's suit accentuated the breadth of his shoulders and all that was masculine about Dylan Wayburn.

With Otis and his son Charlie standing by as witnesses to this breath-stealing moment, the captain began his words and Lily's stomach swooped.

"Dearly beloved, we are gathered here today…"

The ceremony, and the ensuing dinner spent with the crew and all the passengers on board the ship heading to Dawson passed much too quickly for Lily. She wanted the evening to last forever. They would dock until midnight, then leave.

When Dylan finally whispered in her ear, "It's time we go. It's almost twelve, and our suite is waiting," she trembled with sentiment. Could she ever be enough for this man? All that he'd shown her, that he'd fought for, she needed to return.

Ten minutes later, they said their goodbyes. Lily kissed Amanda on the cheek and walked her to her cabin.

They said farewell to Charlie and Otis, for they would be moving to Alaska for a while, they'd said. Closer to the ocean that they both enjoyed.

"God bless you, Otis," said Lily at the railing, brushing her lips across his bristly cheek, watching him blush in return. He was wearing his brand-new silver spectacles, made for a gentleman.

"I knew somethin' was goin' on with you two, but had no idea you weren't truly married on our trip. It makes more sense, now, what you went through. From what I've seen, you'll have a long and happy marriage." He lifted his hat in the wind. "Adios!"

Charlie followed him down to the riverbank and waved so long. "I'll catch up to you one day! My pa and I will see you again! Fare well, my friends!"

And now it was time to face her husband.

She looked up into the handsome face, the smoothly shaven cheeks, the dark eyebrows that gave him such a look of power, the searing eyes that saw and understood who she was and what she needed in this life.

With a nod goodbye to the captain and the crew, Dylan grasped her hand and led her toward their suite.

He unlocked the door and with a swoop of surprise, lifted her and her train over the threshold.

Kicking it closed with his cowboy boot, he smiled and set her down. He frowned at the door.

"What is it?"

"I was expecting something. Something I wanted to give you as a wedding gift, but…I suppose…"

She slid her hands inside his suit jacket, past the holsters he insisted on carrying, and drew him close. "I don't need anything but you."

He murmured and kissed her earlobe, then brushed her neck with his lips. She closed her eyes. Her chest tightened, ready for an evening of Dylan.

"Let's take this off, shall we?" He undid the top button at the point of her high collar. "How many dozens of buttons must I go through before I get to you?"

She laughed quietly as he tugged. Then came a rap at the door.

His dark head lifted from her neckline. With a steady stride, he opened it. No one there.

But there was something left behind. On the floor sat a huge picnic basket covered with a checkered cloth.

"Did you order this?" she asked, drawing closer. "Are you hungry? We could eat—"

"I can't fit another morsel. It's not food."

"Then what is it?" She picked up the basket. It wiggled and she screamed lightly in surprise, then giggled at herself.

He swooped beside her to ensure it wouldn't fall. "Open it."

She pulled back the cloth and sighed in exclamation. Two tabby kittens peered up at her, their tiny faces framed with white fur, their noses a healthy pink.

"Oh, Dylan…"

Dylan touched her chin. "He came through."

"Who?"

"Charlie."

"One for you, one for your sister."

Yelping with delight, Lily picked them up and nuzzled each one. So soft and warm and friendly.

"I must show Amanda!"

"Lily! Wait!"

She kept going.

"But it's our night!" he hollered.

Two crew members walked by, saluted and chuckled. "Problems so soon, sir?"

She wouldn't be long. Just long enough to show the remarkable gift to Amanda. Amanda was equally stunned, then absolutely gleeful.

"Leave them here with me," she begged. "Look, Charlie's left some biscuits in the basket. Please, leave them here with me. You can visit in the morning."

Laughing and cheering and bursting with love for Dylan, Lily made her way back to the cabin, wedding dress, veil and all.

When she opened the door to the opulent suite, he was lying back on the wide bed, boots propped up on the covers, his long feet nearly spanning the entire length, his jacket off and waiting. A lantern glowed beside him, casting a blanket of warmth and invitation to the bed.

"I can't believe what you've done."

"I thought you could use a little company when I go off on my duties."

"Do you know how much I love you?"

"Come here and show me."

She ran to him on the bed, and amid their laughter and muffled groans of endearment, she kissed every part of him she could reach. His mouth, his eyes, his forehead, his throat. His hands and the strong, strong wrist that would bear its scars forever.

"Let's take this off, shall we?" he repeated with that familiar gleam in his eyes she'd come to adore.

He tugged on her buttons, she loving the slow undress of his lazy fingers, as if they had all the time in the world.

And they did, didn't they? They had all their time before them.

"I think this needs to come off, too," she whispered. She removed his shirt and slid her hands up the smooth expanse of his belly. She felt him shiver beneath her fingers, affected by her touch as much as she was by his.

They took their time, till well past midnight, stripping each other and languishing in the heat of their embrace. He pressed his aroused body on top of her thigh, touching the fullest part of her stomach, coaxing a feminine rush of heat straight through her, through her breasts, down her belly and to the sensual swelling only Dylan was allowed to touch.

He drew her out, that innermost part of her, the place of raw desire and erotic pleasures. She trembled with the sensations he evoked. When he looked down again, he found a faint smile on her lips, her breasts straining forward as he cupped them, her mouth parted, waiting to show him how much love she had for him.

No words needed to be said.

* * * * *

*Look for LAST WOLF WATCHING
by Rhyannon Byrd—the exciting conclusion
in the BLOODRUNNERS miniseries
from Silhouette Nocturne.*

*Follow Michaela and Brody on their fierce journey
to find the truth and face the demons from the past,
as they reach the heart of the battle between
the Runners and the rogues.*

*Here is a sneak preview of book three,
LAST WOLF WATCHING.*

Michaela squinted, struggling to see through the impenetrable darkness. Everyone looked toward the Elders, but she knew Brody Carter still watched her. Michaela could feel the power of his gaze. Its heat. Its strength. And something that felt strangely like anger, though he had no reason to have any emotion toward her. Strangers from different worlds, brought together beneath the heavy silver moon on a night made for hell itself. That was their only connection.

The second she finished that thought, she knew it was a lie. But she couldn't deal with it now. Not tonight. Not when her whole world balanced on the edge of destruction.

Willing her backbone to keep her upright, Michaela Doucet focused on the towering blaze of a roaring bonfire that rose from the far side of the clearing, its orange flames burning with maniacal zeal against the inky black curtain of the night. Many of the Lycans had already shifted into their preternatural shapes, their fur-covered bodies standing like monstrous shadows at the edges of the forest as they waited with restless expectancy for her brother.

Her nineteen-year-old brother, Max, had been attacked by a rogue werewolf—a Lycan who preyed upon humans for food. Max had been bitten in the attack, which meant he was no longer human, but a breed of creature that existed between the two worlds of man and beast, much like the Bloodrunners themselves.

The Elders parted, and two hulking shapes emerged from the trees. In their wolf forms, the Lycans stood over seven feet tall, their legs bent at an odd angle as they stalked forward. They each held a thick chain that had been wound around their inside wrists, the twin lengths leading back into the shadows. The Lycans had taken no more than a few steps when they jerked on the chains, and her brother appeared.

Bound like an animal.

Biting at her trembling lower lip, she glanced left, then right, surprised to see that others had joined her. Now the Bloodrunners and their family and friends stood as a united force against the Silvercrest pack, which had yet to accept the fact that something sinister was eating away at its foundation—something that would rip down the protective walls that separated their world from the humans'. It occurred to Michaela that loyalties were being announced tonight—a separation made between those who would stand with the Runners in their fight against the rogues and those who blindly supported the pack's refusal to face reality. But all she could focus on was her brother. Max looked so hurt…so terrified.

"Leave him alone," she screamed, her soft-soled, black satin slip-ons struggling for purchase in the damp earth as she rushed toward Max, only to find herself lifted off the ground when a hard, heavily muscled arm clamped around her waist from behind, pulling her clear off her feet. "Damn it, let me down!" she snarled, unable to take her eyes off her brother as the golden-eyed Lycan kicked him.

Mindless with heartache and rage, Michaela clawed at the arm holding her, kicking her heels against whatever part of her captor's legs she could reach. "Stop it," a deep, husky voice grunted in her ear. "You're not helping him by losing it. I give you my word he'll survive the ceremony, but you have to keep it together."

"Nooooo!" she screamed, too hysterical to listen to reason. "You're monsters! All of you! Look what you've done to him! How dare you! *How dare you!*"

The arm tightened with a powerful flex of muscle, cinching her waist. Her breath sucked in on a sharp, wailing gasp.

"Shut up before you get both yourself and your brother killed. I will *not* let that happen. Do you understand me?" her captor growled, shaking her so hard that her teeth clicked together. "Do you understand me, Doucet?"

"Damn it," she cried, stricken as she watched one

of the guards grab Max by his hair. Around them Lycans huffed and growled as they watched the spectacle, while others outright howled for the show to begin.

"That's enough!" the voice seethed in her ear. "They'll tear you apart before you even reach him, and I'll be damned if I'm going to stand here and watch you die."

Suddenly, through the haze of fear and agony and outrage in her mind, she finally recognized who'd caught her. *Brody.*

He held her in his arms, her body locked against his powerful form, her back to the burning heat of his chest. A low, keening sound of anguish tore through her, and her head dropped forward as hoarse sobs of pain ripped from her throat. "Let me go. I have to help him. *Please*," she begged brokenly, knowing only that she needed to get to Max. "Let me go, Brody."

He muttered something against her hair, his breath warm against her scalp, and Michaela could have sworn it was a single word…. But she must have heard wrong. She was too upset. Too furious. Too terrified. She must be out of her mind.

Because it sounded as if he'd quietly snarled the word *never*.

nocturne™

THE FINAL INSTALLMENT OF
THE BLOODRUNNERS TRILOGY

Last Wolf Watching

Runner Brody Carter has found his match in
Michaela Doucet, a human with unusual psychic powers.
When Michaela's brother is threatened, Brody becomes
her protector, and suddenly not only has to protect her
from her enemies but also from himself....

LOOK FOR
LAST WOLF WATCHING
BY
RHYANNON BYRD

Available May 2008 wherever you buy books.

Dramatic and Sensual Tales of Paranormal Romance

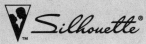

Silhouette®

Romantic

SUSPENSE

**Sparked by Danger,
Fueled by Passion.**

Seduction Summer:
Seduction in the sand...and a killer on the beach.

*Silhouette Romantic Suspense invites you to the hottest
summer yet with three connected stories from some
of our steamiest storytellers! Get ready for...*

Killer Temptation
by **Nina Bruhns;**
a millionaire this tempting is worth a little danger.

Killer Passion
by **Sheri WhiteFeather;**
an FBI profiler's forbidden passion incites a
killer's rage,

and

Killer Affair
by **Cindy Dees;**
this affair with a mystery man is to die for.

Look for

KILLER TEMPTATION by Nina Bruhns in June 2008
KILLER PASSION by Sheri WhiteFeather in July 2008
and
KILLER AFFAIR by Cindy Dees in August 2008.

Available wherever you buy books!

Visit Silhouette Books at www.eHarlequin.com   SRS27586

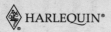
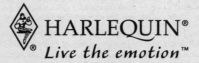

REQUEST YOUR FREE BOOKS!

Harlequin® Historical
Historical Romantic Adventure!

2 FREE NOVELS PLUS 2 FREE GIFTS!

YES! Please send me 2 FREE Harlequin® Historical novels and my 2 FREE gifts (gifts are worth about $10). After receiving them, if I don't wish to receive any more books, I can return the shipping statement marked "cancel". If I don't cancel, I will receive 6 brand-new novels every month and be billed just $4.94 per book in the U.S. or $5.49 per book in Canada, plus 25¢ shipping and handling per book and applicable taxes, if any*. That's a savings of 20% off the cover price! I understand that accepting the 2 free books and gifts places me under no obligation to buy anything. I can always return a shipment and cancel at any time. Even if I never buy another book, the two free books and gifts are mine to keep forever.

246 HDN ERUM   349 HDN ERUA

Name	(PLEASE PRINT)
Address	Apt. #
City	State/Prov.	Zip/Postal Code

Signature (if under 18, a parent or guardian must sign)

Mail to the **Harlequin Reader Service:**
IN U.S.A.: P.O. Box 1867, Buffalo, NY 14240-1867
IN CANADA: P.O. Box 609, Fort Erie, Ontario L2A 5X3

Not valid to current subscribers of Harlequin Historical books.

Want to try two free books from another line?
Call 1-800-873-8635 or visit www.morefreebooks.com.

* Terms and prices subject to change without notice. N.Y. residents add applicable sales tax. Canadian residents will be charged applicable provincial taxes and GST. This offer is limited to one order per household. All orders subject to approval. Credit or debit balances in a customer's account(s) may be offset by any other outstanding balance owed by or to the customer. Please allow 4 to 6 weeks for delivery. Offer available while quantities last.

Your Privacy: Harlequin Books is committed to protecting your privacy. Our Privacy Policy is available online at www.eHarlequin.com or upon request from the Reader Service. From time to time we make our lists of customers available to reputable third parties who may have a product or service of interest to you. If you would prefer we not share your name and address, please check here. ☐

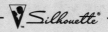

SPECIAL EDITION™

THE WILDER FAMILY
Healing Hearts in Walnut River

Social worker Isobel Suarez was proud to
work at Walnut River General Hospital, so
when Neil Kane showed up from the attorney
general's office to investigate insurance fraud,
she was up in arms. Until she melted in his
arms, and things got very tricky...

Look for

HER MR. RIGHT?

by

KAREN ROSE SMITH

Available May wherever books are sold.

COMING NEXT MONTH FROM

HARLEQUIN®
HISTORICAL

- **WESTERN WEDDINGS**
  by **Jillian Hart, Kate Bridges and Charlene Sands**
  (Western)
  You are cordially invited to three weddings in the Old West this May!
  *Three favorite authors, three blushing brides, three heartwarming
  stories—a perfect recipe for Spring!*

- **NOTORIOUS RAKE, INNOCENT LADY**
  by **Bronwyn Scott**
  (Regency)
  Her virginity would be sold to the highest bidder! Determined not to
  enter into an arranged marriage, Julia could see no way out—unless she
  could seduce the notorious Black Rake…
  *Harlequin® Historical is loosening the laces with our newest, hottest,
  sexiest miniseries, UNDONE!*

- **COOPER'S WOMAN**
  by **Carol Finch**
  (Western)
  A proper lady should have no dealings with a gunfighter with a shady
  past, yet Alexa is bent on becoming Cooper's woman!
  *Carol Finch's thrilling Western adventure will have you on the edge of
  your seat.*

- **TAKEN BY THE VIKING**
  by **Michelle Styles**
  (Viking)
  A dark, arrogant Viking swept Annis back to his homeland—now she
  must choose between the lowly work that befits a captive, or a life of
  sinful pleasure in the Viking's arms!
  *Viking's slave or Viking's mistress? Annis must choose in this powerful,
  sensual story!*